ɟ

JEMCO

The Bards
of Bone Plain

Ace Books by Patricia A. McKillip

THE FORGOTTEN BEASTS OF ELD

THE SORCERESS AND THE CYGNET

THE CYGNET AND THE FIREBIRD

THE BOOK OF ATRIX WOLFE

WINTER ROSE

SONG FOR THE BASILISK

RIDDLE-MASTER: THE COMPLETE TRILOGY

THE TOWER AT STONY WOOD

OMBRIA IN SHADOW

IN THE FORESTS OF SERRE

ALPHABET OF THORN

OD MAGIC

HARROWING THE DRAGON

SOLSTICE WOOD

THE BELL AT SEALEY HEAD

THE BARDS OF BONE PLAIN

Collected Works

CYGNET

The Bards
of Bone Plain

THE BERKLEY PUBLISHING GROUP
Published by the Penguin Group
Penguin Group (USA) Inc.
375 Hudson Street, New York, New York 10014, USA
Penguin Group (Canada), 90 Eglinton Avenue East, Suite 700, Toronto, Ontario M4P 2Y3, Canada
(a division of Pearson Penguin Canada Inc.)
Penguin Books Ltd., 80 Strand, London WC2R 0RL, England
Penguin Group Ireland, 25 St. Stephen's Green, Dublin 2, Ireland (a division of Penguin Books Ltd.)
Penguin Group (Australia), 250 Camberwell Road, Camberwell, Victoria 3124, Australia
(a division of Pearson Australia Group Pty. Ltd.)
Penguin Books India Pvt. Ltd., 11 Community Centre, Panchsheel Park, New Delhi—110 017, India
Penguin Group (NZ), 67 Apollo Drive, Rosedale, North Shore 0632, New Zealand
(a division of Pearson New Zealand Ltd.)
Penguin Books (South Africa) (Pty.) Ltd., 24 Sturdee Avenue, Rosebank, Johannesburg 2196,
South Africa

Penguin Books Ltd., Registered Offices: 80 Strand, London WC2R 0RL, England

This is an original publication of The Berkley Publishing Group.

FIRST EDITION: December 2010

Library of Congress Cataloging-in-Publication Data

McKillip, Patricia A.
    The bards of Bone Plain / Patricia A. McKillip.
        p.   cm.
    ISBN 978-0-441-01957-1
    I. Title.
    PS3563.C38B37 2010
    813'.54—dc22   2010034093

PRINTED IN THE UNITED STATES OF AMERICA

10   9   8   7   6   5   4   3   2

The Bards of Bone Plain

PATRICIA A. McKILLIP

ACE BOOKS, NEW YORK

Chapter One

Phelan found his father at the river's edge. It was morning, early and very quiet. Tide washed softly along the flank of one of the great, weathered standing stones scattered so randomly on both sides of the river that some said they moved about restively at night when the moon was old. That was one tale of the stones. Another was drifting drunkenly behind a pile of rubble from a wall that had collapsed wearily into the conjunction of water and earth.

I was there when they went to war,
The stones of Bek, the stones of Taran,
And the doughty stones of Stirl.
I saw them rage and thunder. I lived to tell the tale.
Who am I?

Phelan knew the answer to that one: there was no mistaking Jonah Cle's rich, ragged voice, with the edge of careless mockery in it honed so fine it could flay. He sighed noiselessly, walked along the sucking mud that clung to each footstep. The mist was thick over the Stirl River; the entire plain seemed silent. Phelan might have been alone in the mist, and the world itself beginning all over again but for his father's voice.

"Who's there?"

"Much you'd care," he reminded the pile of stone, and got a soft chuckle out of them.

"Ah. Phelan. Good. I'm down to my last waterfowl."

Phelan clambered up the broken pile, sat at the top of it, his boots, slimy with mud, propped on a stone at a level with his father's head. Jonah glanced up, gave his son a twisted smile. His handsome, ravaged, stubbled face was pale; his eyes were fire-rimmed. His long, dark hair was clotted with the leavings of the tide line: broken bird and snail shells, soggy pinfeathers, shimmering fish scales. A hooded homespun cloak he must have filched during his wanderings looked as though he had slept in it on the scabrous bank, washing in and out with the tide, for days.

"I have a message for you," Phelan told him.

"How did you find me?" his father asked curiously. "You always find me."

"Maybe I smell you." Phelan picked a twig out of Jonah's hair, snapped it between his fingers. "I don't think about it. If I must go looking for you, I prefer to get it over with as soon as possible."

"Did she send me some money?"

"No. She wants you home." His father rolled a narrowed eye at him; he shrugged. "Don't ask me why."

"Why?"

"Why not? You have a home. You could stay there and drink."

Jonah felt around himself at the suggestion, came up with a broken bottle neck. He grunted, dropped it. "I don't see why I should inflict this on your mother."

"Then why—"

"Why does she want me? Is it important?" He reached out at Phelan's silence, seized his filthy boot, shook it. "You know why. Tell me."

"No," Phelan said flatly.

"Well, do you have any money?"

Phelan ignored that. He shifted out of reach, leaned back, brooding with the gulls along the bank and looking, with his pale hair and gray eyes, something like one. Like them, he watched the water for a ripple, a sign, direction. Water spoke, broke in a delicate froth upon the worthless clutter it had dredged up and laid like treasure upon the mud. Reeds stirred; a breeze had wakened. It would blow off the mist, the marches of that tiny, private patch of timelessness. Already the half-hidden standing stone nearest him, a blunt, creamy yellow tooth three times the height of a man, was losing its blurred edges, blowing clear.

Phelan murmured, scarcely hearing himself, "I watch the comings and goings of water. Birds know me. I came here from the north, from the land of Noh. Look for me there, watching along the edge of the sea. Here I am, and there, since the beginning of words. What am I?"

His father spat out something between his teeth: a fish scale, an inarticulate comment. He said succinctly, "Answer."

Phelan laughed a little, soundlessly, at the blank face of the morning. "You answer it," he breathed. "Tell me what you are. Tell me how I can understand why you are here, sitting in mud and rubble on the river's edge at dawn in this desolate wasteland." He waited without expectation. The mist was fraying, pulling threads out of itself to reveal a glint of light, a dead fish floating by, the slab of yet another stone, which had picked itself up and waded, sometime in the past centuries, deeper into the river. Any hope of an answer shredded away with the breeze. He straightened. "I have to go."

Jonah glanced up at him again, his eyes slitted and glittering under a sudden shift of light. "I won't like it, will I? What she wants me home for."

"You can put up with it," Phelan said wearily. "Take a bath, refill your pockets."

"You won't tell me."

"You know I won't."

"Lend me—"

"No."

Jonah lay back on the rubble, began the litany, intoning it melodically and with charm: "Stubborn, pigheaded, obstinate, iron-hearted, pitiless, remorseless—"

"I know, I know." Phelan rose, scrabbled back over the pile. "Never a doubt I am your son. I'll see you there."

"Where?" the rock pile demanded. He turned his back to it, crossed the weedy road, and nearly fell into his father's latest vision.

The city was becoming riddled with Jonah's obsessions, Phelan thought dourly as he caught his balance at the edge of this one. He paused a moment to peer into the shadow, then turned and found his way through the barrens to the bridge across the Stirl.

Midway across, he stepped out of the clammy ambiguities of fog, gray water, stone, into the full astonishment of light.

A long, roofless vehicle, half car, half wagon, gave Phelan a goose's honk as it passed and sent a plume of steam into the air. He waved, turning for a glimpse of the princess. But the car plunged too quickly into the ribboning mist behind him, carrying the work crew to his father's inexplicable project. He hoped they wouldn't run over Jonah along the way. There was no other traffic on that bridge, ending where it did in the broken memories and weed-strewn ghosts of past so distant no one was left there to remember it. Why his father chose to haunt that bleak smudge in the heart of the city, Phelan had no idea.

The rest of the immense royal city of Caerau, cheerfully colored under the sun with riotous hues of marble, paint, and brick, spread itself across half the plain on both sides of the Stirl River. Merchant ships lined the docks, sails furled, engines silent, busily loading and unloading; others had begun to follow the outgoing tide, unfurling sails bright and individual as butterfly wings, to follow the Stirl to the sea. Fishing boats, elegant barges, swift, slender market skiffs plied the water around them. On the crown of the only hill in the city, Phelan could see his destination: the ancient school, the thick-walled building hugging the broken tower rising out of it, making a dark gray stroke among the brighter walls of later centuries around it.

On the noisy, busy streets at the other end of the bridge, he caught a horse-drawn tram to the school on the hill.

He kept a robe along with his books and papers in the oak cupboards lining the staff room in the pink and gray edifice that had been funded by, and named appropriately for, Jonah Cle. Several other of the younger student teachers were pulling on their robes as well, yawning and muttering comments in the early hour. Like Phelan, they were nearly finished with years of study; they lacked only one last subject to master, a class or two to teach, a final research paper, before they could go out into the world and call themselves bards. The robes they wore over their clothes were still the students' gold and green. But as masters in training, they were allowed to leave them casually unbuttoned, revealing leathers, homespun, silks, brocades, sometimes looking as tavern-glazed and frayed as their wearers.

Phelan heard his name spoken, glanced around absently as he sorted through books and papers.

"Have you got a topic for your final paper, yet?" a young man asked. He was a fine musician, ferociously hardworking except on anything that wasn't music. "I hate history. I hate reading. And above everything, I hate writing. I can't come up with an idea that would compel me to sit for days in a chair with a pen in my hand writing an endless succession of words that nobody but one or two masters will read, and only because they have to. What are you going to write about? Have you decided?"

Phelan shrugged. "Something easy. I just want to get out of here."

"What's easy?" the young man pleaded. "Tell me."

"The standing stones."

"The stones of Caerau?" someone interjected. "That's been done. Once a decade at least for the last five hundred years. What's left to say about them?"

"Who knows? Who cares? Anyway, not Caerau. I'm researching the standing stones of Bone Plain."

A dour young woman who taught beginners to write their notes groaned. "Twice a decade for five hundred years."

Phelan smiled. "You sound like my father; he said exactly that after he asked me what I would write. It's simple: all the hard work has been done, and I won't have to think when I write."

"You haven't started yet?" she guessed shrewdly. Phelan shook his head. She gazed at him silently a moment, asked abruptly, "How can you possess such astonishing gifts and so little ambition?"

He hefted papers and books in one arm, closed the cupboard, and gave her his wry, charming smile, then turned away without bothering to explain that his entire life up to that point was his father's idea.

Phelan had long given up trying to understand him. Enough that Jonah had had his thumb on Phelan's destiny since he was five, when he was ruthlessly ensconced in the school on the hill with a promise of freedom and wealth if he stayed to the end of the long course of studies. The end, after all those years, was a step or two away: one last boring class to teach, the final paper. A hundred times he had nearly walked away from the school; a hundred times he had chosen to stay. The most compelling reason—far more compelling than his father's promises—was that somehow he could, by doing as Jonah insisted, unravel Jonah's convoluted mind and finally understand him.

He had, sometime before, bitterly admitted defeat. Now he only wanted to walk one final time from the school on the hill down to the streets of Caerau and never look back.

The class he taught was held, by tradition, or on days it didn't rain, in the oak grove on the crown of the hill. By the school steward's estimation, the grove was on its fifth generation of oak. Across the lawn, Phelan could see his seven students already sitting under them. The immense, golden boughs that could catch lightning, that created thunder when they broke, flung shadows like webs; the students sitting on the ground seemed obliviously tangled in them. A couple of the hoariest trees had already dropped a bough, huge, moldering bones that the gardeners, with an eye for the picturesque, had let lie.

The students, ranging in age from twelve to fifteen, were midway through their rigorous studies. They blinked sleepily at Phelan, who was beginning to feel the lack of his breakfast. No one, not even the teacher, opened a book or used paper or pen in this class: it was an archaic and exacting exercise in memory.

"Right," Phelan said, dropping down into their circle on the lush grass. "Good morning. Who remembers what we're trying to remember?"

"'The Riddle of Cornith and Corneath,'" the round-faced twelve-year-old, Joss Quinn, answered earnestly.

"Which is about?"

"Two bards having a contest to see who becomes Royal Bard of King Brete." Joss stuck, his mouth still open, Sabrina Penton, a neat, confident girl whose father was the king's steward, picked up the thread.

"They try to guess each other's secret names by asking questions."

"How many questions?"

"A hundred," the irrepressible eldest, Frazer Verge, breathed. "A thousand. How could anyone ever have performed this without everyone falling asleep facedown in their plates?"

"It was a game," Phelan said, pausing to swallow a yawn. "And a history lesson as well. Remember the order of the first letter of each line. There is the pattern, your aid to memory. Around the circle, one line apiece." He looked for the eyes that avoided him; the slight, fair Valerian seemed most uncertain. "You first, Valerian."

The boy gave his line without mishap. The lines began to ratchet like clockwork around the circle. Phelan's thoughts wandered back to the earlier hour. His father would return home as his wife requested, only who knew by what route? A birthday party awaited him; he would not be pleased. At least it wasn't his own.

He became aware, suddenly, of the wind in the oak leaves, the distant clamor of the city. The clock had stopped. His eyes flicked around the circle, found the daydreaming face everyone else was looking at.

"Frazer."

The young man blinked, fell back to earth. "Sorry. I drifted."

"We await the next line." P, was it? Or T? He couldn't remember, either.

"You," he heard Sabrina breathe to Frazer, and memory opened its door, shed light upon teacher and student.

"'Up or down go you at night,'" Frazer recited promptly, "'or by the light of day?'"

Phelan emitted a dry sound from the back of his throat, but no other comment. He shifted his attention to the dark-haired, strawberry-cheeked Estacia, next in the circle, who picked up the rhythm without a falter.

"'Vine are you to twine and bind the branching hawthorn bough?'"

"The clues," Phelan said glibly when they had muddled their way through the rest of the riddles, "will become obvious to those who complete their years of study and training here. The more you learn of such ancient poetry, the more you realize that all poetry, and therefore all riddles, are rooted in the Three Trials of Bone Plain. Which are what?"

"The Turning Tower," Frazer said quickly, perhaps to redeem himself.

"And?"

"The Inexhaustible Cauldron," said the rawboned Hinton, all spindly shanks and flashing spectacles.

"And?"

"The Oracular Stone," answered Aleron the indolent, who was bright enough, but preferred the easy question.

"Yes. Now. Of all the bards in the history of Belden, which bard passed all three tests?"

There was silence again. A dead oak leaf, plucked by the spring wind, spiraled crazily off a branch and sailed away. "Your muses are everywhere around you," Phelan reminded them as the silence lengthened. "Your aids to memory, and creation. Sun, wind, earth, water, stone, tree. All speak the language of the bard. Of poetry." The leaf was flying across the grass toward the great standing stones that circled the crown of the knoll above the river in a dance that had begun before Belden had a name.

"Where," Frazer asked suddenly, "exactly, is Bone Plain? Are we on it?"

"Maybe," Phelan answered, quoting his research. "No one has yet found conclusive evidence for any particular place. Most likely it existed only in the realm of poetry. Or it was translated into poetry from some more practical, prosaic event, which a mortal bard might have a chance of enduring. As we know, stones do not speak, nor do cauldrons yield an unending supply of stew except in poetry. Do you remember the bard who passed the tests?"

Frazer shook his head. Then he guessed, "Nairn?"

"No. Not Nairn. Great a bard as he was, he failed even the least complicated of the trials: the Test of the Flowing Cauldron. Which was what? Anyone?"

"The test of love, generosity, and inspiration," Sabrina said.

"Thereby rendering himself at once immortal and uninspired. Not a good example to follow."

"So where is he?" Frazer asked.

"Who?"

"Nairn. You said he's immortal."

There was another silence, during which the teacher contemplated his student. Frazer's wild face, with its lean, wolfish bones framed by long, golden hair, looked completely perplexed.

"Where is your mind today?" Phelan wondered mildly. "Lost, it seems, along with Nairn in the mists of poetry. Between the lines. He did exist once; that is a matter of documented history. But the exacting demands of storytelling, requiring a sacrifice, transformed him from history into poetry."

"But—"

"Into a cautionary tale."

"About what?" Frazer persisted. "I'm confused. Why a cautionary tale about an illusion, if that's what Bone Plain is? And if not, then where do we go to find the tower that will give us three choices: to die, or go mad, or to become a poet? I want to become a bard. I want to be the greatest bard that Belden has ever known. Must I enter that tower? That metaphor?"

"No," Phelan said gravely, hiding an urge to laugh at the notion. "It's not a requirement of this school. Nor of the Kings of Belden. You can go looking for the tower if you choose. Or the metaphor. At the moment, I'd prefer you just answer my question." Frazer only gazed at him, mute and stubborn. Phelan glanced around. "Anyone?"

"The bard Seeley?" the quiet, country-bred Valerian guessed diffidently.

"Good guess, but no. Prudently, he never tried." He waited.

"No one? You do know this. You have all the history and poetry you need to unravel this mystery. Do so before I see you again. The weave is there, the thread is there. Find and follow."

The students rose around him, scattered, all but for Frazer, whom Phelan nearly tripped over as he turned.

"I have another question," he said doggedly.

Phelan shrugged lightly, sat back down. The boy's ambition was formidable and daunting; Phelan, wanting only his breakfast, was grateful he had never been so afflicted.

"If I can answer."

"I've been at this school for seven years. Since I was eight. You're almost a master. So you must know this by now. How many years must we complete before we are finally taught the secrets of the bardic arts?"

Phelan opened his mouth; nothing came out for a moment. "Secrets."

"You know," Frazer insisted. "What's there. In every ancient tale, between the lines in every ballad. The magic. The power in the words. Behind the words. You must know what I'm talking about. I want it. When am I taught it?"

Phelan gazed at him with wonder. "I haven't a clue," he said finally. "Nobody ever taught me anything like that."

"I see." Frazer held his eyes, his face set. "I'm not old enough yet to know."

"No, no—"

"You've completed your studies. Everyone says you're brilliant. You could go anywhere, be welcome at any court. There's nothing you wouldn't have been taught. If you can't tell me yet, you can't. I'll wait."

He seemed, motionless under the oak, prepared to wait in

just that spot until somebody came along and enlightened him. Phelan yielded first, got to his feet. He stood silently, looking down at the young, stubborn, feral face.

"If such secrets exist," he said finally, "no one told me. Perhaps, like that tower, you must go looking for them yourself. Maybe only those who realize that such secrets exist are capable of discovering them. I lack the ability to see them. So no one ever taught me such things."

Frazer sat rigidly a moment longer. Gradually, his expression eased, through disbelief to a flicker of surprise at both himself and Phelan.

"Maybe," he conceded uncertainly. He rose, blinking puzzledly at Phelan. "I thought if anyone knew, it would be you."

He took himself off finally. Phelan, completely nonplussed, headed to the masters' refectory to fortify himself against several hours in the library archives, as he tried to find a way to say the same thing everyone else had said, twice a decade for five hundred years, only differently.

In his head, he could hear Jonah's derisive comments, even the ones he hadn't made yet. Phelan ignored them all, as he had so many others, and walked into the oldest building, under the shadow of its broken tower, to seek his breakfast.

Chapter Two

Across a thousand years of poetry, we have come to know Nairn the Wanderer, the Fool, the Cursed, the Unforgiven intimately through hundreds of poems, ballads, tales. We know his adventures, his loves, his failures, his despair. We have explored his most intimate passions and torments. He is named in any given century; he wears the face, the clothes, the character of those times. Even now, he speaks through our modern voices as he inspires new tales of love and loss, of his endless quest for death. His trials become ours and not ours: we seek to avoid his fate as we are equally fascinated by it.

But of the man behind, within the music and the poetry, who cast his unending shadow across a millennium and more, we know astonishingly little.

He is first named in the records of the village of Hartshorn as the son of a farmer in the rugged wilds of the north Belden known then as the Marches, during the reign of its last king, Anstan. That much at least is documented. Between his birth and the next documented

*detail of his life, we can only rely on later ballads, which give him
the name "Pig-Singer" as a child for his astonishing voice, which he
exercised frequently while tending to his father's pig herd. According to more ribald versions of the "Ballad of Nairn the Unforgiven,"
he was often pelted with pig shit by his older siblings for spending
more time sitting on the sty posts and singing than attending to his
other chores. How the pigs responded to his remarkable gifts of voice
and memory has not been documented outside of poetry. He vanished, probably with good reason, out of village life and into folklore
at an early age, to surface again in history, a dozen or so years later,
in a tavern on the edge of the North Sea, where he was pressed into
service as a marching bard for the final battle of King Anstan's
doomed reign: the Battle of the Welde.*

> *Dark his hair, darker his eye,*
> *Sweet as cream and honey his voice,*
> *O the charm in it, O the lure of it,*
> *He could wile a smile from the moon.*
>
> FRAGMENT OF "BALLAD OF THE PIG-SINGER," ANONYMOUS

Nairn was the youngest of seven sons, and a hardscrabble
lot they were, scraping a living with their fingernails out
of the rocky, grudging soil of the mountains in the southern
Marches. He learned to dance early: away from that foot, this
elbow or great ham hand, one or another careless hoof, or some
cranky goose's beak. His mother took to a corner of the hearth
after he was born and refused to budge. Hers was the first singing voice he heard when the crazed house was empty, and he

could finally hear beyond the thunder of his brothers' clumping boots and shouts and laughter, their father's harsh rasping bark that could cut short their clamor like the sound of the blunt edge of an ax head smacking the side of an iron pot. So young Nairn was then that he still lay at his mother's breast as he listened to the high, pure voice threading word and sound into something he could not see or touch or taste, only feel.

Later, when he could separate words into tales and drink out of a cup, his mother went away, left him alone with his bulky, milling brothers as oblivious to their flailing limbs as cows were to their tails and hooves. A woman as round as the moon, with hands as big and hard as theirs, came to cook and mend for them. She sang, too, sometimes. Her voice was deep, husky, full of secrets, odd glints and shadows, like a summer night. She held Nairn spellbound with her singing; he would stand motionless, wordless, his entire body an ear taking in her mysteries. She would laugh when she saw that, and as often as not slip something into his grubby hand to eat. But she clouted his brothers when they sniggered at him, and her swinging fists were not always empty; they learned to dance, too, away from cleavers and the back sides of spoons. One day, standing so ensorcelled, Nairn opened his mouth suddenly and his own singing voice flew out.

It was worse than the time his brothers caught him in the barnyard one night trying to peel the moon from a puddle of water. Far worse than when they heard him trying to talk to crows, or drumming the butter churn with his mother's wooden clogs. It was standing in the muck of the pigsty, singing to the pigs while his brothers made bets on which would knock him over first. It began to dawn on him then that his brothers had a skewed vision of the world. They couldn't hear very well, either. The pigs seemed to like his singing. They crowded around him, gently snorting, while his brothers laughed so hard that they never noticed their father banging out of the house to see what the racket was about until he came up behind them and shoved as many as he could reach off the fence and into the muck. Nairn went down, too, drowning in a rout of startled pig. His father pulled him up, choking and stinking, tossed him bodily into the water trough.

"Time you went to work, Pig-Singer," he told Nairn brusquely. "Sing to the pigs all you want. They're your business now."

So he did, and got a scant year older before his voice, drifting over hedgerows and out of the oak wood, attracted the attention of passing villagers and, one day, an itinerant minstrel. He showed Nairn the instruments he wore on his belt and slung over his shoulder.

"Follow the moon," he advised the boy. "Sing to her, and she'll light your path. There are places you can go to learn, you know. Or maybe you don't?"

Nairn, speechless, spellbound with the sounds that had come so easily out of wood and string, as easily as his own voice came out of his bones, could not answer. The minstrel smiled after a moment, blew a ripple of notes out of his smallest pipe, and gave it to Nairn.

"Maybe not yet. Give this a try. The birds will like it."

Later, when he had found all the notes in the pipe and could flick them into the air as easily as his voice, a passing tinker, pots and tools on his wagon chattering amiably in the sun, pulled his mule to a halt and peered into the oak trees.

"You must be the one they call Pig-Singer," he said to the scrawny, dirty urchin piping among the rooting pigs. "Let me hear you."

Nobody had ever asked him that before. Surprised, he lost his voice a moment, then found it again, and raised it in the first ballad his mother had ever sung to him. The tinker threw something at him when he was done; used to that, Nairn ducked. Then, as the wheels rolled on, he saw the gleam of light among the oak leaves under his feet, and picked it up.

He looked at it for a long time: the little round of metal with a face on one side and hen scratches on the other. Such things appeared in his father's life as often as a blue moon and vanished as quickly. And here he sat, with one of his own in his hand, and all for doing what he loved.

He piped the pigs home and wandered off into his destiny.

He found his way, year by year, as far north as he could get without falling into the sea and living with the selkies. Somewhere during the long road between his father's ramshackle farm in the southern Marches and the bleak sea with its voice of golden-haired mermaids and great whales, he grew into himself. He had walked out of that skinny, feral urchin with his singing voice so pure it could set the iron blade of a hoe humming in harmony. Slowly, through the dozen and more years of wanderings, odd jobs, stealing when he had to, charming when he could to keep himself fed, finding and learning new instruments, and listening, always listening, his stride lengthened, his face rearranged itself, his voice turned deep and sinewy, his eyes and ears became vast doorways through which wonders ceaselessly flowed, while his brain worked like a beehive to remember them.

Stepping onto the sand on the farthest northern shore, he left a trail of footprints broadened by travel. He stood at the waves' edge, watching the foam unfurl, flow over the smooth gold sand, fray into holes and knots of lacework. It touched the tip of his sandal and withdrew. He shrugged off his pack, his harp, his robe, and ran naked after the receding song.

Later, coming up out of the roil, he heard a tendril of human song.

He dressed and followed it.

The noise came from a hovel near the sea: half a dozen crofters and fishers banging their tin mugs on a table and bawling out a ballad he'd never heard. He picked it up easily enough on his pipe; a few songs later, he switched to his harp. That got him his first meal of the day: ale and cheese and a stew of some briny, gritty, slithery pestilence that, by the last bite, he was trying to scrape out of the hollows of his bowl.

"Oysters," the one-eyed tavern keeper told him, kindly fetching more. He added, incomprehensibly, "They make pearls. Where are you from, lad?"

"South," Nairn said with his mouth full.

"How far?" one of the shaggy-haired men behind him growled. "How far south?"

Nairn turned, sensing tension; he fixed the man with a mild eye, and said, "I've been wandering around. Never beyond the Marches. I go where the music is. Yours brought me here."

They snorted and laughed at the thought. Then they refilled their cups and his. "That old song," one said. "My granny taught it to me. My dad sang it, too, while he mended his nets. So you haven't seen what's going on, south of the Marches." He paused at Nairn's expression. "Or even heard?"

He shook his head. "What?"

"War."

He shook his head again. All he knew of war was in old songs. But as he stood there in the ramshackle place, the plank door groaning in the wind, the endless, wild roar without, the spitting, fuming fire within, he suddenly felt the eggshell fragility of the stone walls. Something beyond fire, wind, tide, there was to fear. Something he, with all his footsteps leaving crisscrossing paths across the Marches, might not recognize until it was too late. He shivered slightly; the men, watching him around one of the two battered tables in the place, nodded.

"Best stay low, boy. The king will be looking for warriors to defend the Marches, even this far north."

"I'm a minstrel. I carry a knife to skin a hare for my supper or carve a reed for my bladder-pipe. Nothing more."

"You're a strong, healthy man with two feet to march with, two ears to hear orders, and enough fingers to wield a sword or a bow. That's what they'll see."

"What's a bladder-pipe?" someone wondered.

He pulled it out of his pack. "I heard it played in the western hills. They use it to call their families together across the valleys. The songs differ, but the sound could blast the feathers off a hawk."

He played it, had them groaning and pleading for mercy in a minute. He threatened to keep at it until they sang for him again. By evening's end, they were slumped against one another, humming softly to his harping. The tavern keeper came up to him, where he sat by the fire, dreamily accompanying the song sung in the dark by the moon-tangled tides.

"Stay," the man suggested softly. "There's a loft up in the eaves where my daughter slept before she married. I'll feed you, give you a coin when I can. And all the oyster stew you can hold. It's safer than roving around in the kingdom, just now."

"For a while, then," Nairn promised.

It was a shorter while than he intended, but sweeter than he expected, especially after he met the tavern keeper's daughter, with her eyes the silver-green of willow leaves and her rare, rich laugh. She came early to get the cooking started for the day: the bread, the pots of soup and stew, the slab of mutton turning on the hearth. She clouted Nairn when he first turned the full, dark depths of his wistful gaze upon her. But she was laughing a moment later. For days after, he felt her eyes when she thought he wouldn't notice: little, curious glances like the frail pecks of hatchlings tapping at their boundaries.

Then, one morning, she came in the wee hours, slid next to him on the pallet in the loft.

"Himself is out with the early tide," she whispered. "And my father's sleeping with his deaf ear up. Just don't think this is more than what it is."

"No," he promised breathlessly, embarking upon yet another path with no end in sight. "Yes. Of course, no."

He spent his evenings playing in the tavern. His days were his own. He roamed the coastal barrens, searching out the tiny stone huts of fishers and shepherds, coaxing songs from their toothless grandparent stirring the fire, the child chanting over its game of driftwood and shells, the wife rocking a babe in the cradle with one foot and singing as she churned. Ancient words, they sang in this part of the world; his quick, hungry ear picked up hints of far older tales within the simple verses. Sometimes they'd tell him tales of magic and power, the toothless, dreamy-eyed old ones, as they hugged the hearths for warmth. All true, they assured him. All true, once, a long time ago . . . Children taught him their counting rhymes; older girls showed him their love charms, bundles of tiny shells, dried flowers, locks of hair, tied up with colored threads. They told him where to bury them, what to sing as he did.

"This one you cover with sand in the exact center of the Hag's Teeth. You'll see. The dark stones down the beach that look like fangs."

"This one you give to the Lady Stone as the full moon rises."

"This one you burn at the King Stone, on top of the hill across from Her. There's a charred circle around it, old as the stone, some say. So many have burned love-gifts there, it must be true, don't you think so?"

He found the stones.

They watched him, he felt a couple of times, these immense, battered old shards of time set deep into the earth by who knew what fierce, single-minded urgings. He played to them, leaning against them; he saw what they saw: sunrise, moonrise, the tides rushing in, rushing away. They watched him, looming over him when a young mother brought her sleeping baby with her, let it lie in a hollow of sea grass and strawberry vines while she fed the wanderer wild strawberries between her lips. They watched.

So little time, such scant weeks passed, that none of the men had yet offered the honey-voiced wanderer a flat-eyed glance, a comment less than friendly, before the next stranger entered the tavern following a song.

The fishers crowding the tables looked upon him suspiciously enough. But he carried no arms, only his harp in a fine, worn leather case. His robe and cloak were simply fashioned, embroidered here and there with once-bright threads. His lean face was lined, his red hair, streaked with white along the sides, was cut short and neat as a fox's pelt. His strange eyes were gold as a snow owl's. They went first to the harper on his bench by the hearth. Then he nodded to the men, and they nodded back silently, not knowing what to make of the stranger in their midst, especially one verging, in such an unlikely place, on the exotic.

He bought them all ale immediately; their first impressions changed, and their tongues loosened. He had a strange accent, an odd lilt to his sentences, but that was explained easily enough when they asked. He wasn't from the Marches but from the smaller, mountainous kingdom to the south and west, whose king, everybody knew, lived on a crag with the eagles to keep an eye on his rambunctious nobles.

"My name is Declan," he told them. "I am the court bard of Lord Ockney of Grishold. We received word from the King of Grishold that a stranger is trying to overrun the five kingdoms, take them for himself. The barbarian, who calls himself King Oroh, sailed up the Stirl River with his army and challenged the King of Stirl, whose own army was massed across the plain on both sides of the river. The battle was fierce and terrible. The Stirl, we heard, ran red. The King of Stirl surrendered to the invader, who has now turned his eyes west of the plain toward Grishold. The King of Grishold sent several of his nobles, Lord Ockney among them, to plead with your king Anstan and his nobles for help, men, arms. With the plain taken, we are cut off from the other kingdoms, Waverlea and Estmere. We were forced to find our way north up the rugged western coast to get here. If King Oroh conquers Grishold, he won't stop there. He'll come north to the Marches, strike while the weather is fair."

"I thought the barbarian king was already nipping at us," a fisher said heavily. "That he's just over the border hills of the Marches."

The bard shook his head. "No. He was moving his army toward Grishold when we left. It's rough country, and the nobles there are contentious. It may not fall so easily to him as the kingdom on the plain."

"What are you doing all the way up here," another asked, "if your Lord Ockney wants the king? Court's in the south."

"My lord stopped in your western mountains to plead for help from the hill clans." He paused, added with wonder, "They have some very strange music there," and the men laughed. "He sent me up here to seek out the great, rich courts of the northern coasts, to soften the nobles' hearts with my music, so that when he came begging, they would be generous."

There was more laughter, brief and sardonic, at that. "Not much up here besides the fishing villages," the innkeeper explained.

"Ah."

"Surely you didn't come up here alone? The northerners are generous, but they don't bother to bar their doors, that's how little they have. They'll give you their best for the asking: chowder and a moldy pallet. You won't find an army here, and the only nobles we have are the standing stones."

Declan smiled. "I offered to come. I've heard the bladderpipes of the hill clans. I wanted to hear what strange music has grown along the edge of the world."

They studied him curiously, all suspicion gone. "Another wanderer," one decided. "Like Nairn."

"Nairn."

They gestured toward the young harper. "He can play anything; he's been everywhere around the Marches. He's heard it all."

The golden eyes, glinting like coins, studied Nairn. Nairn, meeting the unblinking, dispassionate gaze, felt oddly as though his world had shifted sideways, overlapped itself to give him an unexpected vision of something he didn't know existed. The feeling echoed oddly in his memories. Astonished, he recognized it: the other time he had wanted something with all his bones and didn't know what it was.

Declan smiled. Wordless, Nairn tipped his harp in greeting. The older bard came over to him, sat on the bench beside him.

"Play," Declan urged. "Some song from the sea."

Nairn shook his head slightly, found his voice. "You first. They're all tired of listening to me by now, and so am I. Play us something from your world."

The men rumbled their agreement. Declan inclined his head and opened his harp case.

The harp came out dancing with light. Uncut jewels inset deeply into the face of the harp glowed like mermaid's tears: green, blue, red, amber in the firelight. The men shifted, murmuring with wonder, then were dead still as the harper played a slow, rich, elegant ballad the like of which Nairn had never heard. It left a sudden, piercing ache in his heart, that there might be a vast sea-kingdom of music he did not know and might never hear. The wanderer who had enchanted the pigs with his voice and had callused his feet hard as door slats had glimpsed the castle in the distance, with its proud towers and the bright pennants flying over them. Such lovely, complex music was no doubt common as air within those walls. And there he stood on the outside, with no right to enter and no idea how to charm his way in. With a bladder-pipe?

The ballad ended. The men sat silently, staring at the harper.

"Sad," one breathed finally, of the princess who had fled her life on her own bare feet to meet her true love in secret, only to find him dead in their trysting bower with her husband's wedding ring lying in the hollow of his throat.

Another spoke, after another silence. "Reminds me of a ballad my wife sings. Only it's a sea-maid, not a princess, and her husband is seaborn as well, but her own true love is a mortal man, drowned by a wave and found in the sand with a black pearl on his throat."

Nairn saw a familiar kindling in Declan's eye. "Please," the bard said. "Sing it for me."

"Ah, no," the man protested, trying to shift to safety behind his friends. "I couldn't. Not for you."

"I'll sing with you," Nairn suggested promptly. "I know it."

You see? their faces told Declan as Nairn began. He knows everything.

They were all singing it toward the end, all the villagers with their voices rough as brine-soaked wool, trying to imitate the older bard's deep, tuned, resonant voice. Declan listened silently, harp on his knee, hands resting upon it. He was hardly moving. Maybe it was his breathing that kept the harp moving imperceptibly, the jewels glittering with firelight, then darkening, then gleaming again, catching at Nairn's eyes as he played. For the first time in his life he saw some use for what he only knew as words in poetry: gold, jewels, treasure. He was born poor; he took his music for free; it cost no more than air or water. But there were other songs, he realized, other music, maybe even other instruments secreted away where only those who possessed gold, wore jewels, were permitted to go.

The jewels, fair blue as sky, green as river moss, fire red, teased him, lured his eyes when he ignored them. He met Declan's eyes once, above the jewels; they told him nothing more than mist. He had stolen things in his life, but only to keep on living: eggs out of a coop, a cloak left on a bush to dry, a pair of sandals when his feet grew bigger than his shoes. Things he needed. Never anything like this. Never anything he wanted, mindlessly, with all his heart: these jewels, useless, brilliant, indolent creatures, doing no one any good, just flaunting their wealth and beauty on the face of a harp whose supple, tender voice would not change so much as a tremor if the jewels vanished.

He heard Declan's voice then, softly pitched to reach him beneath the singing.

"Take them. If you can."

He met the bard's eyes again, found them again wide, unblinking, oddly metallic, the pupils more like coins than human eyes. Like the jewels burning on his harp, they lured, teased, challenged.

Nairn dropped his eyes, pitched every note, sang every word of longing and passion in the ballad to all the music he had never heard, might never hear, the treasure hoard of it, hidden away like forbidden love behind windowless walls, within indomitable towers.

He scarcely noticed when the ballad came to an end; he

heard only the longing and loss in his heart. His fingers stilled. He heard an ember keen, a twig snap. No one spoke, except the fire, the wind, the sea. Then, as he stirred finally, he heard an odd ping against the flagstones, then another, as though, beneath his feet, some very ancient instrument were turning itself.

Another.

He looked down, found the jewels had melted like tears down the harp face, slid to his feet.

He stared at Declan, whose eyes held a pleased, human smile. The men at the tables were beginning to shift a bone, draw a breath.

"They go where they are summoned," the bard said. "Take them. They came to you."

Nairn felt his skin prickle, from his nape to the soles of his feet, as his view of that tiny piece of the world expanded to contain inexhaustible questions. He whispered the first one.

"What are you?"

"Good question." The bard bent, picked up the jewels, pushed them into Nairn's hand. The tavern keeper cleared his throat, gripped the crockery jug to refill their cups.

The door flew open as though the wind had pushed it. Nairn's hand locked painfully on the jewels. He recognized the strangers entering by their swords, their chain mail, their gaunt, tired, merciless faces. They ignored the rigid villagers, the aging bard watching them out of his yellow eyes; their attention homed instantly onto Nairn.

"You," one said to him. "Get your things. There's an army coming at us from Stirl Plain, and King Anstan needs a marching drum. And a bladder-pipe to call the clans if you've got one."

Finally, one of the fishers spoke, said bewilderedly to Declan,

"I thought you told us the army is on the move south toward Grishold."

"I was wrong," he said, rising and putting away his harp. When Nairn came down from the loft with his pack, there was no sign of the bard; he had vanished back into the blustery night.

Chapter Three

The king's daughter Beatrice, who drove the graceless, snorting steam wagon over Dockers Bridge, narrowly missed hitting Jonah as he loomed out of the mists in the middle of the road. The work crew, tools of every kind prickling around them like pins in a pincushion, shrieked in unison. Beatrice's feet hit the pedals hard; the vehicle skidded on the damp and came panting to a stop inches from Jonah. A rubber mallet continued its flight out of somebody's tool belt, bounced off the hood, and landed magically in Jonah's upraised hand.

Jonah laughed. Beatrice closed her eyes, opened them again. She unclenched her fingers from the steering wheel, managed a shaky, sidelong smile.

"Good morning, Master Cle."

"Good morning, Princess."

"So sorry—this mist. Are you all right?"

"Of course I am. What it takes to kill me has not yet been invented." He stepped to the side of the steam wagon, proffered the mallet to his work crew. Curran took it, his face beet red under his already flaming hair.

"Sorry, Master Cle," he said gruffly, his country vowels elongating under the stress. "Thought we were jobless, there for a moment."

"Can I give you a ride to wherever you're going?" Beatrice asked.

"I've been summoned home," Jonah said a trifle acerbically, "though why eludes me."

"Oh, yes. We passed Phelan on the bridge." She paused, blinking at another illumination. Jonah's shrewd eyes, black as new moons in his ravaged face, seemed to see his fate in her thoughts.

"You know why," he said flatly, and she nodded, her long, slanted smile appearing again, partly apologetic, partly amused.

"Yes. I'm afraid it's my father's birthday party." She waited until he finished groaning. "Shall I drop off the crew and come back for you, take you home?"

He ran his hands over his face, up through his disheveled hair, picked what looked like a small snail out of it. "Thank you, Princess," he answered heavily. "I'll walk. There's always the chance that someone else will run over me."

"All right, Master Cle," she said, slipping the car into gear. "I'll see you at the party, then."

She continued into the fog and found her way to the appropriate hole in the ground in that blasted wilderness without mishap.

She had known Jonah Cle all her life. The museum he had built to house his finds from throughout the city had fascinated her since childhood. Antiquities of Caerau, mended, polished, and labeled, carefully preserved behind glass in their softly lit cases, gave her random details, like a trail of bread crumbs, into a story so old even the bards on the hill had forgotten it. Whose blown-glass cup was this? she would wonder. Whose beaded belt? Whose little bear carved out of bone? Surely they had names, these faceless people; they had left footprints when they walked; they had looked at the stars as she did and wondered. That and a peculiar fondness for holes, underground tunnels, forgotten doors, and scarred, weedy gates, rutted bits of alleyway, for notic-ing and exploring small mysteries no one else seemed to notice, had finally translated itself into a direction. She would go here, study that, do this with her life. The king, himself captivated by the history Jonah unburied, found no particular reason not to let her do what she wanted. Having three older children as potential heirs made his demands on his youngest a trifle perfunctory. Her mother assumed nebulously that Beatrice would quit clambering down holes and playing in the dirt when she fell properly in love.

She had, several times, by her own reckoning; so far that hadn't stopped her from shrugging on her tool vest and follow-ing the dig crew down the ladders into Jonah's latest whim. Great hollowed caverns of burned-out walls loomed around them in the thinning mist, watching out of shattered eyes. They were scarcely centuries old. What might lie hidden under layers of past in this particular hole, Beatrice guessed, would have its links to the far older stones: the monoliths among the ruins, watching them as well.

So far, this site had yielded little more than broken water pipes. The tide had gone out far enough that they didn't have to use the pumps. Both Curran and wiry Hadrian cautiously wielded shovels to loosen the dirt. Beatrice, tiny blond Ida, and Campion, with his wildflower blue eyes, used the smaller tools, trowels and brushes, to comb through the rubble for treasure. Baskets of earth were slung on rope and hoisted up and out on a winch after it was picked through. So far, Ida had uncovered a plain silver ring, probably flushed down a pipe; Hadrian had unearthed a broad bone that Curran had identified as ox. Beatrice and Campion were working their way across an odd line of something, possibly a brick mantelpiece, that so far was only a vague protrusion of packed earth in the wall. Curran's great find had been a layer of broken whelk shells, more likely from someone's dinner than from an ancient intrusion of sea-life across the plain.

"Why here?" Curran wondered at one point, standing at the foot of the ladder, staring around blankly, sweating from winching up a basket of earth. He didn't seriously want an answer; Jonah's foresight was legendary, startling, always inexplicable.

But at that point, Beatrice thought, it seemed a fair question.

"There are five standing stones around us," she said, brushing as much dust onto her face as off the protrusion. "We're exactly in the middle of them."

"They walk around at night," Campion said. "Don't they? They'll be somewhere else tomorrow. And we'll be still here digging up drainpipes."

Hadrian shrugged. "We get paid. And the glory, if we find the gold he's seeded this with to raise the property values in the neighborhood."

Curran chuckled. "Doesn't need gold to raise them. They've fallen so far here, rumor could raise them. The word alone."

"Rumor?"

"Gold."

They were scarcely listening to one another, just tossing out words to pass the time. It was nearly noon, Beatrice guessed from the merry blue sky above and the light spilling over the lip of the site. She had to leave soon, go home, and turn into a princess for her father's fifty-seventh birthday. Jonah would be there, she remembered.

"I'll ask him," she promised. "When I see him at my father's party."

She recognized the quality of the silence around her: the sudden suspension of thought and movement as they remembered the princess among them, disguised in her dungarees and boots, her curly hair swept up under a straw hat, her nails grimy with dirt. They had all been students together; they had gotten used to her years earlier.

Only some juxtaposition of incongruous detail—the king's birthday, she and their employer together at the royal celebration—could still catch them by surprise.

Then Curran spoke, breaking the spell. "Will he tell, do you think? Will he know, even? What he's looking for, honeycombing Caerau with all his diggings?" Or at the bottom of a bottle, he did not add. But they all heard it anyway. "You talk to Phelan, too. Does he have a guess?"

She turned tiredly away from the outcrop and smiled at them. "He's never said. I don't know either of them well enough to pry. Jonah pays us; we find things. Eventually."

Campion smiled back at her, making her one of them again. "Inevitably," he sighed. "We find wonders. But it never happens unless we complain first."

Their spirits were raised considerably when Curran unearthed a copper disk with his shovel. The find, half the size of his broad palm, was green with age, stamped on one side with a worn profile and on the other with what looked like broken twigs. A little quarter moon attached above the blurred head indicated the chain or the leather ribbon from which it had hung. They all crowded around it as he brushed crumbs of earth carefully away from it.

"Master Cle will love this . . ." Ida breathed. "Oh, Curran, you are the lucky one."

"Whose face is that?" Campion wondered. "Doesn't resemble any coin I've seen. Is that a crown?"

"Could be a coin," Hadrian said dubiously. "Those markings might signify worth. But it looks like it's meant to be worn."

"Runes," Beatrice said, feeling time stop in that sunny moment underground, as they stood face-to-face with a message out of the distant past. "Those twiggy things—"

"Hen scratches," Curran suggested, as one intimately acquainted. He turned the disk in his hand to catch light in the little grooves.

"Early writing. Secret, sometimes." She touched one of the twigs wonderingly, very gently, as though she might wake it. "I wonder what it says."

"It's a love note," Ida said. "That's the face of the lover. It says—"

"My heart is yours forever," Hadrian intoned. "Meet me in the old oak grove beyond the cornfields and let me prove how much I love you."

"All that in three twigs," Curran marveled. He turned it; they studied the face again.

"Not," Campion decided, "a love token. Look at that weird chin."

"Love is blind?" Ida suggested.

"Mine never is."

"Campion, you are such a romantic," Beatrice murmured. "Still. There is something . . ."

"Maybe it's not a person," Curran guessed. "Maybe a bird? It's a beaky thing for certain, and that would explain the chin. The no chin."

"Wouldn't explain the hair."

"Is that really hair?"

"Some flowing plumage, you think?"

"It's a hood," Beatrice said suddenly. "It's hiding the chin. I've seen that profile in my father's collection . . . But where?" she wondered, as they looked at her expectantly.

"Ask him," Curran said simply. "This afternoon. Take this—"

"No, Curran. You found it. You should be the one to show it—"

He grinned. "Shovel found it. Anyway, we all want to know, and no telling when he'll loom at us out of whatever fog he's in again." He folded her hand around the mystery. "Of course, you might mention my name."

She slid the disk into her pocket and, a little later, drove back across the bridge, leaving the others to catch the trams, since no one else knew what to do with a car. She left it under the jealous and attentive care of the royal chauffeur, who had taught her how to drive.

Peverell Castle, named after the ancient line of Belden's rulers, had been a drafty, thick-walled, narrow-windowed, many-turreted fortress when it was first built near the bank of the Stirl a couple of centuries after the school on the hill had opened. The realm of Belden had been pounded together by tooth, nail, sword, and bow after the upstart invader, Oroh, had gotten lost looking for another land, anchored his ships in the fog on the Stirl, and led his army ashore. His bard, Declan, wandering across the land with the king and memorializing his battles with an infusion of glory and proper rhyme, had fallen in love with the plain. He returned to it upon relinquishing his position, went to live in an ancient watchtower on top of the hill among the oak and the standing stones, where he was sought out by would-be bards for his great gifts. So the school on the hill had come into existence, built to house students and teachers over the frigid winters on the plain. The rulers of Belden took their time settling somewhere. Moving from court to court across the realm periodically exhausted the coffers of their hosts and kept them from spending their money on armies. Finally, the realm quieted. Irion, the seventh of the Peverells to rule Belden, looked about for a place to keep his court and built it along the Stirl.

The original castle had long been swallowed up in many layers of changing fashions. Beatrice had explored all of it in her early years. The servants got used to finding the princess anywhere at all: in the laundry room examining water pipes, following the line of an ancient wall into the butler's pantry, in the wine cellar with her face smudged, her hair veiled with cobwebs, trying to see the blocked-up archway behind the wine racks. Her father, King Lucian, encouraged her, finding books and old maps for her in his library, showing her secret passageways and where the dungeons had been bricked over for a plumbing sluice. At formal court functions, she found him often in conversation with the sour-eyed Jonah Cle, who, otherwise impeccable, always looked as though he had just dunked his head in a bucket of cold water. Their words, glinting, mysterious references to history, old ballads, to a past older than she could yet imagine, invariably sent her back to her father's library. Somehow—maybe asking the right question, venturing a little-known detail of her own explorations—she began to be included, welcomed into their discussions.

And now, she thought with wonder, digging the disk out of her pocket before the chambermaid disposed of her dirty clothes, she worked for Jonah Cle.

Showered, freshly coiffed, and dressed in what she called her marzipan clothes, pastel and sugary, she put the disk back into a pocket, where it sagged in the thin, creamy silk frock like cannon shot. She took it back out; she and her lady-in-waiting studied it doubtfully.

"A ribbon?" she suggested.

"Must you, Princess Beatrice?"

"Yes, I must. Or else back into my pocket it goes."

"Well, we can't have that." She picked a thin gold chain out of Beatrice's jewel box, threaded it into the disk, and clasped it around the princess's neck, where it hung gracelessly within her rope of pearls. They studied it again, the tall, rangy Beatrice with her gold-brown hair and lightly freckled face, her calm cobalt eyes, and the willowy, elegant Lady Ann Never, with her critical green eyes, her black, sleek hair, and her unfailing sense of fashion.

"Can't you hide it in your shoe?" she asked, pained. "It's really dreadful."

Beatrice laughed. "My father will love it."

Her mother did not. Queen Harriet, standing next to the king in the reception line, looked at it incredulously, then closed her eyes upon it and her daughter. It was a rather moldy shade of green, Beatrice knew, and it had fallen chicken-track-side up above her beaded neckline. The frothy afternoon frock didn't show it to its best advantage. But the king didn't care.

"Happy birthday, Father," she said, kissing his cheek.

"What in the world is that?" he asked, his eyes already riveted.

"I have no idea. Curran unearthed it with his shovel this morning."

"I hope you are giving it to me as my birthday present."

"I would love to, but I believe Master Cle should make that gesture."

"He's not here yet," the king murmured, turning the disk to its hidden side. "He'll never know."

The queen cleared her throat, indicated the long line of well-wishers that Beatrice had effectively brought to a standstill. She moved out of the way, joined the group of her siblings, their various guests, mates, and children.

"Hello, Bea." Harold, oldest son and heir, handed her a glass of champagne off a passing tray. He was quite tall, big-boned, and red-haired, a throwback, their father said, to the primitive Peverells. "Been digging up the city again? And wearing it, I see." He raised his own glass toward the latest of the succession of appendages on his arm. "Do you know Lady Primula Willoughby? My sister Princess Beatrice."

"Yes, of course," Beatrice and Lady Primula said together, both smiling hugely and both wondering, the princess guessed, where on earth they had met. Lady Primula, with apple cheeks and corn-silk hair, looked alarmingly full of crisp country air, and Beatrice, who spent her life in holes, could barely find her way out of the city. They were diverted by the young son of Beatrice's sister, Charlotte, plopping himself abruptly on the floor and beginning to crawl away between feet.

"Marcus!" Charlotte cried, making a dive for him. "Come and kiss your auntie Beatrice." She swooped him up and deftly plunked him into Beatrice's hold, where he promptly began teething on the disk. "Ah, no, Marcus!" Charlotte chided ineffectually. She took after their mother: ivory skin and hair, all cheekbones and fluttery blue eyes. She took a swallow of champagne and a closer look at what her son was biting. "Nasty thing—whatever is it, Bea?"

"I don't know," she answered. "Something we just dug up."

"What a peculiar thing to have around your neck. Do you mind Marcus chewing on it?"

"Well, it's been buried in a hole under some plumbing pipes for at least decades," Beatrice answered amiably. "I doubt that much could hurt it now."

Charlotte's eyes widened. She downed her champagne, plucked the boy from Beatrice's arms, and winced at the sudden bellow in her ear. Beatrice drank what Marcus hadn't kicked out of her glass and looked around for Jonah Cle.

The hall was filling rapidly. Musicians played softly in the gallery above the hall, sweet notes from flute and violin echoing purely within the ancient walls. Only the vastness of the room and the massive stone hearth, big enough to hold hundred-year-old oak logs and guarded by dragons, was left of King Irion's great hall, where his knights had tossed bones to the hunting dogs as they ate their supper. The walls had gone through various transformations through the centuries. They were overlaid with wood now, painted, and hung with the framed faces of every ancestor the present royal family possessed, it seemed. Past watched the present goings-on with varying degrees of interest and approval. Couches and chairs and potted plants were scattered everywhere; everyone stood around them, talking across them with a great deal of vigor, clusters growing deeper as the reception line dwindled. A tiered cake half as big as the hearth stood on a table at the other end of the room. An army of servants, bearing trays of champagne and elegant little savories, followed their own mysterious patterns through the crowd. Beatrice, listening absently to her other brother, Damon, and his beautiful, garrulous betrothed describe endless wedding plans, finally saw Jonah's harrowed, sardonic face across the room. His charming wife, Sophy, hand on his arm, was drawing him toward the end of the reception line. Phelan flanked him on the other side, his expression imperturbable while his eyes searched the room for escape. Only Sophy, tossing comments to friends as they passed, sailed with oblivious good humor through the crush.

Beatrice waited a few minutes, until they had greeted the king. Jonah lingered there; Phelan, his face loosening as he sighted a friend, plunged one way into the currents; Sophy, waving, went another. Beatrice moved then, as the long line finally came to an end, and the king turned to speak to Jonah.

The king had evidently asked about the peculiarity adorning his daughter; they were both looking for Beatrice before she reached them.

"Princess," Jonah Cle said a trifle tiredly, as she came up. He looked very pale and very well scrubbed. "You look lovely. I would scarcely have recognized you."

"Thank you, I think, Master Cle. And so do you."

"What have you found for me?"

"Curran found it," she said, feeling for the chain clasp. "He asked me to give it to you."

"I was hoping," the king interposed, "you might consider it my birthday present." He had his own fine collection of oddments, many given to him by Jonah. "It would be a gracious gesture and very much appreciated."

"We have already left a very expensive present on your gift table."

"But this is merely a trifle, I'm sure. You probably have dozens of them."

Beatrice slid the stained copper disk off the chain, put it into Jonah's hand. The runes were up; he studied them silently a moment, then turned it over to reveal the hooded face.

Beatrice saw his eyes widen. Then his fingers closed abruptly over the disk; he threw back his head and laughed, an open and genuine amusement that caused heads to turn, Phelan's startled face among them.

He opened his hand again, offered the disk to the king. "Take it, with all my good wishes. Happy birthday, Your Majesty."

"But what is it?" he demanded.

"What does it say?" Beatrice pleaded.

Jonah was silent again, weighing words along with the disk on his palm. Then he gave up, flipped the disk lightly in the air, caught it, and held it out again to the king. "You both enjoy a challenge. The weave is there, the thread is there. Find and follow."

"But—" Beatrice and her father said at once. But the queen was suddenly among them, drawing the king's attention to the Master of Ceremonies at her side.

"Your Majesty," he said softly. "The guest bard from the school is about to sing. Then Prince Harold will make his toast to you, and you will speak after. Then the Royal Bard will sing his birthday composition to you, after which they will cut the cake."

"We all must gather near the table," the queen said.

"Yes, my dear." The king took the disk, dropped it resignedly into his pocket, and held out his arm to her.

"Come along, Beatrice."

"Yes, Mother."

"I need a drink," she heard Jonah mutter, as she turned to follow in the royal wake, then, in the musician's gallery, the guest from the school stroked her harp and loosed her voice like some rich, wild, haunting echo out of the singing bones of the plain in a ballad about the Peverell kings that was as old as Belden.

Chapter Four

History next records Nairn's presence, unlikely as it seems, at the ceremony after the Battle of the Welde during which Anstan ceded the Kingdom of the Marches to the invader, King Oroh, who was busily amassing the five kingdoms that would become Belden. Oroh's bard, Declan, was also present. The exact nature of his extraordinary gifts is nebulous, and most often a matter of poetry rather than record. Whatever they were, his place was always at the king's side. An odd tale rippled down the centuries from that ceremony, in ballads, in poetry fragments, and as metaphor: Nairn returns to Declan the jewels he had taken from the older bard's harp. In some tales, he throws them at Declan. How he acquired them is also a matter of folklore, especially of the Marches. Some say he stole them; others that he took them with magic; though that is never adequately explained, certainly not to the historian. After that, Nairn once again vanishes from even the footnotes of history.

He reappears, a few years later, at the bardic school that Declan started after King Oroh finished his campaigns. Pleading age and long years of service, Declan relinquished his duties as Oroh's bard and returned to Stirl Plain, now under Oroh's rule. There, on a small hill crowned with ancient standing stones and a watchtower overlooking the Stirl River, he retired to a life of contemplation. It did not last long, as bards and would-be bards from the five conquered kingdoms were drawn by his great knowledge and abilities to learn from him. There, on that hill, Nairn steps back into history.

> There he stands between two kings,
> The bard with his bitter eyes.
> His hand he lifts, and down he flings
> The jewels as he cries:
> "What worth are these from a bard who sings
> Treachery and lies?"

FROM "THE BATTLE OF THE WELDE" BY GARETH LOMILY BROWN

> Fickle as jewels on a harp.

NORTHERN SAYING

The Battle of the Welde lasted three days. By the time it started, Nairn, who had beaten a marching rhythm for Anstan's army through the western mountains of the Marches, and summoned the clans with his bladder-pipe, then drummed the army east and south to meet the invader, had calluses on his calluses. He had never traveled so quickly or played so hard in his life. The Welde, a broad, lovely river valley along the border between the Marches and Stirl Plain, had laid down a soft carpet of creamy yellow wildflowers. So Nairn saw it at the beginning of the battle, when he blew the long, coiled, battered cornu someone had handed him and told him to sound. By the end of the battle, there were a few flowers left untrampled and about as many of Anstan's warriors. King Oroh sent his bard, Declan, across the field to meet the king's emissary and demand that Anstan surrender his kingdom.

Anstan, furious and heartsick, answered with what he, not being particularly musical, considered a last, futile gesture of contempt. He sent his bedraggled drummer on foot across the ravaged, bloody field where nothing moved, nothing spoke except the flies and the flocks of crows, to meet with Oroh's bard.

Declan rode a white horse. He was dressed in dark, rich leather and silk; he carried his harp on his shoulder. As always, he was unarmed. He reined in his mount at the center of the field between the two royal camps and waited for the young, grimy minstrel in his bloodstained robe and sandals with one sole tied to his foot with rope where the laces had rotted during the long march. He still carried the cornu over his shoulder, the last instrument he had played to call retreat.

Nairn stopped in front of the bard; they looked at one another silently.

"You asked," Declan said finally, "what I am."

The taut mouth in the stained white mask of a face moved finally, let loose a few words. "Yes. I asked." He was silent again, his bleak, crow eyes moving over Declan, narrowing as memory broke through, a moment of wonder instead of bitterness. "You're Oroh's spy," he said tersely. "And his bard. But what else? I didn't sing those jewels out of your harp. You gave them to me."

The strange eyes glinted at him suddenly, catching light like metal. "You took them," Declan said, and raised his eyes to ask of the sky, "Is this entire land ignorant of its own magic?"

"What?"

Declan tossed a hand skyward, relinquishing a comment. "I'll answer that when you've learned to understand the question."

"You'll forgive me if this is the last I ever want to see of your face."

"You may not be given the choice." Nairn, staring at him, drew breath to protest; the bard didn't yield him that choice, either. "Since you brought the matter up, we should deal with it. King Oroh will accept Anstan's sword and crown and his pledge of fealty at dawn tomorrow."

"Dawn," Nairn interrupted recklessly. "What makes you think King Anstan will still be around?"

"Because I will be watching," Declan answered softly, and Nairn, staring again, felt the short hairs prickle at his neck. "In return for Anstan's pledge, he may keep one holding in the Marches for his family. As to other matters, the size of his retinue, tributes to King Oroh, such things will be left to the king's counselors. For tomorrow, the king will be content with the sight of an unarmed, uncrowned man with one knee in the dirt in front of him. That is the price of peace."

"I can't tell King Anstan that," Nairn said flatly. "He'd kill me."

"He should honor you."

"For what? Blaring a retreat out of this poor dented wheel of a horn?"

"He should honor you," Declan repeated, "for all that you should have been able to do for him."

"What—"

Again, the bard's hand rose, inviting Nairn's attention to the disaster around them.

"Who do you think you fought?" There was an odd note of exasperation in the fine, calm voice. "This entire field is ringed with King Oroh's army. Most of them just stood and watched you flail at one another in the mist."

Nairn felt his heart close like a fist, the blood vanish out of his face. The bard turned his horse, but not before Nairn glimpsed his weary revulsion.

"King Oroh's tent," he reminded Nairn without looking back. "At dawn."

"You're a bard," Nairn pleaded to the retreating figure. "Put some poetry in the message, or I'll be out among the dead at dawn, with the crows picking at my eyes."

Declan glanced around at that, his expression composed again. "I've heard what you can do. Find your own poetry in that."

Stumbling back across the darkening battlefield, ignoring the black clouds of crows scattering up around him as he passed, Nairn managed to fashion King Oroh's demand into words more akin to a preference. Anstan, slumped on a chair in his tent, surrounded by his generals, listened wordlessly to Nairn's message. He gave an inarticulate growl, seized his crown with both hands, and flung it out the tent door. Then he followed it, stopping at the threshold long enough to say,

"All of you. Here with me before sunrise."

He went out to mourn under the moon. So did Nairn, in an opposite direction, carrying his harp, which he hadn't played in weeks. Whether the grieving king heard the sweet, melancholy harping, or he played only to the moonstruck faces of the dead, Nairn didn't bother to wonder. He only hoped that the tin-eared king wouldn't mistake him for Declan and send a knife after him in the dark.

But Anstan surprised him in the predawn hour, when Nairn made his way into the king's tent.

"Bring your harp," Anstan said tersely. "You honored the dead of the Marches last night." He flicked a glance over the unkempt bard and gestured to a servant. "Find him something decent to put on. And wash your face. You look half-dead yourself. There must be some reason," Nairn heard him grumble to his generals, "that barbarian gives his bard such status. Not that I can see it. We can at least pretend we have what he has."

Later, kneeling beside Anstan in the mist-soaked mud churned up by constant comings and goings outside the new king's tent, Nairn watched an earthworm undulate between two clods of dirt and felt that even it had more status than he. Anstan's crown and sword appeared in a corner of his vision, laid as low as they could get, on the mud at Oroh's feet. It was then that he opened his clenched fist, let the jewels fall out of it to smolder like embers in the muck.

"What's this?" Oroh demanded. He was a tall, brawny man with tangled red hair and a deep, rumbling voice. A line of toggles made of boar tusks kept his loose tunic closed over his shirt and the flaps of his boots fastened. His crown was a jagged circle of golden tusks. He picked his words with less certainty than Declan did; Nairn heard the same unfamiliar lilt to his phrases.

"Jewels from your bard's harp," Nairn said, too dispirited for courtesy. What king would expect good manners from a worm? "I took them from him."

There was a moment's utter silence on the field. Not even a crow commented.

Then Oroh hunkered down in front of the young bard, to his astonishment. "Look at me," the king said. "Give me my title."

Nairn raised his head. The king's eyes were the color of hazelnuts; they held Nairn's for a long time, studying him, until Nairn heard himself say, "Yes, my lord."

Oroh turned his head finally, shifted that piercing, unblinking gaze to Declan. "How did he take them?"

"They came to him, my lord."

"Indeed," the king breathed, and straightened. "You are fortunate in your bard, sir."

"Yes," Anstan agreed blankly, and added with bitter precision, "my lord."

"Perhaps too fortunate. He's a weapon, and I will add him to the salvage of battle. Rise."

"He's only a marching bard," Anstan protested bewilderedly as he got to his feet.

"Well, you won't need him now." Oroh turned, gesturing them to follow him into the tent. "Where I am from, bards are valued highly, and you will receive compensation for this one. He may go back now for his other instruments and possessions." He nodded to a pair of guards, then raised a brow at Declan, asking a silent question.

"They'll do, my lord," Declan said briefly. "His ignorance is abysmal."

"Ah? His misfortune is now our fortune." He turned his curious gaze from Nairn to the guards. "Go with him."

They took him back across the field. While they walked, Nairn watched warriors searching for the wounded startle sudden, whirling black clouds of crow into the air. Nairn's own thoughts whirled as darkly. He had failed, in Declan's eyes, at some portentous task that might have turned the tide of yesterday's battle. How, exactly, he could not imagine. Because Nairn had failed so miserably at that, Declan expected nothing more than failure from him. Singing the jewels out of the harp had been an aberration: an impulse of deep, impossible desire in which there was no hope, only longing. He felt very much like that again: filled with desire without a gnat's worth of hope to get himself as far from that sad, smeared disaster and as far from Declan's eerie eyes as he could get.

If he could crawl like a snake through the dead, if he could fly among the crows . . .

Lacking any better ideas, he left the guards rummaging through Anstan's possessions and walked into the back partition of the tent, where he had left his things scattered among the useless paraphernalia of war. Neither the marching drum nor the battered cornu would fit into his pack, so he left them there reluctantly. He slit a seam along the floor of the tent with one of the generals' swords, slid himself, his harp and pack and a pair of somebody's boots out the back of the tent. He made his way quickly among the morning campfires of the remnants of Anstan's army. The glum warriors watched him leave, raised a cup or two for luck. Then Nairn imitated the earthworm, slithering on his belly among the unburied dead, and made his way with more haste than caution to the thick trees along the river.

No one rode him down, dragged him back. But someone watched him, he realized as he stood at the water's edge. He felt that eerie prickling of awareness glide all through his body, chilling his skin, stiffening his bones. He looked behind him, then abruptly up, and found a snowy owl on a branch, staring down at him out of wide, golden eyes.

A voice out of nowhere filled his head, at once lilting and sinewy.

You found me once. You found me twice. The third time is the charm.

A shout leaped out of Nairn that must have opened the eyes of the dead, and he began to run.

He ran for days, it felt like, weeks, months, before he began to feel safe again and slowed a little. He disappeared into the southern forests of the Marches, keeping to small villages, the less ostentatious manor houses, crofters' cottages so ancient their stones must have put down roots. As the bedraggled marching bard of the last king of the Marches, he was given sympathy and honor. Ballads he composed about the Battle of the Welde opened doors for him, gave him shelter, for events were so new few realized, in those quiet, unchanging places, that the ancient court of the northern kingdom was no more. Nairn managed to stay ahead of King Oroh's soldiers and officials, hiding in isolated corners of the realm, where the oldest words, tales, and musical instruments might linger for centuries, and gossip tended to be a season or two older than events. So he learned, sometime after the facts, that Oroh had taken the last of the five kingdoms and had named his realm Belden.

By then he had been roaming during fair seasons and finding places to winter in comfortable manses owned by farmers and merchants who had managed to elude the new king's attention. As always, he paid for his lodging with his music and ferreted out ancient, unfamiliar songs while he was there. He scarcely noticed the passing of time, only that the king's name, his face on coins, became more and more Oroh's instead of Anstan's, even in the timeless backwaters and pockets of the land. The old kings were easily confused in places that distant from the ancient court, whose rulers were known mostly as names in ballads about the battles they had fought. Imperceptibly, the shape of the world changed during Nairn's travels, until there were no longer five kingdoms, only one, and Oroh was its king. Nairn was not paying much attention to where he was in the world one late summer when he passed out of the pleasant fields and woodlands of east Belden and onto Stirl Plain.

He recognized it by the vast, flat green sea of grass he walked across, which began to flow and swirl into gentle hillocks and knolls around him the farther he wandered into it. Strangely colored standing stones had been planted here and there across the plain, some crowning knolls, others marching along the river a ways, then stopping for no reason. Solitary trees grown huge and snarled with age stood sentinel on other hills. The Stirl River, welling up somewhere out of the northern mountains, cut the plain in two as it meandered toward the sea. No one lived along it except the stones, an unexpected, creamy yellow, all of them, in a place where stones in the river, boulders thrusting up through the grass, were drab as slate.

Nairn was alone on the plain, it seemed after a day or three. Mountain and forest transformed into distant brushes of dark on the far horizons. By day, the world was soundless but for the wind, leaves chattering in the tree he rested under, the occasional passing greeting of a hunting falcon or a lark. By night, the only lights he saw glittered high above his head, too far for shelter or comfort. He played to the stars, his only audience. When he slept under a tree or a stone, wrapped in his cloak, head on his pack, breathing the scents of grass and earth and the great, worn lichen-stained slabs, he heard the wind whispering into his dreams, in a language as ancient as the standing stones.

Sometimes he heard fragments of an unfamiliar, haunting music: from the singing wind, maybe, or the river water, or perhaps the voices of the standing stones resonating to the shifting fingers of moonlight as it drifted over the plain. The music would fade as he woke, struggling to open his eyes, glimpse the elusive musician, and finally seeing that no one else was there; he was alone on the plain, playing to himself in his dreams.

One night, he saw the blurred, red glow of firelight on a distant hill. He walked in that direction the next day. That evening, he saw it again: a handful of red stars spiraling upward as though behind the windows of a tower. Another day brought him close enough to see the crown of standing stones upon a hill beside the river, and within the ring, a dark stone tower. As he neared the hill, he saw it clearly: a broad spiral of fieldstones shaped into what might have been a watchtower, left from sometime beyond memory, when there was something worth protecting on the plain. Through the narrow windows winding up the sides, he had seen its night fires; they had beckoned to him across the plain.

Newer stonework, huddled up against the tower, was still growing. Piles of stone pulled out of the earth and from the river-bed lay among stacked logs. A well-trampled path between the top of the hill and the river had worn away the grass to uncover dark, rich soil. The logs, he guessed, would have come from the thick forests to the north and west, carried down by water to stop at this unlikely place, where no one but mice and meadowlarks seemed to live. But as he made his way toward the path, he saw other stone walls among the trees along the riverbank. A village was growing there, he realized with surprise. For no particular reason he could see: it was no less lonely and isolated than any other bend in the river. But people were building there. He caught the sweet, dank, familiar smell of broken earth, uprooted grass from fields and gardens he couldn't see across the river. And then another familiar whiff: pig. People had come to stay. Curious now, and hungry as well, for his stash of bread and cheese had dwindled to a crust and a rind, he quickened his pace, turned onto the path running up the hill.

As he walked between two of the bulky, sun-warmed standing stones, he heard, from within the half-finished building or the tower, a piper piping.

After a breath of silence, a scattering of pipes joined it, raggedly but with spirit. Nairn stopped. It was a marching tune, one of the many he had played to get Anstan's army through the mountains to the Welde. It had been well-known there: a folk song of the Marches. But here, on Stirl Plain, it sounded in his ear like a wrong note, a warning. The song should have stayed north where it was born, not traveled down here in the mind of someone else who had heard it, perhaps again and again, as the army slogged mindlessly, doggedly toward its bitter defeat.

He gazed at the closed plank door with the sheep's bell dangling from the latch, a breath away from turning, walking down the hill and vanishing among the trees along the riverbank, for no clear reason, just a prickling of old, sour memory. Then wind blustered over him, blown from the open back of the building, engulfing him in smells of meat cooking, hot bread, burning sap.

He turned, followed it helplessly.

It brought him past the newer walls expanding outward and around much of the tower, to a door opening into the bottom of the tower itself. He looked in. A young woman with long, pale, curly hair stirred a cauldron over an ancient hearth. She turned at his step across the threshold. Her face stopped his heart.

It was a perfect oval, skin luminous as spindrift and pearl, cheekbones like half-moons, and a mouth, in all that pearl, as full and sweetly red as strawberry. Her eyes were pale green. The expression in them as she saw the lank-haired stranger with his harp and his pack and the hollows of hunger in his face was both discerning and reserved; it made her seem older than she looked.

She spoke, and his heart started up again, erratically thumping. Low and melodious, her voice sounded like some fine, rare instrument. In that moment, he glimpsed the proud towers, the pennants, the rich tapestries in which such voices might be heard, and knew why, in all his wanderings, he had never encountered such music before.

"Take a bowl from that stack," the wondrous instrument said. "They'll be finished playing and down in a moment. You've come just in time to help finish the roof. There's water in that pitcher, and bread— Ah, you found it."

"Thank you," he said huskily around a bite. He forced his eyes from her face and found her hands. Two poems, he thought, entranced: long, tapered, graceful fingers, the nails a bit work worn, but warmly suffused with rose, while in the veins along her ivory wrists, the blood ran blue.

He asked with an effort, not really caring, just trying, now, to drag his attention from her fingers, "What is this place?"

"You don't know?"

"I'm on my way across the plain. It's a broad, lonely stretch of nowhere, with no one to talk to but those great stones. I saw the firelight on a hill a few nights ago and came looking for it. Then I smelled your stew."

She smiled; he watched the pale skin glide like silk over her bones. "I am still learning how to cook," she said, ladling stew into a bowl. "We all do what work we can, and I'm no good at lifting stones or shaping logs." She dropped a spoon into the bowl and handed it to him. "Be careful; it is very hot. When I saw your harp, I assumed that you had come to join the school." A hot bite rendered him mute; he could only raise his brows at her until she enlightened him. "Declan's school."

He swallowed too quickly; the pain made his voice harsh. "Declan."

"King Oroh's bard. You harp; you must have heard of him. He came here to live when he relinquished his position at King Oroh's court two years ago. He fell in love with this plain. He says that wind and leaves and stones here speak the oldest language in the world and that he can teach us to understand it. By then, he had played everywhere in the five—Belden, it is now. He wasn't alone here long. Rumor found him, and then we did."

"How?" His voice still sounded seared. "How did rumor find a way across this emptiness?"

"Who knows? A bird told a fox who told a tinker's mule . . . Word traveled. Declan played for my father, Lord Deste, at his court in Estmere when I was fifteen, six months after my brothers battled King Oroh for Estmere. I left home to come to Stirl Plain the day I learned Declan was here. My father and brothers tried to stop me, but . . . His music has that effect. I wasn't his first student, and more musicians kept coming after I did.

Winter here is pitiless, and this tower grew too small for us. So we began to build around it."

A ragged flow of voices preceded the clatter of feet down the ancient watchtower steps behind her. Nairn shifted his eyes, a bite of mutton frozen between his teeth. The lean, fox-haired bard spiraled into view first, his harp over his shoulder, and a shepherd's pipe in one hand. He looked back at Nairn without surprise.

"You took your time," he commented.

Nairn, still transfixed, stared at him, as the students, a motley crowd of men and women of varying ages and circumstances, jostled past them. He felt his skin constrict suddenly, as he guessed that those owl's eyes must have watched every step he had taken across the plain, and maybe even down his secret, crooked path before that.

"The third time," he whispered, hearing the charm behind him begin to ladle stew for the others. "How did you know I would find you?"

"Where else," Declan asked, his voice mingling patience and exasperation, "in this utterly oblivious land, could you go?"

It was a while before Nairn understood that question, a little longer than that before he realized how right the bard was, and far too late when he understood at last how wrong.

Chapter Five

The guest bard, Zoe Wren, was cooking breakfast for her father in the ancient cavern of the tower kitchen when Phelan knocked and walked in. She broke off midline of the ribald song she had encountered at the Merry Rampion sometime in the wee hours after the king's birthday and reached for a couple more eggs without bothering to look. She knew the sound of his knuckle and the sound of his knock in exactly the middle of which slat in the door ever since they were both five, and the knock was a lot lower down on the door. They had known each other that long. Wood wailed against stone as he pulled out a chair. The scarred deal table creaked as his knee hit a leg; the glass teapot and butter dish lids trembled; one elbow thumped as she broke an egg. It splashed, as the other thumped, into the bowl of liquid, floating suns.

He spoke then. "Someday," he warned. "Someday you'll think it's me, and it won't be—"

"Nonsense. I feel you come in like an old familiar song, only without the sound." She turned finally, laughing at herself. "You know what I mean."

"No. I don't." He was smiling, maybe at the sight of her bare feet, the sleeves of her school robe shoved back to her elbows over yesterday's silks, a strand of her rumpled dark hair trying to join the eggs in the bowl. "Late night?"

She nodded, gazing at him a moment longer, sensing things awry, hidden behind his smile. She turned back to the old iron stove, dropped a lump of butter into the pan heating on it. Her own elegant face, lean and brown, hid little and flashed color, from her shrewd green eyes and her holly-berry mouth. Phelan's pale coloring had first caught her curious gaze when she had come out of the refectory kitchen upstairs where her mother was cooking, and saw the small boy with his duck-fluff hair and his wide eyes as opaque as mist, sitting silently, expressionlessly beside his father.

"I stayed with Chase," she said over her shoulder. "Some bards out of the north came down to hear what kind of music the students play. They taught us some wonderfully rowdy songs. I just got back. How is your father?"

"Why?"

"You have that expression on your face."

She heard him lean back hard in his chair until it creaked. He answered dispassionately enough. "I found him in the wasteland across Dockers Bridge at dawn yesterday. That gave him a few hours to get cleaned up for the king's party. He was sitting in the mud by the river, singing to the standing stones. He wonders how I find him, but even he is predictable. I just look around his most recent dig site." He paused, added restively, "I don't know what he's looking for. I wish I did. Once I thought he was wandering around Caerau digging graves, trying to find his own death. But he keeps finding treasures instead . . ."

Zoe upended a chopping board full of onions, chives, sausages, into the frothing butter. She stirred them, said slowly, "Death is easy enough to find. Isn't it? If you truly want it. So he must want something else."

"He has everything else," Phelan said, then paused. His mouth crooked. "Except music. But if he put me in this school to make up for his own abysmal failure here, it makes no sense to let me turn my back to all I've learned and walk away—"

"No," Zoe said pointedly, rapping the spoon on the pan for emphasis. "No more than it makes sense for you to want to."

He ignored that. "He's rich in so much else. Everything he touches turns to gold. The King of Belden calls him friend despite his eccentricities. Even my mother still loves him."

She glanced back at him. "Even you do."

He flung up a hand. "But why?"

Zoe thought, but had nothing to add to the familiar litany of conjectures about Jonah that they had strung together through the years. She added salt to the mix, stirred it, sent the smells swirling through the kitchen.

"How was your class this morning?" she asked to get them off the labyrinthine subject. "Everyone awake?"

"Except me. I've started them memorizing the ninety verses of the 'Catalog of Virtues.' It's enough to drive everyone to slavering mayhem in the streets of Caerau. Except for Frazer. He's inhaling it all in through his pores. He thinks there's magic between the lines."

Her eyes widened at the word; she stared hard into the pan, turning things mindlessly with her fork until the onion fumes bit at her eyes. She blinked. "Magic."

"I don't know what he's talking about. Except what you did yesterday at the king's party. That song—I swear it nearly melted the expression on my father's face. That was magic."

She smiled. "Thank you."

"Where did you find it? It sounded as though you dug it out of a barrow."

She nodded, peppering the eggs vigorously. "It's very old. Quennel taught it to me."

"The Royal Bard? That Quennel?"

"Yes."

"He wouldn't part with a song if you held fire to his feet."

"He likes me," she answered cheerfully. "He says I'm what the plain would sound like if it sang, wind, bird, bone, and stone. Don't ask me. That's what he said. What exactly did Frazer say to you?"

"Exactly, I don't remember. Something about secrets. The secrets of the bardic arts. When he would be taught them."

"Strange," she breathed. "Maybe you should do your research paper on that."

"On what? A connection between magic and poetry?"

"When Oroh fought his only battle in the Marches, according to the 'The Lament for the Marches,' his bard Declan raised a fog with his poetry that blinded King Anstan's army so badly they could not recognize one another's faces. Anstan's army fought itself; Oroh's mostly stood and watched." Phelan was silent behind her. "The magic was in the words. The words were the magic."

"That's one reference," he said dryly. "I just want to get out of here, not spend half my life tracking down obscure incidents of bardic magic. Let Frazer write that paper."

"Maybe I'll write it," she said recklessly. She beat the eggs until they frothed, then added them to the pan, musing over the question. "I wonder what caused Frazer to ask."

"I think something he read."

"Well, what?"

"I have no idea." His voice shrugged the subject away. "Some old ballad, probably. He'll figure it out, whatever it is he wants to know. He's bright enough."

She drew breath to speak, then stared down into the pan again, without moving, wondering what in her head had leaped at the word without understanding the question at all, and what in Phelan, with all his gifts, failed to resonate with any interest whatsoever.

She heard her father's steps on the tower stairs and reached for a spatula to turn the eggs. The smells had wafted to him, pulled him out of the ancient room he used for his office. The chambers of the school steward were as old as the school itself: the four tower rooms up the winding stairs, the hoary kitchen at the bottom, with its huge maw of a hearth that could roast an entire sheep in the days when one sheep could feed the entire student body. Zoe loved the tower. The smoke-stained walls, their stones dug out of field and river, still spoke, she thought, of a time so long ago that the school on the hill with its broken tower and the tiny village called Caerau were surrounded only by grass and fields and the great standing stones so old nobody remembered when or how they had come to the plain.

Now the oldest school building housed the masters in elegant rooms pieced together out of the hive of tiny stone cells the early school had occupied. The masters' cook was upstairs in the pristine modern kitchen, supervising their breakfasts. Zoe's mother had been the cook there until she died. She taught her very small daughter this and that when she was very young, to keep her from running underfoot in the busy kitchen. Even then, tiny Zoe's singing, vigorous and pure as she stirred the flour and butter and pan juices into gravy, riveted the masters' attention.

She pulled plates out of the cupboard, lined them on the table, and divided the eggs between them. The butter was on the table, the fruit in its bowl, the bread already cut on its board. She sat finally. Her father, a tall, spare, graying man with the tidy habits becoming to a steward, greeted Phelan without surprise and asked about his paper. Zoe watched their faces together: the son her father hadn't gotten around to having, the intelligent, calm, unambiguous father Phelan wished he had. Her thoughts strayed. The Royal Bard had invited her to sing again, during the visit of Queen Harriet's brother. He was Lord Grishold, Duke of what was once one of the five kingdoms, in the mountains of west Belden. His new bard would be traveling with him. Zoe had never met him. The previous bard in Lord Grishold's court had forgotten his verses, or mistuned a string, or otherwise embarrassed himself, and had relinquished his position several months before, pleading age. He was upstairs now, eating breakfast in the masters' refectory, preferring to live out his years in the genial city rather than among the gloomy crags of Grishold.

She mentioned as much to Phelan as they lingered over cups of tea and coffee, trying to delay the day.

"I've been asked to sing during the formal supper for the guests from Grishold. Are you coming?"

He looked blank. "I can't remember if we've been invited. I hope not."

Bayley Wren set his cup down, asked gently, "Is he missing again?"

"Vanished like the dew upon the sloe berry, after the birthday party. I don't think he even went home to change his clothes. I'm not sure where I'd look for him so soon. It's easier to find him when he's running out of money."

The steward raised his cup an inch, his pale eyes lowered, then set it down again. "You might try looking in the school's household records."

"For my father?"

"Well. I was thinking more of your paper."

"For some legendary stones?" Phelan said, still bewildered. "What would they be doing among the price of beer or a mended hole in a master's boot?"

Bayley gave his slow, thin smile that bracketed his mouth with lines inscribed, Zoe thought, by decades of such painstaking entries. "You'd be surprised at the odd things you can find in those records. They go back centuries, all the way to the first summer, when the first students began to put up the stone walls around this tower."

"But Bone Plain—it's likely no more than a poem. A legend. A communal dream that got handed down from imagination to imagination through the centuries. That's what most of the papers about it say. There's no proof it existed in any real place. Every standing stone in Belden has been linked to Bone Plain in one paper or another, and every argument to prove it circles back to poetry. More myth and dreams."

"Is it?" He sipped his cooling coffee. Zoe wondered, not for the first time, what was on his mind. "You said you'd picked it for an easy topic. It doesn't sound easy at all."

"It will be," Phelan insisted. "I'll write it with my eyes closed as soon as I figure out how to begin."

He took himself off to the library soon after. Bayley refilled his cup and carried it up into the tower. Zoe surveyed the mess in the kitchen, decided that it wasn't going anywhere, and went to give singing lessons to half a dozen beginning students.

They attracted an audience, the children with their pure, fluting voices, and Zoe tempering her own to roam in a high, sweet descant above theirs. A shadow crossed the open doorway of the small classroom, lingered. She flicked her eyes along it to its owner: the young, golden-haired Frazer, with his wolfish jawline and his light blue eyes burning with impatience, longing for mysteries, bewildered by his impulses and his own changing bones. Her voice had lured him, she realized; he was entranced, his eyes wide and cloudy, staring at her without recognition as though she had just sprung fully formed and unnamed from between the floorboards.

He waited there until she finished the lesson and sent the students flowing out the door around him. Then he stirred, and finally spoke.

"Zoe." Like Phelan, she was on that indeterminate border between student and master, given authority but as yet untitled. "I was wondering . . . I wanted to ask you something."

"About magic?" she guessed, and he flushed, his face tightening.

"I thought it was secret," he protested.

"It's so secret I don't know anything about it either. What

made you ask Phelan? I mean—I know why you would choose Phelan to ask, but what made you ask at all? Something you read?"

He was looking at her incredulously by then; he wandered into the room toward her, pulled by some private, wayward path. "How can you ask me that? I hear it in you. Every word you sing says magic. Says power. How could the word itself exist if it means nothing?"

She gazed back at him, startled, trying to imagine what he felt, what he meant.

He came closer, his burning eyes haunted with a passion he could scarcely name. Somehow, in the way she could sense Phelan before she saw him, or her father, she felt Frazer's blind hunger, his frustration, like something unruly, undefined, blundering its way into being.

He passed it to her, like a gift or a curse, she couldn't tell; she only knew that in that inexplicable, wordless moment, she recognized what it was he wanted.

He spoke finally, huskily. "Tell me what it is."

"I don't know." Her own voice had vanished. "I have glimpsed it, here and there, within the notes of ancient ballads, between the lines: the shadow, the footprint, of something ancient, powerful. Memories, maybe. Resonances."

"Yes," he said urgently. "Yes. Where do I go to learn more?"

"I don't know."

Still, his eyes clung to hers, wanting, willing answers out of her. You see it, too, he told her without words. You want it, too.

"Who will you ask?" she heard, and was uncertain which of them had spoken aloud.

She stepped back finally, drawing breath deeply as though she had been submerged in some timeless, nameless realm and had, for a moment, forgotten that she was human.

"I don't know," she said a third time, feeling at once shaken and inordinately curious. "We may—we may be seeing only the remnants of something long gone from this world. Maybe you and I were just born with primitive eyes. Or hearts. Born with a gift for something that doesn't exist anywhere any longer, and the recognition, the longing for it is all we'll ever know."

He swayed toward her, as though she, understanding it, had become part of his longing. His face, at once ardent and tentative, looked suddenly very young. She had learned to dance around such impulses; she slipped past him, was at the door as he turned, surprised, searching for her.

She said simply, "If I do stumble into an answer, I'll tell you. And you must tell me. Promise."

He nodded after a moment, said finally, "I promise," and she left him there, still wondering, from the look on his face, what had or hadn't happened.

She returned to the tower, went upstairs to take off her robe in her room, and downstairs again to see if the kitchen had somehow cleaned itself. It hadn't. But something of Frazer's chaotic impulses still clung to her thoughts; the chaos in the kitchen seemed to mirror them. She turned abruptly, went outside, across the school grounds, scarcely seeing the tranquil gardens, the lawns, the gnarled oak, the dreaming stones. She walked down the hill until she spotted a lumbering steam tram, and took it to the bottom. There, along the noisy waterfront, she walked again, on ancient cobbles past docks and fish markets and every kind of shop, until she reached a doorway with a painted sign above it: blue lilies cavorting in a ring beneath the sun's smiling face. The Merry Rampion, the sign proclaimed, and she went in.

There she found Chase Rampion drying glasses behind the bar. He noticed her and smiled like the sun, cheerful and benign, golden rays of his uncombed curly hair petaling out around his face. She went behind the bar, threw her arm around his neck, and kissed him, feeling like the parched traveler in the desert stumbling into the unexpected spring. When she loosed him finally, the world within her head had straightened itself out, grown familiar again. The handful scattered among the little wooden tables were chuckling; so was he, when he could finally speak.

"Good morning to you, too, love. What was that for?"

"I don't want to talk about it," she said, and sat down with him awhile to talk of everything but.

She found a note from the Royal Bard on the kitchen table next to the crusty frying pan when she got back.

A day later, she went down the hill again and walked in the opposite direction along the river to Peverell Castle. She wore her students' robe over the finest of her silks, long skirt and tunic and a colorful filmy scarf chosen to match the colors of the oak leaves dying and reviving on her robe. "I have several suggestions," Quennel had written in his fine, antique hand, "as to what you might sing for the Duke of Grishold's supper. Bring your harp."

He met her in a little antechamber off the minstrels' gallery. Decades ago, he had been a student at the school, then, briefly, a master, until the Royal Bard had suddenly and fortuitously died. Custom, which Declan himself had brought into Belden, demanded a competition of all bards interested in the position. In Declan's own turbulent times, after he had retired from Oroh's court and opened the school, the competition to choose his successor's successor had been fierce.

The numbers Quennel had bested were legendary: bards had come from all over the realm vying for the highest position; countless more had come to watch and listen. He had sung one song and everyone had put down their instruments in defeat. Or all their harp strings had snapped. Or one by one, over forty days and forty nights, he had picked them off, put them to shame, sent them packing. The truth of the matter depended on the ballad. Now he was aging, but still vigorous, a hale old man in a long robe the kingfisher blue of his eyes, his short ivory hair still springy and apt to curl if he neglected to prune it.

"Thank you for coming," he said, smiling fondly at her. He had brought his own harp with him, itself a thing of legend. The uncut jewels on its face were said to have fallen out of Declan's harp at his death. They had wandered the realm in the pockets of thieves, in the crowns of queens, having their own extraordinary adventures until chance or story found them a haven in Quennel's harp.

"I'm honored," Zoe answered, sitting on a bench beside him. Musicians waited their turns to play, or tuned their instruments in this room. As she took her harp from its case, she could almost hear centuries of overlapping notes echoing around her, resonating in her strings.

"Yes," the old bard agreed cheerfully, "you are. But so are you rare and wonderful, and I do all that I can to manipulate events so that I can hear that astonishing voice of yours. Have you had any thoughts about what you would like to sing for the duke?"

"A ballad about Grishold, I think. Beyond that—" She shook her head, guessing that he had already chosen for her.

"Yes," he said. "Yes. Of Grishold, most certainly." He hesitated disingenuously, continued, "I wondered if this perhaps had suggested itself to you: 'The Duel of the Kestrels.' Two rivals for the Duke—well, in the ballad they called him king, back then— the King of Grishold's daughter. You know it?"

"Of course. They had a competition with their falcons for the privilege of courting her. The one whose bird killed first would win her. It's a lovely song, wheeling and turning like the birds high in the air, crying out as they see what the nobles cannot: the princess in the distance, riding off with her true love." She plucked a string, added dubiously, "Do you think he might be offended? Considering that the princess's true love trounces her father roundly when he attacks to get her back."

"Offended by such a confection? It's a trifle, a fantasy, and your voice would make it a marvel, a shining jewel out of Grishold's past." He paused again. "There is, of course, the question of the different endings. Which do you prefer?"

"My favorite," she said, attuned to what was on his mind, "is the one where the kestrels fly in the opposite direction, for the language of birds is the language of love, at least once in their feathery lives, and they lead the scheming nobles away from the lovers."

"Yes," Quennel exclaimed happily. "My favorite as well."

"Though I do like the long, dark notes of the ending where nobles chop off her true love's head."

"Oh, no. Indeed, no."

"Too dark."

"Another supper, perhaps. Though," he said, lowering his own sinewy voice as though the nobles were listening, "I do love those notes, too. Yet so rarely is there an appropriate occasion for them . . ."

Zoe smiled, answered as softly, "We could sing it now, together. The hall is empty; the guards will never tell."

They tuned their harps, began the centuries-old ballad, with its unhappy ending most likely as close to the truth of the matter as a bard ever got.

They hadn't yet reached it themselves when the great hall began an eerie counterpoint of its own: voices, a great many steps, some slowing, others tapping away in a spiderweb of directions, laughter, exclamations, all tangled together and becoming noisier. Quennel, looking both annoyed and perplexed, finally laid his hands flat on his strings, signaling silence. Zoe set her harp down reluctantly, regretting the unsung ending. She followed Quennel into the gallery, where they could look over the oak balustrade down into the hall.

"He's early," Quennel murmured with surprise.

A formidable bald man in brocade and black leather was kissing the queen, whose voice was raised in surprise as well. Courtiers hurried across the hall to join her; pages were running out to summon others; the duke's wife and their entourage crowded in behind him, while footmen slipped behind them and out to see to the luggage. Zoe hung over the rail, watching the colorful crowd, the gathering of the king's children hurrying through this door, that, to greet their uncle. The cacophony reached a lively crescendo before she saw the face in the crush watching her.

A young, big, restive man with dark eyes, his long hair black and gleaming like a racehorse, had tossed his head back to scan the gallery. He heard us, Zoe thought with astonishment. All that noise around him, and he looked for the hidden musicians.

"Who—" she began, and stopped herself, knowing who, of course, he must be, even before she spotted his harp.

The duke's bard smiled at her as though he had heard, through the tumult, even that fragment of a question. Her hands tightened a little on the wood. She amended her first impression.

"Who is that kelpie?"

She realized, at Quennel's dry chuckle, that she had spoken aloud, and, from the glint in the midnight eyes, the sudden flash of teeth, that the kelpie had heard her as well.

Chapter Six

Neither history nor poetry adequately explains why Nairn decided to stay at Declan's school. Aside from any ambiguous feelings about Declan, which are examined with great enthusiasm in ballads but rarely documented, the choice was unexpected. Most likely, Nairn had never been to a school in his life. They were few and far between in the Marches and of rare interest to a crofter's son. Nairn was born to wander; he learned his craft on the road, and though he had roamed widely before reaching Stirl Plain, he still had much of Belden to lure him onward, new instruments to discover and learn, much music, in both taverns and courts, he had never heard.

And yet, on Stirl Plain, he stopped and stayed.

As a teacher or a student, no one is certain. Ballads tend to focus on the relationship between Nairn and Declan. The school itself becomes a backdrop for their competitions, their feuds, their friendship. They are thrall to the whims of changing story; truth becomes whatever suits the tale. They challenge one another to lengthy bardic riddle-games; they fall in love with the same woman (this apparently despite the difference in their ages); Nairn seeks revenge for Declan's loyalty to the king who conquered the Marches. If there is any truth to these incidents, history remains mute. The most coherent documented references to Nairn at this time are in the household records of the school.

For the scant year in question, they are noted daily by the first school steward. He began his records in the spring before Nairn joined the school, perhaps watching, as he wrote in his high tower room, the building going up around the tower beneath him that grew to look, by summer's end, much as it does today.

"Accounts rendered this day to Hewn Flout, cobbler, for six pair of sandals for various students and masters, and for patching Nairn's boots."

"Accounts rendered this day to Lyth Holme for a breeding sow, chosen by Nairn."

"Accounts received this day by cloth merchant, Han Speller, his daughter and his servant for lodgings and for stable, and for one crockery washbasin broken by said daughter against a door Nairn closed behind him."

And so on, prosaic entries rarely referencing even an echo of the tumultuous ballads, all signed: "by my hand Dower Ren, Steward."

> *I leave the footprint of the fox behind me,*
> *I ride the night with owls' wings,*
> *I am the key that opens the heart of a jewel,*
> *I am the heartwood of the sounding harp.*
> *Who am I?*

FROM "THE RIDDLING OF DECLAN AND NAIRN," ANONYMOUS

Her hair the froth of windblown wave,
Her eyes the ancient woodland green,
Pale hands that shape the music from the pipe,
And stroke the wild sweetness from the harp.
They loved her, the two great bards,
Old and young, they loved her both.
They went to her and bade that bright mouth tell
Which of them she loved best? She spoke:
"Play for me, and my heart will hear
Who truly loves, and who loves only love."

FROM "THE PRINCESS OF ESTMERE" BY MRS. WELTERSTONE

He would have walked away from Declan's school without one last glance at his unfinished stew, but for that one unexpected thunderbolt: Lord Deste's daughter. He had sung a thousand times a thousand tales and ballads about love and never felt it once. It was, he realized starkly the longer he lingered, like singing about fire without ever experiencing its warmth and wonders, its pain, its absolute necessity. He had strewn the word as freely as wildflowers along his path through the world, tossing it here, there, like a small, pleasing gift that cost nothing and would be forgotten even before it withered. He had never before come up against his own absolute ignorance of it.

Declan tended to dwell on the question of Nairn's ignorance as well, though he seemed to be complaining about something entirely different, when Nairn bothered to pay attention to him. Mostly he did not. He did whatever he was asked: he carried stones, shaped wood for beams and rafters, shared songs of the Marches with the other students, learned their songs, learned to read, without thinking about much of anything but the long-fingered, green-eyed beauty in the kitchen. Why Declan wanted him to learn his letters eluded him. His memory was faultless and inexhaustible. If the words were already in his head, why bother learning to write them? But he did what he was told, only for the privilege, twice or thrice a day, of putting himself next to Odelet, receiving a plate, a cup from her hands, and taking the memory of her expression, her low, sweet, voice, whatever words she spoke, away with him to contemplate during the rest of the busy, meaningless day.

Declan snagged his attention once, when he told Nairn not to show his writing or speak of it to anyone. It seemed a suspicious request since the purpose of writing was to be seen, shared. But turn the request every which way and on its head as he did, Nairn made no sense of it.

"You're far too old to be learning to read and write," Declan told him briskly when he finally asked. "But it must be done, so do it quickly and quietly, and no one you care about will laugh at you. I have asked a few of the others to learn, too," he added. "They will keep it secret as well, as I require."

It seemed easy enough to master. A few straight twiggy ink scratches turned this way and that fashioned a word that meant "shirt" or "egg" or "eye" depending on the pattern. They had other meanings as well, Declan told him, but did not say what, only that the meaning at its simplest contained its power.

That much Nairn understood: he was learning daily the peculiar, poignant turmoil of the simplest, most common of words.

"Heart" for instance. He was vaguely aware, from its rhythms, of the position of his heart in his body. But for the first time in his life, he was stumbling, will he, nil he, into an awareness of why so many emotions and abstractions in song and poetry were attached to that faithfully thumping organ. It acquired an unusual life of its own. It expressed itself in odd ways, pounding almost painfully at an unexpected view of Odelet in the kitchen garden, her graceful hands searching through green leaves for pea pods. At the sight of her emerging from the henhouse with an egg basket, her slender neck bending gracefully under the lintel, his heart would send the blood flashing through him with all the force and silent thunder of distant lightning. Around her his throat dried, his palms sweated, his feet grew enormous. He whispered her name to anything that would listen: the sun, the moon, the carrot tassels in the garden. Practicing his secret writing one morning, he felt an overwhelming urge to watch her name flow out of his quill. But none of the words he had learned from Declan came close to it.

How many twiglet-strokes and in what pattern would mean "Odelet"?

He could not ask her, and he would torment himself into oblivion before he opened his heart to Declan. His heart, a delicate object those days, would not permit him to bring the matter anywhere near Declan. It would shrivel within him at the bard's amusement, cringe like a cur, and try to slink out of sight behind some stronger organ. No matter how he shaped the request, even at its simplest it would bring to life an impossible image: the lowly Pig-Singer casting his eyes at the daughter of an Estmere noble. Even in ballads, such tangles rarely ended happily. Usually someone died. Nairn doubted that Odelet, who seemed obliviously unruffled around him, would burst into the traditional storm of grief over him. She might, he imagined, let fall one cool pearl of pity at the idea of his torment, then promptly forget all about him.

He finally remembered the one man who could write everyone's name, and did, routinely, without paying the least attention to the complications of the heart, as long as they affected neither accounts rendered nor received.

Nairn had never gone farther into the ancient tower than the kitchen. Somewhere up there, Declan taught his classes; somewhere up there, the school steward kept his records and himself. The students slept in a jumbled warren of tiny rooms whose walls they built themselves under the completed portion of the new building's roof. There was little Declan taught that Nairn didn't know, and he tried to stay out from under the bard's yellow gaze: strange things happened when their paths crossed.

But for the sake of seeing Odelet's name flow out of the ink in his quill nib, he would venture into the unexplored regions of the tower.

Odelet was chopping a chicken with a cleaver when he crossed the kitchen. She didn't notice him until, watching her blade pierce the pale, plucked, hapless breastbone, Nairn walked into the edge of the open tower door. He winced and rubbed his nose, then glanced at her furtively to see if she had noticed his bumbling, just as she turned her face hastily away from him and gazed impassively down at the chicken. She raised the cleaver; he slipped across the threshold and up the stairs.

The narrow windows spiraling up the walls gave him glimpses of the long summer evening, the plain turning and turning around him as he moved. Yellow-gray sky at one horizon where the sun had gone down changed in the next elongated frame to the river winding its way to yet another horizon, trees along its banks bending protectively over the mystery of water. Moonlight spilled across the next window, silvering the distant sky. Beyond the next, massive stones watched the guttering end of day, watched for the stars. The next slit sparked with a sudden glow as someone lit a lamp at the tavern door beside the river. Nairn passed Declan's chambers, then: the lower, where he taught, the higher, where he slept. Both doors were closed. At the next window, Nairn heard someone harping in the twilight, softly, dreamily: Declan, perhaps, sitting in the ring of stones and watching moonlight crust the dark, massive tower on the field below, rising so high it seemed crowned with stars.

Nairn stopped. He clung to that meager opening with both hands, trying to widen it as he pushed his face to the stones and stared at the tower. He blinked. It vanished as he opened his eyes; he saw the familiar emptiness below, rapidly misting into night. He let go of the stones finally, stepped back, still staring. A moon shadow, he conceded finally, flung by the watchtower itself across the grass. He turned, continued his climb up the seemingly endless steps, the harper's music drifting along with him.

He reached the steward's door at last, somewhere near the roof, and marked by the book and quill he had sketched beside a series of incomprehensible shapes. He knocked.

The steward called out from within. Nairn found him at his table, quill in hand, looking up from his massive book, his eyes still full of numbers. He was around Nairn's age; other than that, the two young men might have been born on different stars. Ink ran in the steward's veins, Nairn guessed. His heart beat by rote: it would go on counting one number after another until it stopped. Still, the steward was a kindly young man, for all his gravity. He asked no questions about Nairn's odd request, just began flipping pages in his book.

"Odelet. I remember an entry, just before you came here."

Nairn looked over his shoulder, watched as the steward settled on a page and ran his fingers down the lines.

"Here. Accounts received for three nights' lodging and stable from Berwin Deste, brother of Odelet Deste." He pointed to a flowing fragment within the line of knots and coils. "This word spells her name."

Nairn studied it. He brushed at the hair over his eyes and studied it again. "What is that?"

"What?"

"That." He ran his hand through the air above the page. "What came out of your quill."

"It's writing."

"No, it's not."

The steward raised his head abruptly, met Nairn's eyes. After a moment, he pushed the book toward Nairn, dipped his quill, and offered it. "Show me. There in that blank space. What your writing looks like."

Entirely ignoring Declan's requirement for secrecy, Nairn leaned over the page, arranged four twiglets into a pattern.

"Ah," Dower said softly, gazing at the twigs. "I understand why you are confused. That's an ancient way of writing. I don't know it, though I've seen it here and there, carved into standing stones. No one writes like that anymore. I should say: I didn't know that anyone still does."

"Then why is Declan teaching it to me?"

"I don't know." The steward's head was still lowered as he studied the word Nairn had left in the margin. "You'll have to ask him. What does this mean?"

"Onion. Yes. I will ask. Can you show me—" He took another look at the onion-shaped circle that began Odelet's name, and shook his head hopelessly. "Never mind. It doesn't matter. I mean: not to her."

Dower was silent, flicking the feathered end of the quill at the page. He looked up at Nairn finally. "Why don't you just tell her?"

Nairn's heart spoke first, sent the blood roiling through his body. That language, he realized, was clear. "I'm terrified," he mumbled, his tongue stumbling over the word.

The steward straightened, dipped his nib again, wrote a word on a corner of the page and tore it carefully free. "Here. That's how she would write her name."

Nairn took the tiny paper triangle wordlessly. In his chamber, a cell in the hive containing a pallet, a couple of dowels shoved between stones in the wall for hanging clothes and instruments, and a rough table for his candle and oddments, he studied the word, repeating it over and over until he remembered every curve and angle, every spike and cross. Then he pushed the paper through the hole in the sound box of his harp, where it would tremble and resonate to all the music he played.

Then he went to talk to Declan.

The bard was easily found: Nairn stuck his head out the door into the night and heard his harping. He followed it to where Declan sat in his favorite place, leaning against one of the great standing stones on the crown of the hill and playing to the moon. It must have been his harping that Nairn had heard as he climbed up the tower; it stopped as Nairn halted beside him, glancing puzzledly down the hill for the outlines of the unfamiliar tower in the dark.

Then he felt Declan's eyes on him, and he said brusquely, "You lied to me again."

For a moment, the bard was silent, motionless. Then he set his harp beside him in the grass and answered evenly, "Then you spoke of what I asked you to keep secret. How else would you know?"

"It's such a small thing—Why would you lie about something that unimportant?"

"Whom did you tell?"

"Dower Ren. I went to him to ask him how to spell one word—"

"Why didn't you come to me?"

Nairn felt himself redden, said shortly, "It was private."

"You barely know the steward."

"I knew he would tell me the truth, how to spell the word I wanted, not give me some other word like 'bell' or 'butter' instead of 'O—'" He stopped, clamped his mouth down on the word, but too late.

A sound came out of the bard's nostrils, a snort, a laugh, or just a passing spore, expelled. "Odelet?"

Nairn's fists clenched. "I knew you'd laugh. You keep your secrets and laugh at everything. You came as far north as you could go in this land just to spy on fishers and shepherds and lie to them—"

"I'm not laughing," Declan interrupted sharply. "I would not laugh at the only thing that keeps you here. Do you always tell the truth?"

"Yes. No. When it's important. That's not the point—" He

stopped, thinking back at his piecemeal life, all that it had taken to bring himself here to sit on a hill with the greatest bard in five kingdoms.

"Music doesn't lie," the bard said after a moment. "If you play a false note, it sounds. But words can shift their meanings so easily, weigh so lightly one moment, fly like a star, or drop like a stone in the next. How many times have you spoken the word 'love' and meant anything but that?" Nairn, staring rigidly down at him, blinked. "And now that you finally think you know what the word means, you find it impossible to say. Who would believe you?"

"That's not—" he protested. "That's not exactly— She— Anyway, I didn't come to talk about that. How do you know? I've never said anything to anyone—"

"Your face speaks every time you look at her. Your feet speak when you trip over them in her presence. Your fingers speak when they tremble on a pipe note. You talk about her all the time, in ways that I would wager my harp strings that you, with your gifts and your comely face, have never had to speak before."

Nairn was silent, gazing back at the eavesdropping moon. He drew breath finally, loosed it. "True enough. Am I that pitiful a creature around her?"

"You're not the only one."

"I hadn't— I hadn't noticed."

"You haven't been paying attention to anyone else. According to her brother, she left a very wealthy noble waiting for an answer to come here."

"Oh," he said, deflated.

"You might talk to her now and then."

"Maybe. She makes all the words vanish out of my head. And

so do you," he added restively. "This is not at all what I came out here to talk about."

"At least you are talking to me," Declan breathed. "What did you come to talk about?"

"Why are you teaching me to write 'water' with scratches that are as ancient as the standing stones and that nobody understands anymore?"

"Because it's the language of secrets, the language of power, the language of lost arts. The word only looks like 'water.' Beneath the surface, it becomes something else entirely. And you have the gift to use that power. You told me that in the grubby tavern by the sea when you took the jewels from my harp." He turned its face; they glittered with a familiar warmth and beauty at Nairn. "They recognized you."

Nairn gazed back at them expressionlessly, remembering with what power and what innocence he had taken them. He shifted his eyes to Declan's barely visible face, the cold tear of moonlight in his owl's eyes.

"Why do you want me here?" he asked slowly, sensing he would not like the answer. "Why are you teaching me this?"

"I am learning this as well," Declan reminded him. "I took the language from your ancient stones. It's the forgotten power of your land I am trying to waken. The kings of my land know how to use their bards; the greatest of the musicians are the most powerful mages. I can teach you what you will need to know to become the Royal Bard of Belden."

Nairn took a step back, nearly lost his balance and tumbled down the hill. "No," he said harshly. "No. I will never work for that usurper."

"Think," Declan said softly. "Think. Of what your status would be in the king's court. Of the music you have never heard: the court music of the five lost kingdoms and of King Oroh's land. Of the instruments you could play. Of the knowledge that would come your way. The advantages of wealth and rank, as the king's most honored bard, would open every court in Belden to you. Even Lord Deste, Odelet's father, would welcome you under his roof."

Nairn whispered, trembling, "How do I know—"

"That I'm not lying to you again? This was the final request of the King of Belden to me when I left his court: that I find and train the bards most capable of magic in this land. I am doing so. Think about all this. Then decide to stay or go. If you stay, that is what I offer you, in the name of the king."

"You didn't answer—"

"You'll never know, will you? If you leave."

Nairn stood, mute again, gazing down at the shadowy figure as Declan picked up his harp, ran his fingers down it, shook a glitter of notes into the moonlight.

He said haltingly, as Declan began to play again, "When I— when I went up the tower steps to talk to Dower Ren, I saw, out of one window, a great, dark tower on the flat land at the bottom of the hill, rising so high that it seemed to stretch into the stars, and they became part of it. Is that what you mean by the power of the land? You must have seen it, too. You were out here playing, then."

The harp stilled midphrase; it seemed, for a moment, that Declan's voice had frozen with his fingers. Nairn heard him draw breath, hesitate; he answered finally, looking up at Nairn, his face in shadow but for his moonstruck eyes.

"I was out here, yes. I was watching the moonrise and thinking about the music of my own land, wondering how much of it will be remembered without its history, how much will wither on this foreign soil. The bell jangled when you opened the front door. It pulled me out of my memories; I began to play, then.

"I saw no tower. I heard no harping but my own. All the magic was for you."

Chapter Seven

The formal invitation to the queen's supper in honor of her brother, Lord Grishold, reached Phelan, as usual, in haphazard fashion. He had wandered out of bed after a long night at the Merry Rampion to be faced with the impending day, which offered nothing, no matter which way he looked at it, but a vast, empty blankness of paper upon which he was expected to write. His father's house stood on the bank of the Stirl, not far above Peverell Castle, where the city streets, broad and lined with huge old trees, grew quiet. The water traffic there tended toward rich barges and sailboats; working vessels rarely came that far beyond the docks except to pursue a run of fish. The house, built of fieldstone centuries earlier, retained a few of its early eccentricities, including a pair of unmatched windows inset on a side wall as awkwardly as flounders' eyes. Inside, time sped forward into oak and marble walls, thick rugs and carpets, softly glowing lamps that revealed Jonah's enormous collection of oddments from everywhere in the world, including several places that Phelan couldn't find on a map. His mother, Sophy, herself an heiress with family connections to the Peverells, favored all the modern conveniences, only drawing the line at keeping a car. They were slow, she said, and noisy, and you couldn't tell them what to do.

Sophy, fully dressed and wrestling with a skintight glove as she came upon the yawning Phelan in the living room, left a kiss somewhere in the vicinity of her son's jaw and asked briskly, "Have you found your father?"

"Am I looking for him?"

Sophy nodded vigorously. Phelan had inherited her pale hair and gray eyes, even her charming smile, but not, he realized early, her stubbornly temperate disposition, which provided a formidable barrier to any questions about Jonah's behavior. "I told you, didn't I?"

"No."

"Oh, dear. Well, you must find him for Lord Grishold's supper—" She stopped, loosed a chuckle. "Not that the duke is planning to take a knife and fork to him, but we must all attend. The king wrote a tiny note on our invitation that he expressly desired Jonah's presence, to finish a certain conversation."

"When?"

"When, what, dear?"

"The supper?"

"Oh. In a day or two—I've forgotten—" She smiled at him brightly, patted his cheek. "Just find him, Phelan. You're always so good at it. The invitation is around here somewhere. I must rush away. We are knitting socks today for Caerau's poor, and then Ursula Baris's cook's grandmother will teach us how to divine the future in a bird's nest."

She left Phelan wordless, awake at last. He moved finally, stepped toward the cluttered desk in her study to look for the invitation, then veered abruptly at the door. It didn't matter: clean, fed, his pockets clinking again, Jonah might be anywhere in the city. Phelan would either stumble across him in time for the occasion or not. He had a paper to write; his father could wait.

He did turn from his chosen path, walking across Dockers Bridge again for a quick search around the dig site, before he buried himself in the school library. In the clear morning light, the desolation lost its mystery and became simply the sad ruins of an earlier century, walls slumped into one another, charred window frames staring empty-eyed at the colorful buildings across the river, ruined warehouses and broken pilings haunting the abandoned waterfront. Fire had gutted it; everyone had gone to more prosperous parts of the city; no one had found a need to rebuild the waste. Still, in the eerie silence, Phelan heard voices, brisk and cheerful, with no visible owners and seemingly from underground.

He walked to the edge of Jonah's latest project and looked down at the top of a head ascending. It was covered with a soft cloth hat; he couldn't see the lowered face talking to someone below.

He did recognize the voice.

"Princess Beatrice," he said, and the head came up abruptly. She smiled at him; the hat slid, its tie catching at her throat, loosing a burnished curl or two from her rigorously pinned hair.

"Phelan." She accepted his hand briefly, politely, as she stepped off the ladder, then let go and beat a cloud of dust from her clothes. "Sorry," she added as she stepped back, laughing. "I'm not fit for civilized company after I've been down here. Are you looking for your father?"

"Yes. Have you seen him?"

"He was here earlier for just a few moments; then he went off."

"Do you have any idea where?" he asked without hope.

She pulled pins out of her hair, shook it again as it fell, releasing more dust. "I don't." She paused, thinking. Behind her, below ground, Phelan could hear the soft whisk of brushes, the cautious tink of a pick, an occasional word. The princess's calm eyes shifted from Phelan's face to the city beyond his shoulder. They were, he realized, the same inky blue as the asters growing out of a nearby midden. "I know he's been asked to court, but that's no help to you if that's why you're looking for him." She turned abruptly, called down, "Does anybody know where Master Cle might have gone?"

There was a faint, ragged chorus of amusement; Phelan's mouth crooked.

"Ah, well. I'll find him. If you see him—"

"Yes, of course. I'm driving home now. Lady Hartshorn is giving a lunch for Lady Grishold that I couldn't get out— I promised I'd attend. Can I drop you somewhere along the way?"

"Yes," he said before he thought, then changed his answer reluctantly. "No. I should stay, look around here a little; it's where I found him last. And I can spot him better on foot. I know a few of his favorite places."

"If I do see him, can I give him a message?"

"Thank you, Princess. Just tell him we need him home."

He sat at a table in the school library later, thinking idly of the encounter, then of Jonah, and then ruthlessly clearing his head to think of nothing at all. He gazed intensely at a sheet of paper, breath suspended, a word on the quivering point of his pen poised and waiting to fall. Monoliths of books and manuscripts rose around him. All were crammed with words, words packed as solidly as bricks in a wall, armies of them marching endlessly on from one page to the next without pause. He forced the pen in his tight grip a hairsbreadth closer to the paper so that the word stubbornly clinging to it might yield finally, flow onto the vast emptiness. Point and paper met. Kissed. Froze.

He sat back, breath spilling abruptly out of him, the pen laden with unformed words dangling now over the floor in his lax fingers. How, he wondered incredulously, did all those books and papers come into existence? In what faceted jewel of amber secreted in what invisible compartment of what hidden casket did others find that one word to begin the sentence that layered itself into a paragraph, that built itself into a page, that went on to the next page, and on, and on?

He straightened again, dropped the pen, reached randomly for beginnings from the piles around him.

"Does Bone Plain exist?" a recent paper inquired simply and succinctly. An older book introduced its argument murkily but more sonorously: "On the farthest horizon we can glimpse, back through time to the dawn of the five kingdoms, the place where history and poetry meet on Bone Plain." Phelan snapped it shut, picked up another book, a thin, limp volume bound in fine leather. It began: "For centuries poets, bards, and scholars have run through rivers of ink arguing exactly which of the standing stones of Belden are also the standing stones of poetry enclosing the Three Trials of Bone Plain."

He closed that one, put it back on its pile, and dropped his brow onto the stack, hoping without hope that the words he searched for would somehow seep through flaking parchment and antique leather into his brain. The library, oak floors carpeted with lozenges of light from the windows, tall mahogany bookcases, the priceless collection of scrolls and first editions donated by Jonah Cle installed under glass on various stands, was relentlessly sunny and dead quiet. Everyone else in the world had something better to do on that bright spring day than agonize over ancient history. Maybe his father was right, he thought resignedly. Everything had been said. There was nothing more to say, which was why he could not find a single word to add to the subject.

He got up finally, examined his father's collection. Jonah had evidently considered the subject so tiresome that he gave away everything that had fallen into his hands. Phelan found, among other things, the earliest version of the tale written on parchment instead of stone, as well as an essay about Nairn by an obscure scholar who seemed to think that the bard, after failing the trials, was still wandering the earth a thousand years later. Phelan summoned the archivist from the depths of the library. The archivist, who would have thrown himself bodily across the doorway to keep the priceless manuscripts from leaving, said finally, in the face of Phelan's desperation, that he could take them out as long as his father didn't see them.

Of all the places Phelan might run into his father, home was the least likely, so he took them there. No one else was around; the house was silent except for an occasional distant noise from the kitchen. He settled on the sofa with the manuscripts, and began to read.

On a plain of bone
In a ring of stone
The Three Trials, the Three Terrors,
The Three Greatest Treasures of All:
The Oracular Stone
The Inexhaustible Cauldron
The Turning Tower.
The bard whose voice melts stone and makes it prophesy
The bard whose heart fills the cauldron and feeds the world
The bard who forges death into song,
    madness into poetry
    night into dawn
That bard will possess the most ancient powers of all
    language.
These are the Three Trials of Bone Plain
The Three Treasures
Beware the Three Terrors:
The bard who fails to wake the stone
    will sing stones henceforth
Who fails to fill the cauldron
    will go hungry henceforth
Who fails to turn the night to poetry
    will be broken on the shards of language
    and taken by the night.
Who fails the Three
    will find no song, no peace, no poetry,
    no rest, no end of days, and no forgetting.

The written poem was followed by an account of the wonders
and tribulations of bards who had dared the trials for the sake of

such power over their words, such glory in their world. Very few could be tracked, like Nairn, out of poetry and into history. Most of the unfortunates had been invented to bear the tales of their failures. Despite the dire consequences predicted, the more noble-hearted of the adventurers were given chances to mitigate their fates. They returned home scarred only with the memory, and rewarded with a tale that would be embroidered more colorfully and grow in detail with every telling.

The manuscript itself was so old that Phelan held his breath as he turned the pages, lest a parchment word flake away into the air of a distant century. The scribe or bard who plucked the poem out of common memory and wrote it down saw no reason to add a name or a date or a place of origin. The tale itself was far older, Phelan knew from various scholarly papers on the subject. In itself, it gave no clues to where exactly a bard had to go to find Bone Plain. But Phelan knew that already, having memorized the entire poem by the time he was ten. He had taken the manuscript on the chance that seeing the ancient written words might spark some thought, some recognition, maybe even some impulse to pick up a pen.

It was there, sprawled on a sofa with both manuscripts on his chest, that he glanced up at a faint stir of carpet threads and found his father.

Jonah eyed the priceless manuscripts, grunted in recognition, and dropped into a chair near Phelan's feet. Phelan could see his face. It looked predictably pale and curdled, but there was a peculiar expression in his eyes, and he seemed, in broad daylight, astonishingly sober.

"Is something wrong?" Phelan asked tentatively. "Did you kill somebody? Accidentally get married again?"

"No."

"Find a gold mine in one of your digs?"

Jonah shook his head. He shifted, started to say something, stopped and started again. "That supper," he managed finally. "When is it?"

Phelan stared at him, amazed. "Why do you care? Anyway, how did you know about it? You never pay attention to those things."

"Don't give me grief, boy, just tell me."

"I would if I knew." He paused, studying his father, found the words finally, for what he saw. "You look like you've seen a ghost."

"I may have," Jonah breathed. "I may have, indeed."

Phelan started to sit, caught the manuscripts sliding off his chest. Jonah raised a brow at them; he said quickly, "I hid them under my school robe; nobody saw me take them."

"Don't try to be noble; it only makes you sound unctuous," Jonah said with so little bite that Phelan frowned. He sat up, still gazing at his father, laying the manuscripts carefully on the sofa beside him.

"Whose ghost?"

Jonah shook his head irritably, but the subject haunting the air between them refused to go away. "A particularly noisome bit of past," he said finally. He held up a hand as Phelan opened his mouth. "Just leave it. It's mine; I'll deal with it."

"But where did you see it?" Phelan demanded. "Him. Her."

"Riding through the river park in Lord Grishold's entourage. I was just stepping into the Arms of Antiquity, after checking some things in the Royal Museum. I looked back and there it was, the ghost behind Grishold, all in black and grinning like the sun. When is that supper again?" he added restively.

"A day or two—Does this mean I won't have to roam all over the city searching for you?"

"I'll be there," Jonah promised, his voice so thin and dry that a dozen questions leaped to life in Phelan's brain, all clamoring together. He gazed, fascinated, at his father, suddenly looking forward to what had sounded like a long and tedious evening. Jonah, forestalling his curiosity, shifted the subject adroitly, reaching for the manuscripts. "Are these of any help?"

"They may be," Phelan answered with no great hope. "I've read nearly everything else."

"I told you—"

"I know, I know."

"Your heart's not in it," Jonah said, carefully turning pages. "How can you find Bone Plain when nothing in you wants anything to do with it?"

"It's only a paper," Phelan said with unaccustomed sharpness. "Of course, I don't want to go there. That's got nothing to do with anything. It's what I want to leave that's everything to me." Jonah sniffed but otherwise refrained from comment. "Anyway, I haven't read the piece about Nairn, yet. It might inspire an idea."

"It's hard to imagine that damp squib inspiring anything," his father muttered. He sat back, brooding at the work in question but did not open it. Phelan watched him, wondering, as always, in what torturous labyrinths of Jonah's brain his father continually lost himself. Jonah rose abruptly under Phelan's scrutiny, gave a wrench to a sturdy bell rope.

"Where is Sagan? I sent him to the cellar an eon ago."

"I beg your pardon, sir," the butler said, gliding like a phantom across the carpet, his hair and the tray upon which the bottle stood glowing silver in the sunlight. "I had to search the racks for this one."

"Thank you, Sagan." He glanced a question at Phelan, who shook his head.

"I'm working," he said shortly, and stretched out on the sofa to read about Nairn while his father and the dusty amber bottle vanished somewhere into the depths of the house.

"Nairn," the essayist had begun without preamble some three or four centuries earlier, "the Wandering Bard to whom the solace of death had been long forbidden by his abject and unforgiven failure at the Three Trials of Bone Plain, was seen at the Bardic School at Caerau, as was cited in the school records by Argot Renne thusly: 'This day: Accounts paid to Colley Dale for three wheels of cheese, five crocks of butter, and ten gallons of milk. Accounts paid to Merlee Craven for nine wool blankets and two lambs. Accounts settled by one guest, a stranger, who paid for his supper by his dishwashing afterwards. Though he carried a harp, he would not play it, claiming that the last thing we needed in this place was another harper. Nor would he give his name. But considering this steward's daughter's description of the boulder inside the ring of stones on the hill turning abruptly into a man carrying a harp, and considering the craggy agelessness of his face, the unremitting dark of his eyes, and that he knew my name, Renne, though he had been stone all our lives, and considering above all, his astonishing question concerning the existence of the ancient Circle of Days, the secret conclave that vanished from history centuries before, I believe him to be the bard in search of his death: Nairn. By my hand, Argot Renne, School Steward.' This being," the essayist continued dryly, "by far the wordiest entry of any of the stewards heretofore on record."

Phelan blinked. The raw silk of the sofa beneath him seemed to breathe beneath his nape, along his backbone, like something quickening unexpectedly to life.

"Circle of Days," he whispered, and saw in his mind's eye the path out of the interminable years at the school: the Wandering Bard, the Unforgiven, who once had a secret, been included in a mystery.

Phelan moved before he realized it, gathered the manuscripts, and stood for the journey back to the school archives. Something tugged at him before he took a step: his father with his head cluttered like a museum basement with brilliant facts and fantastic shards of past that rarely if ever emerged into the light of day.

What might he know about such mysteries?

Then Phelan laughed, which was all Jonah would do at the question, tell him he wasted his time; it was nonsense, a figment, and anyway, it had all been investigated, answered, written down centuries before Phelan drew his first breath, bellowed his first opinion at the world.

He left his father in the company he most preferred, and went to track a bard who was neither living nor dead, and to find where a circle began.

Chapter Eight

The winter that killed the bard who replaced Declan at King Oroh's court seems to have been one of the harshest on record. The Stirl froze nearly all the way from the sea to the tiny village on the plain, which had grown enough to become a coherent entity, and which named itself Caerau. Court records of nobles all over Belden are filled with the sufferings of high and low. Even the king, who liked to keep his court in restless motion in order to exhaust the hospitality and the coffers of potential rebels, hunkered down for the season in the slightly milder climate of Estmere with Lord Deste, whose ample fields and woods provided food, game, and firewood enough even for the king's entourage. His household books record the deaths of the very old and the very young: most succumbed to what was only known then as "fever." The king's own records also list the illnesses and deaths of aged courtiers as well as assorted riding and hunting accidents in the icy fields and woods. The death of his bard, Loyce, was listed among the hunting accidents: he was vigorously sounding the hunting horn when his galloping horse slipped on an icy patch buried under the snow. "Both horse and rider there died," the records say tersely, disguising what must have been a poignant incident. Other sources across Belden record a "rain of birds frozen in their flight," tree limbs overburdened with snow cracking and falling on hapless travelers and rooftops, bodies discovered frozen beneath the ice in rivers, ponds, and wells, bands of the poor, the outcast, and the outlawed living in caves and converging on the unwary "like a great swarm of crows upon the dead." References to children stolen from their cradles by hungry animals are common; on rare occasions, but very likely true, they are eaten by their desperate neighbors.

For every death recorded, a dozen or a hundred probably went unnoticed by history, from the rough northern fishing villages and mountain clans who had little use for writing and kept everything in memory, to the isolated villages in the western crags, and in the southern marshlands of what was once known as Waverlea. As for the school, records list three students who fled the stark life to return to their more comfortable homes. There are accounts payable to a local healer for poultices and herbal remedies, as well as for a futile visit to a student who was struck by an icicle that plunged down from the tower. His death passed with perhaps untimely swiftness from a matter of household record into the speculations and wild surmises of ballad.

What the household records do not divulge is how a couple dozen students spending a deadly winter surrounded by snow-covered plain and cold stone, inadequately washed, living on monotonous winter fare, constantly in one another's company, managed to deal with one another without a continual drain of "accounts rendered to Salix of Caerau, healer . . ."

This day at sunrise:
we make bread.
At noon by the river
we clean the clothes and pots.
Until the waning light of day
we weave our baskets
and bead the hunters' armbands.
At the rising moon
we speak our dreams,
we sing to the dead.
We sleep.
We dream.

FROM "CIRCLE OF DAYS" TRANSLATED FROM THE ANCIENT RUNIC BY
HERMIA CREELEY-CORBIN

Nairn, opening his eyes the morning after his moonlit conversation with Declan, drew his first waking breath and did not think of Odelet. He pulled on his boots without thinking of her. In the kitchen, he took a bowl of porridge from her hand so absently that even she was startled. Her widening eyes, her faint, delicate flush penetrated his distant thoughts; he gazed back at her, perplexed, as one who has been spellbound might remember his enchantment like a sweet, strange, fading dream.

He was still ensorcelled; only the spell had changed.

Now the words that haunted him were fashioned of twigs and meant mysteries. He breathed them in; he drew them in dirt, scratched them on stone, traced them with a forefinger whenever he touched the outward face of one: "egg," "grass," "hill," "knife," "bread." They took fire in his mind as once Odelet's name had burned, relentlessly bright, feeding on an inexhaustible fuel of possibilities. What lay beneath the prosaic images of language might lie dormant within the world itself: the busy egg within its shell, the seeded earth. Somehow music could bridge that great, hidden power between a word and what it truly meant. But Declan had not yet explained the method.

The Circle of Days, he called his lists of ancient language. Indeed, it seemed that commonplace, like someone's early household records. "Sun" and "moon," they learned, "wash," "arrow," "king," "owl," "smock," "fish," and "hook," "needle," and "eye." Nairn had no idea who among the students belonged to the enchanted circle destined to learn such wonders. They would know one another, Declan said, when they were ready.

Oddly enough, distracted from his humiliating passion by the fascinating otherness weighing in his brain, Nairn finally learned to talk to Odelet. The magic had left her, invaded other things. She still caught his eyes at every movement, charmed his heart with her voice and music. But, no longer spell-ridden, he could finally see her more clearly: the highborn lady who had learned to boil an egg and keep the fire burning under a cauldron of lentils for the sake of her music.

Nairn lingered in the kitchen now instead of sneaking through it; he chopped carrots and onions just to listen to her, stayed to scrub pots after a meal. He was awed by her courage in coming to that isolated hillock on the plain, and he wondered if she, too, had been drawn there by more than music.

He drew an ancient word in spilled flour one morning while

she was making bread: three twigs that she brushed away without a glance, so he guessed that she was not a part of Declan's secret group. But they did have one thing in common: both had run away from home.

"I had a horse, and I knew where I was going," she observed wryly. "You had nothing but your feet."

They had gone outside after supper to sit on the hillside and play songs of Estmere and the Marches to one another, she on her harp, he on a pipe. The long summer had drawn to an end; the oak leaves were turning. Somewhere in the dark, Declan played, down by the river maybe, like them watching a full moon as golden as his eyes detach itself from the earth and drift. A tangle of music and voices within the walls behind them seemed engulfed by the vast, cloud-streaked dark.

"It's easier doing something when you're that young and don't know what you're doing," Nairn answered. "And look what you chose to leave: wealth, servants, a loving family, a soft bed, to come here where you cook for everyone and sleep on a pallet on a makeshift floor. All I left was a crusty father with a backhand like the wallop of an iron shovel, and brothers who would toss me into the pigsty as soon as look at me."

"I left to follow the music. So did you."

"Declan's music," he said softly, with a latent touch of bitterness.

"Yes. All the beauty of it. We both came to learn that from him."

He glanced at her, found her eyes full of that rich moonlight. "I didn't follow him," he said softly. "But in the end I found him."

She pulled her fine cloak close around her against the chill night wind just beginning to rouse and send the yellow leaves spinning out of the oak boughs.

"I have no illusions about my talents," she said simply. "I'll return home when I'm ready, marry, and teach my children what I learned. I know that my father is tearing his hair over me; my brother Berwin has come here twice to tell me that. They are angry with me for so many things, not the least for preferring the company of the usurper's bard to theirs. But I am angry, too, at my father. He loves me, I know. I also know that I'm worth more to him now than I will be again. I might as well be sitting on a scale he looks at every day to weigh the gold I'll bring him, calculate the property. My mother told me that he can't help it; fathers are made that way. No matter how they start out, one day they look at you despite themselves and only see what they can get for you."

"I think you would be worth a great deal to someone who truly loves you," Nairn said soberly. He saw her eyes flash toward him in the dark, felt the question in them. But he stayed silent, for once in his self-indulgent life, for his only true hope of her lay at the end of a long and complex road. And he knew that Declan had told him one true thing at least: he had no idea what love meant.

He took his harp up to the tower roof to play late one night, when most of the students had gone to bed. Leaning against the battlements, he played back at the gusty winds, the brilliant, icy stars, the owls, the dry, chattering leaves that the winds gathered and tossed and let fall again like some largesse from the dead. He was naming and remembering as he played, envisioning the twigs in his mind for "owl," "leaf," "wind." They burned brightly in his head, but they did not sound; no one knew how to say them anymore. They would not open, either, not even to his harping, though he coaxed them as sweetly, as passionately as he could. They remained mute instruments. He let his harp fall silent finally except for one note under his thumb that he stroked softly, absently like a slow heartbeat while he pondered how to hear a language spoken, for so many centuries, only by stone.

A dark figure took shape against the stars across the roof. He started, his thumb careening across the strings, wondering what he had summoned out of the night. Then he recognized the tall, cloaked, wind-blurred form.

"I heard you playing," Declan said. "I came up to listen to you. You didn't notice."

"I was thinking about the words," Nairn told him after a moment. "About how to waken them. Hear them."

"I know. I heard you."

Nairn stared at him across the dark. "What else can you do besides hear my thoughts?" he asked, his voice harsh with uncertainty, "and blind a king's army with a fog until it slaughters itself? What else does it take to become a Royal Bard in your country?"

"It took a great deal more than a simple fog," Declan answered slowly. "Anstan's army was neither that blind nor that inexperienced. What it took, I did: I blurred minds, I roused ghosts, made memories real . . . They fought with courage and skill, those warriors. Not all the dead were on your side. Belden is at peace, now. It's unlikely that King Oroh's bard will be asked to do such things for some time. The bard who took my place in his court is a fine musician, but not so adept in other ways. We hope he will not need to be, now that Belden is united and all King Oroh's determination is bent toward peace. A Royal Bard in peaceful times opens the king's court to the finest music and musicians, uses other arts only to keep the peace."

Nairn was silent, trying to hear what Declan wasn't saying, what might lie within his words. He gave up. The bard was too subtle and he too ignorant to understand much more than his own seedling ambitions.

He said finally, haltingly, "And learning these simple words might—"

"Yes," the bard said intensely. "Yes. Their power will open your path to King Oroh's court. The language you are learning is rooted in his land; that power was born here, belongs here. You will use it, in his court, as you see best."

"How can you possibly think—"

"I don't think. I know. You have no idea of your own powers. Even King Oroh, who has few abilities in that direction, recognized yours. We let you flee that day on the Welde because I knew that you would find your own way back to me. Power recognizes itself, even in those most oblivious to it. You recognized what, beyond music, I have to give you."

Nairn stood wordlessly again, unable to summon any argument, only wonder at where the path out of the pigsty had led. The harp spoke for him, his thumb picking at the single string again as he mused. When he looked up finally, Declan had gone.

Winter howled across the plain and stripped it bare. Along the dark, sluggish river, stone cottages seemed to huddle in the snow among the leafless trees. Declan, who said he felt the cruel season coming in his aging bones, had raided his coffers, gifts from the king, and laid in supplies and firewood for a siege. The world shrank daily, lost its far horizons. Days began and ended in the dark. Tempers grew short; noses ran; nerves frayed. Lovers quarreled by day and tangled again in the night for warmth. Nothing existed, it seemed, beyond the plain; its blanched earth, its vast silence, ringed the tiny island upon the hill like an eternally frozen sea.

Nairn, who regarded seasons with a lover's eye, watched winter's changing moods, its astonishing expressions, and learned to write its ancient words: fire and ice, breath and death, dark, night, end. The full moon hanging so clearly among the frozen stars that it seemed to take on dimensions was a word in itself, he thought; it spoke a silent mystery that was somehow connected to the list of patterns lengthening daily under his nib. The glittering path of its light across the dead white plain turned to music in his head; he fashioned its fiery white brilliance with his fingers, played it back to the moon.

He went into the kitchen one morning and found, instead of the tall, calm beauty stirring the porridge, someone darker, slighter, with a tumble of untidy hair and eyes, when she glanced toward him, of a light, startling gray beneath level black brows. She filled a bowl for him briskly without explaining herself.

"Where is Odelet?" he asked, ladling bites into his mouth as he stood there, the way he was used to since they had become friends.

"Upstairs," was the laconic answer, meaning: in the room with the great hearth and the tables where the more civilized students were eating.

"Who are you?"

"I'm Muire." She took a poker to the fire under the cauldron with a great deal of energy, until the listless flame leaped to embrace all the wood it could reach. "Salix's granddaughter. She sent me up here to help out."

He nodded. Odelet, of the fairer climes in east Belden, suffered in the cold; her eyes and nostrils had been red-rimmed for weeks, and she had begun to make bullfrog noises, coughing in the night.

"Good. Do you know how to cook?"

Muire smiled thinly, as though he had asked if she knew how to gut a fish or milk a cow or pluck a hen or any other of a hundred things any idiot knew. "I can cook," she said. He stood there chewing absently, watching her as she shook a lump of dough from a bowl, dropped it onto a patch of flour on the table, and pummeled it with her fingers until it lay round and plump as a cushion. She took a knife to it, slashed it delicately with one long line across its surface and a shorter line to each side of that, three twigs, he realized slowly, in the ancient pattern for "bread."

"Do you know what that means?" he asked abruptly. "Those lines?"

She considered them, then him, her dark brows peaked. "My grandmother always does that," she explained. "To me, it means 'bread.'"

What other magic words had traveled down from ancient days to her? he wondered. Or to Salix? He took to visiting the kitchen when he had a moment, doing the odd task for Muire: bringing in firewood, scrubbing out the cauldron, hauling in water from the frigid well. He left her messages: a twig-word in a dusting of flour on the table, in a spill of gravy. A few she noticed and understood; others she swept up without question with her cloth. Declan, he knew, would have been appalled at him scattering secrets everywhere. But what the bard didn't know he didn't have to think about, and how would he find out anyway?

"How do you know these things?" Muire asked him, after he carved the twiglet-pattern for "willow" on top of the butter in the crock. "Salix puts signs like that in her jars and boxes. I thought she made them up for herself because she can't write."

"They're very old," he answered absently, his mind already traveling down the hill ahead of him. "I wonder where she learned them. I'd like to see your grandmother's signs."

Muire paused in the midst of chopping the pile of carrots and parsnips he had brought up from the root cellar. She pushed hair out of her eyes with the back of her wrist, said simply, "Follow me home, then, whenever you want. She won't mind." She resumed her quick, vigorous strokes with the cleaver, running down a foot of carrot in a breath, while Nairn eyed her silently, curiously. Her eyes had been lowered as she spoke, and she didn't look back at him now, though she must have felt his swift attention. Another message, maybe, in the complex language of the body. Or maybe not.

He plucked a bite of carrot out of the wake of the flashing blade. "I will," he said.

He did, a few days later, after supper on an evening so clear that stars and the half-moon hanging above the village shone luminous and upside down, like a migrant school of glittering fish, in the black waters of the Stirl.

Salix was a rangy, muscular woman with a cascade of white curls and eyes as dark as whortleberries. Her cottage by the river smelled oddly of smoke, rotting eggs, and lavender when they walked in. She laughed as she stirred the mass in her cauldron, and they reeled back out, pushing their weeping faces into the cold again to drag at air that burned like fire and gave them no relief.

"It's a good poultice for wounds," she said. "Graf Dix missed his chopping stump and came close to cutting off his foot with his ax this morning. I'm making a great pot of it for him. Nairn, isn't it? You were scaring the wolves away from my granddaughter on her way home?"

"Something like that," Nairn agreed.

"He wanted to see your pots, Gran," Muire said, untying her cloak. "He's learning your signs."

The spoon spiraling through the morass in the cauldron briefly stopped. "Is he now?"

"He says they're very old words. You never told me that."

"You never asked. They're just some odd things passed down from my grandmother." The spoon was moving again; Salix's eyes, no more expressive than the dark face of the moon, considered Nairn. "And who might be teaching you? Surely not the bard who came with the barbarian king? Why would he have paid any attention at all to such distant past?"

"The stones," Nairn told her. "He saw that writing everywhere on the standing stones across the kingdoms." He gazed back at her, feeling something flow out of her to meet him midway in the flickering lights and shadows of her cottage. "You know," he breathed, scarcely hearing himself. "You know what they are."

Her face, the skin clinging so to her bones that it seemed ageless, softened into reminiscence. "Once. Once maybe, when I was your age, I caught a glimpse inside them. What they truly mean underneath what they say they are. But my gran died, and there was no one else to teach me."

"But what are they?" Muire asked bewilderedly. "If they're not what they mean? I never knew they meant anything at all but what you called them: 'comfrey' and 'mandrake' and such."

"That's all they are to me now," Salix said, "those ancient words." She gave the spoon a turn or two silently, her eyes going back to Nairn. They smiled faintly; she added softly, "I can feel them in you, wanting to speak. Isn't that strange?"

"Yes," he said breathlessly. "How do I—"

"I have no idea. But that bard knows, or he wouldn't be teaching it to you." She lifted the spoon, rapped it against the iron rim. "Is that a good thing or a bad thing? I don't know that, either. Come and let me know, will you, when you find out?" He nodded wordlessly. "You'd best go back up now; the wild things are out tonight, hunting under the moon." She chuckled. "Though they'll give you a wide berth when they catch a whiff of you. Muire, make him a brand to light his way."

She slipped out with him, for another clean breath, she said, as she handed him the torch. But the air between them spoke, brittle as it was, and then her smile did, in the firelight. He wondered, as he bent to catch her kiss, what pattern of twigs that lovely word might make.

When he climbed back up the hill, he found the snow around the school churned by wagon wheels and horses. The broad room the students used both as refectory and study was full of wealthy travelers and guards dripping at the hearth. A young man with Odelet's grace and coloring stood at the hearth, talking earnestly to Declan. The students around them softened their playing so they could hear the news. Nairn, taking off his cloak and watching Odelet come from her chamber wrapped head to heel in a great quilt, realized what they had come for.

"I sent for Odelet's brother," Declan explained to the students. "Her health is frail; she needs to be cared for at home."

Her wan smile, in a face as pallid as eggshell but for her raw nose, seemed genuinely grateful. Nairn bade farewell to her reluctantly the next day, for the band of courtiers, guards, and hunters wanted to get back across the plain before the storms returned.

"Perhaps you'll come to play in Estmere someday," she told Nairn. "I hope so."

He gazed mutely at her lovely face, felt his suddenly heavy heart overladen with wishes, promises, resolves. He saw himself on a fine white horse, riding beside King Oroh to her father's castle, trumpets sounding, doors opening at their approach. "I will come," he said huskily; his eyes clung to her as she turned, a shapeless bundle of furs helped into the well-appointed wagon by her ladies.

As the students gathered around the retinue, a couple piping their farewells, Odelet's brother stopped his mount beside Declan.

"Thank you," he said. "This is most likely the only way she would have permitted herself to be taken home." He paused, shook his head like a restive horse, and added, "I forgot. I was asked to give you a message from King Oroh, who is staying with my father. The bard you chose as your replacement died in an unfortunate accident. The king wants you to find him a new bard." He paused, squinting into the rare winter sunlight and pulled words slowly out of memory. "You know what he needs, the king said, and he will be patient. This must be a bard to bring honor to the new realm of Belden, and he has utmost trust in you that you will recognize the bard he needs."

He raised his hand in farewell and shouted to the wagon driver, leaving the old bard still as a standing stone in the snow, and even more wordless.

Chapter Nine

Princess Beatrice found the face on the disk in her father's private collection of antiquities. It lay in a case of rosewood and glass, this time on the page of an open book. She could not read the language; it was all in chicken-track runes, probably carved on stone originally, and comprehensible only to those chosen few who kept its secrets. Whoever had copied them had sketched the disk as well: the hooded face on the circle, its beaky profile already grown nebulous with centuries. The book had lain there, open to that page, for years. She must have glanced at it many times in passing until it imprinted itself into her memory, and the memory had stirred to wake when Curran's shovel brought the face to light at the bottom of the dig site.

But who was it? she wondered. Or did that matter? Was it simply the recognition of a symbol among those in the know that mattered?

She rang a little bell hung to one side of a shadowy oak corridor to summon the curator. He appeared out of his mysterious warren of offices, workrooms, storage closets. He was a tall, bulky man who always dressed in black; his portentous and slightly annoyed expression melted away when he saw Beatrice.

"Princess," he exclaimed, smiling.

"Good morning, Master Burley." He had been down that corridor all her life, looking much the same, beetle-browed and bald as a bedpost, even in the early years when she had to stand on her toes to see into the cases.

"On your way to work, I see."

"Yes," she agreed, cheerfully. Her digging clothes appalled her mother, so Beatrice usually made a point of fleeing out the nearest door of the castle as soon as she had pulled on her dungarees and boots. But she had taken the detour on impulse that morning, guessing that her father, occupied with business and guests, would not have had time to delve into the mystery yet. "I wonder if you could tell me something about this face?"

Master Burley followed her through the dustless, softly lit, spaciously enclosed spoils of history: jeweled chests and weapons, pipes and harps, coins and clothes, ornately carved cups and platters, to the case in the corner.

He looked at the face, and said softly, "Ah."

"What does 'ah' mean? Master Cle laughed inordinately when he saw it. What would make him do that?"

"Really? I had no idea he knew how. That particular face—what we can see of it—has appeared here and there through the centuries, on the odd metal disk or coin at its earliest; later on this seal, as the frontispiece of this book, even stamped into the silver guard of this sword." He moved as he spoke, taking her from case to case, from century to random century. "Here we see it even on this delicate ivory cameo. So we must conclude that the face is suggestive of many different things: secrets, scholarship, violence, love, power."

"All that," she said, entranced. "But, Master Burley, who in the world is it?"

"No one," he answered with more complacency than she could have summoned. Apparently, he had learned to live with this mystery. "Scholars have suggested various possibilities. The only thing they agree on is that the importance seems a matter not of identity—the owner of the face, or the original artist having died centuries ago—but of symbolism. Of recognition."

"Of what?" she demanded.

"We don't know that, either, Princess. Perhaps of the language. Or the secrets it hides."

"So if you recognize the face, you are one who knows the secrets?"

"Roughly," he agreed.

"Well, then, what does the secret language say? Surely somebody has translated it."

He nodded. "There have been several translations."

"And?"

"Well." He passed a hand over his smooth head, looking bemused. "Scholars agreed on a common title for the work: 'The Circle of Days.' It seems to be a sort of journal of the daily lives of early dwellers in this land. Cooking, planting, chipping arrowheads, making clothes, washing them—"

"Laundry?" she said incredulously.

"That sort of thing."

"Who would keep a journal about laundry when you have to whittle the letters onto tree bark or stone?"

"That has come up in scholarly debates."

"The secrets," she guessed abruptly, "are hidden in the laundry. Cooking, carving—they all mean something else. Something secret."

Master Burley nodded. "Exactly, Princess. And there we stand. At the edge of the mystery, without a clue as to what anything might mean."

She pondered that and smiled a little, reluctantly. "I suppose that's why Master Cle laughed. He recognized the face of the inexplicable. So that's as far as we can go."

"Until the scholar is born who can understand the riddles inherent in primitive methods of laundry, we are indeed at a standstill."

"How extraordinarily peculiar." She stood a moment longer, reluctant to give up on the question but having nowhere else to go for a better answer. "Well. Thank you, Master Burley. My father will probably be in to ask the same thing. I'll tell him what you've told me, of course, but he'll think I've missed something, or you have, or generations of—"

The doors opened suddenly, and there he was, the king, strolling through the cases with an entourage of guests: Lord Grishold, his wife, Lady Petris, assorted courtiers and elderly cousins at whose names Beatrice faltered, and the big, dark-eyed man who was Lord Grishold's bard, come, no doubt, to view the antique instruments. And here she was, the princess remembered suddenly, dressed like a bricklayer in yesterday's laundry, for all the world to see.

She quelled a laugh and an urge to hide herself in the curator's closets. It was too late, anyway. Her father saw her face above the cases, and, as he grew closer, the rest of her. His expression didn't flicker; most likely he didn't notice, having a broad tolerance for peculiar objects. Lady Petris did: her painted brows tried to leap off her face.

"My dear," she said, bravely dropping a kiss near Beatrice's face. "How unusual you look."

"Don't I? I'm just on my way to dig."

"To dig. Yes."

"My daughter has unusual interests," the king said briskly. "She drives herself across the Stirl and vanishes underground for much of the day, then comes home, if we are fortunate, with forgotten pieces of history. Such as this." He flashed the disk he was carrying, and the aged cousins murmured. Lord Grishold leaned in for a closer look. The king added to Beatrice, "Your uncle has taken an interest in antiquities."

"Yes, they are always plowing up the odd bits in my fields," he murmured. His bard was taking a long look at the disk as well. Beatrice found herself taking a long look at him as he did so. She couldn't tell immediately if he was unusually handsome or simply compelling, the way he seemed to inhabit more space than he physically needed. Perhaps, she thought, he just inhabited, in some spirit, more of his burly, big-boned body than most were aware they possessed at any given moment. Even his long hair, left fashionably loose as musicians wore it, seemed to glow, like a well-groomed horse pelt, with black light.

He raised his eyes abruptly from the disk, met hers. They, too, held that black light; it seemed, for an instant, to flow into her. In that brief moment, the vigorous young man seemed insubstantial as air, as time, little more than a mask for the nameless, ancient piece of past that had found its way under her father's roof. She was used to looking at old things; something in her recognized him as yet one more.

She blinked herself free after a heartbeat, remembered to breathe. She saw his compelling face again, looking back at her gravely, curiously. She felt the blood surge through her, then, color her brightly from breastbone to brow. She shifted her gaze with an effort; even then she felt his eyes.

Or she imagined it: when she lifted her eyes again, he had turned his attention to her father, who was saying to the curator, "Yes, Beatrice has brought us a mystery, as she told you. This is what came out of the dig."

What was the bard's name? She tried to remember. He had not yet played formally for the court though she had heard soft strains of harping from the minstrels' gallery the evening before. He would play that night, she knew, at the supper for Lord Grishold.

"Beatrice?"

They were all looking at her. She felt herself flush again, and smiled apologetically. "I'm sorry, Father. I—my thoughts strayed." She backed a step. "I should go. The tide is low now, and the others are waiting to be picked up."

"Wait, wait," he said, laughing. "Before you rush away, tell us where this was found."

"Oh. Across Dockers Bridge, among the standing stones near the river."

"Really. And what inspired Master Cle to go exploring among the blighted ruins there?"

"Father, nobody ever knows what inspires Master Cle."

"True enough. Well, if you must go, you must. Do try to dig up something suitably astonishing that you can show us all at supper tonight."

"Yes, Father."

Maybe she felt the bard's attention again as she opened the

door; maybe it was only her own inclination that made her turn her head, look back before she crossed the threshold. He was watching her, his face a clear reflection of the surprise and interest in her own.

She found herself, through the day, puzzling over that broad, clean-cut face, which somehow exuded energy and enigma at the same time. There seemed a wildness about it. Well, not exactly wildness, nothing the least feral; maybe it was only a suggestion of unpredictability, as was suitable for the court bard of the harsh and moody Grishold landscape. He would have plucked his music from high and low, lord's hall and hovel, wherever he heard it. Maybe . . . It kept coming between her eyes and her brush, that face, her eyes and her small pick, as she and Campion worked along the line of protruding stones, Campion whistling intermittently, sometimes asking questions about the disk that she barely heard herself answer.

She did hear the sharp exclamation he gave toward the end of the afternoon. She looked at him, startled; he had dropped his brush and was rubbing his eyes.

"You flicked your dust cloud right into my face, my lady," he complained, half-laughing, half-snuffling at the dust up his nose.

"I'm so sorry," she exclaimed, groping for her handkerchief. "Here—use this—"

"I can't blow my nose on the monogram of the Peverell kings."

"Or course you can; I do it all the time."

He managed, despite his protest, with a great deal of enthusiasm; he mopped his streaming eyes, then tossed her a shrewd glance as he picked up his brush.

"You haven't heard a word anyone's said for hours. Are you in love?"

She stared at him, dumbfounded. "How can I be?" she heard herself say. "I only saw him this morning."

Such amusement erupted from the depths of the hole that must have unnerved even the hardened denizens of the ruins, she thought a trifle sourly, had there been any besides Master Cle.

"Kelda," Lady Anne said that evening, helping the princess dress for supper. "The bard's name is Kelda."

Beatrice, who had tortured a good quarter hour of conversation bringing it around to the harper, felt a moment's solace. "Odd name."

"Something musty out of Grishold history, I would imagine. Yet I've been hearing it all day."

Beatrice eyed her in the mirror as she dangled sapphires along the princess's green satin neckline, then amber. "Really."

"Everyone's been asking. All the queen's ladies and most of yours are suddenly fascinated by the harp and have been paying visits to the minstrels' gallery for lessons."

"Oh." Deflated, she gazed at her tidy reflection, then studied Anne's exquisite, aloof face, the arch of her fine nostril. "Not you, I take it?"

"Too raw by far for me, Princess Beatrice. He's spent his life in the wilds of Grishold, and he looks like a pony. A rather willful pony at that." She held an elaborate, fussy, and quite hideous collar of gold roses twined around chunks of amethyst against Beatrice's collarbone without, it seemed, actually seeing it. "Still. Something besides all that rustic homespun, a decent pair of boots, and a good haircut, he might just possibly . . . especially with those shoulders . . ." She caught the princess's clear, speculative eye upon her and actually blushed, Beatrice saw to her amazement: a tint of old rose like something in an antique painting. "I beg your pardon, Princess; I was distracted. Well." She snatched the necklace away quickly. "That won't do at all."

"No."

"Worse than your medallion, the other day. Did you find out what it was?"

"In a way. Once it meant a great deal, and now it means nothing to anyone."

"A bit like—" She hesitated, considering the subject.

"Yes. A bit like love. I think the sapphires."

"I think you're right. The color offsets the pale green of your dress and complements your eyes."

"But what is it about him?" Beatrice wondered. "Is it something he does deliberately, or something he can't help?"

"I don't know yet," Lady Anne said slowly, clasping the necklace and settling the tiers of gold and deep, sparkling blue around the princess's shoulders. "But may I suggest, Princess Beatrice, that finding out might be far more trouble than he's worth?"

Which, considering the troubling events of the evening, Beatrice thought later, proved her lady-in-waiting's shrewd eye for it.

It began predictably enough. Guests in their finery gathered in the long antechamber before supper to greet Lord Grishold and his family. Bottles were uncorked; platters carrying morsels of edible art followed trays of gleaming crystal in their labyrinthine paths through the crush. Flutes and viols sent their voices genially from the distant minstrels' gallery to weave among the conversations below, all of them getting progressively louder as more guests were announced and added their own voices to the throng. Beatrice, drifting and making agreeable noises here and there, found her gaze straying through the gathering, searching, she realized, for the young, energetic face that had riveted her attention that morning. She felt herself flushing at the memory and pulled her attention resolutely back to the face in front of her: her brother's affianced, she discovered, describing, inch by inch, the lace, piping, pearls, and ruches on the sleeves of her wedding gown.

Beatrice smiled and nodded and drifted again as soon as politely possible. A dark head caught her eye. But it was the back of Jonah Cle's head, not the bard's. He was standing on the edge of the crowd, a glass in his hand. His son, who tended toward the opposite side of whatever room his father was in, stood unexpectedly next to him. Even more unpredictably, they seemed to be talking, at least until someone in the crowd caught Phelan's attention, and he vanished into it.

Beatrice, remembering the hooded face appearing at odd places in her father's collection, put on her brightest smile, pretended to be deaf, and made her way to the fraying edges of the party.

"Good evening, Master Cle."

His crabbed expression remained unchanged, but she did cause him to blink.

"Princess. You clean up astonishingly well."

"Yes, don't I? I wanted to ask you about that disk. I went to consult Master Burley this morning, and he pointed out the hooded face on several different pieces from entirely different centuries. He said that beyond the fact that it meant a secret, no one knows what the secret was. Do you have any idea?"

He was still looking at her, but his heavy-lidded gaze had become fixed and very dark, as though his attention had shifted imperceptibly beyond her. As she glanced around, something equally dark loomed to her other side. She turned her head quickly, and there was Lord Grishold's bard, all in black as usual, and smiling upon them.

"Princess Beatrice," he said, bowing his head to her. His deep, warm voice seemed to resonate in her bones, set them thrumming like harp strings. "Master Cle. We have not met, but I had the privilege of seeing many of your finds this morning in the king's collection. I understand you also studied at the bardic school on the hill?"

It seemed to take forever for Jonah to answer. "Once," he said finally, so dryly that Beatrice expected the word to puff into dust in the air.

Then the bard turned to her once more. Tall as she was, his big bones made her feel oddly birdlike, more swallow than her usual stork, as though he could carry her on his fingers. She felt her skin warm beneath the sapphires as he spoke; again, she sensed the odd, jarring, intriguing juxtaposition of ancient mystery and youthful exuberance.

"Princess, my name is Kelda. It's an old crofter's name in Grishold. What my father hoped I would become, except that he kept finding me sitting on the sty and singing to the pigs after I fed them."

"Charming," Jonah breathed to one of the ancestors hanging around the room, and the bard's smile turned rueful.

"We in Grishold are a plainspoken lot. I learned my ballads in some rough places, where folk still sing the most ancient songs of the realm. I thought that, considering what you were wearing this morning, Princess, you would know something about earth."

"Yes," she answered a trifle dazedly. "I do. In my other life, I dig things up for Master Cle."

"Forgive my ignorance, but isn't that an unusual occupation for a king's daughter?"

"I suppose, judging from old ballads, you would think that we all sat around doing needlepoint and waiting for our true loves to ride up to our door. Doors." She was gabbling, she felt, under his smiling eyes, and wished she had pulled a glass off the champagne tray disappearing beyond him.

"Of course I do," he answered with disarming candor. "Tales are all I know of princesses, in Grishold. But why do you like old things?"

She flushed again, as though the question were somehow intimate, and he knew it. She answered more slowly, studying his face helplessly as she spoke, entranced by the ambiguities in it. "I like—I like recognizing—I mean finding—what's lost. Or rather what's forgotten. Piecing people's lives together with the little mysteries they leave for us. I like seeing out of earlier eyes, looking at the world when it was younger, different. Even then, that long ago, it was building the earliest foundations of my world. It's like searching for the beginning of a story. You keep going back and back, and the beginning keeps shifting, running ahead of you, always older than the puzzle piece you hold in your hand, always pointing beyond what you know."

He nodded vigorously, his flowing hair catching rivulets of light. "That's what I feel when I come across a new ballad," he exclaimed. "I keep listening for the older form of it, the place where language changes, hints at something past, the place where the story points even farther back."

"Yes," she agreed quickly, and noticed Phelan, then, coming to a stop beside the bard and gazing at her, entirely oblivious to the tray of wine intruding in front of him. Jonah took a glass promptly, and she saw it then, the older story: the flick of perceptive amusement in the young bard's face, the faint, narrowed, teasing glance, the odd familiarity with the man he had never met. She stood with her mouth left hanging gracelessly open, forgetting even to reach for wine herself. Then Phelan greeted her, and she closed her mouth again quickly.

"Princess Beatrice," he said, looking so innocently amazed, she could have kissed him. "You've stepped out of an old fairy tale."

"Let me guess," she heard herself babble breathlessly, just to keep her startled eyes off the bard. "The one about the maiden who cleans hearths by day and dances with the prince by moonlight."

He nodded, smiling. "She rises from the ashes, phoenixlike, under the fires of the moon. I suppose that tale would be apt, though ash bins were farthest from my mind."

She felt the bard's dark gaze drawing at her as Phelan spoke; somehow, in that crush, she heard his indrawn breath, gathering words to speak, to force her to look at him. But another voice blundered into his, deep and jovial, trained to command attention and overwhelm the competition.

"Ah, good. Here you are, Master Kelda. I would like you to meet Zoe Wren, whose voice you will hear tonight. She is a young bard from the school, nearly finished with her studies there. We are, of course, also eagerly anticipating your own performance."

The impervious Royal Bard Quennel, his white hair tufted

like a skylark's crest, beamed upon the gathering. Zoe, in flowing, twilight-colored silks, greeted the princess first with her usual courtesy, then shifted her sharp, lovely eyes to the bard. She seemed oddly impervious to his charms.

"Master Kelda," she said briskly in her strong, sweet voice. "I do look forward to your playing. I expect you will work magic in the great hall."

That caused Jonah Cle to snort in his wine for some reason. Kelda regarded Zoe with interest, as though she were an unfamiliar species. "I have heard your voice," he remarked. "Very clearly, when we all arrived. It was, as Master Quennel says, astonishing."

She smiled cheerfully. "Yes, I suppose it was."

A platter of tiny glazed tarts shaped like scallop shells carrying an oyster beside a black pearl of roe presented itself and was ignored, except by Beatrice, who nibbled when she was unnerved by undercurrents, and by Quennel, who swallowed the briny mouthful whole and engulfed them all again in his pleasure.

"Tell us, Master Kelda, do you travel often beyond Grishold? I don't believe we have seen you before in King Lucien's court. Nor, indeed, in his father's, though you might have been a student then. I have been here in this court so long I lose track of the years."

Kelda shook his head, causing Jonah to emit another peculiar noise. "I travel rarely. And I have never been in the ancient school on the hill."

"You must go, then!"

"Yes, tomorrow. The masters have invited me, and Lord Grishold will not need me. But surely, Master Quennel, you have played for three kings in this court: King Lucien's grandfather as well."

"Ah, yes—I became Royal Bard just before he died. I'm surprised that you remembered. I did not."

"We listen greedily in Grishold for news of Caerau. It takes the chill out of the long winter evenings. I'm in awe of your stamina. Your musicianship. You have been in this position for so long that surely you are tempted, now and then, to yield such strenuous duties to a younger bard?"

"Never," Quennel said complacently. "I have the voice and fingers of a far younger man, and a memory rigorously trained in the school on the hill. I forget that I am old when I play."

"You make us all forget," Phelan murmured, glancing askance at the visiting bard and the turn he had given the pleasantries. That brought him Kelda's attention.

"You are also at the school, I believe?"

"I am," Phelan answered, sounding like Jonah at his most arid. "But I have no ambitions and no interest at all in trying to fill Quennel's boots. He is a very great bard, an example to us all, and I can only wish him to keep playing for the Peverell kings as long as he himself wishes."

"Which would be," Quennel added, smiling, "until I draw my final breath between lines and leave one last verse unsung to haunt these old stones forever."

"Admirable," Kelda said with enthusiasm, and stopped a tray of toast points bearing minute molds of salmon, with capers for eyes. "We can all learn from your example."

"You see," Quennel began affably, and paused to pop a salmon into his mouth before he continued. He swallowed, paused again, swallowed again. Beatrice, working on her own fish, saw his face flush the hue of well-cooked salmon, then of uncooked beef. She nearly inhaled her own bite. Jonah said something sharply to Quennel, who was beginning to sag oddly against the startled Zoe. She struggled to hold him upright. As he slid, Jonah threw out his arm; it struck the old man hard below his ribs. The wine in Jonah's hand splashed all over Quennel, and the salmon flew out of him like the final word on the subject before he slumped to the floor at their feet.

Chapter Ten

Given the mysterious nature and gifts of the bard who honored King Oroh's court and sat at his right hand at councils, the king had handed Declan a conundrum. Declan had replaced himself, the first time, with someone he already knew and trusted, a skilled musician, presumably with the kinds of talents Oroh expected. This bard had also traveled in the king's company from their native land. The court chronicler's notes on the matter indicate that the bard's sudden and completely unexpected death was indeed a stunning loss for the king. In his own land, the bard might have been easily replaced. In the new Kingdom of Belden, bards were trained far differently, and what King Oroh had come to expect in his Royal Bard simply did not exist. "The young bard left no one in this wild country to replace him," the chronicler wrote. "King Oroh has no choice but to summon Declan back to him if he can find no other of such necessary skills."

What exactly were these "necessary skills"?

Either they were kept secret, or alluded to between the lines, or everyone so easily recognized them that there was no need for explanation. Any of these are possible, since nobody ever explained why a gifted bard native to any of the five lost kingdoms would not have suited Oroh as easily. References are made to Declan's unusual powers, both in historical records and in ballads. But in records, the references are brief, subtle, and sometimes barely there.

"The mist that flowed that third day over the adversary [at the Battle of the Welde] Declan raised with his skills, and thus was the King of the Marches brought low."

Is Oroh's chronicler actually telling us that Declan raised a fog that blinded only King Anstan's army?

If so, such gifts that died with Oroh's latest bard must have been extremely difficult to replace. Indeed, the terse passage casts a glance askew at all of King Oroh's victories, and explains, in some occult fashion, his swift, triumphant usurping of the powers of five kings. He anchored his fleet in the foggy waters of the Stirl in early spring; by the next spring he declared himself King of Belden.

The modern historian can only suspend disbelief and conclude that the king, requesting that Declan find a successor to a bard with like powers, must have been well aware of the extremely hard nut he handed to the aging bard to crack.

And back he came, her faithless love,
In the night from the village below.
She stood upon the tower above,
Heard him singing in the snow.

Hot tears spiraled down the ice,
Whittled it sharp as love and lack.

She called him once, she called him twice,
He heard the deadly crack.

He looked up and saw her eyes,
Then he felt the blow.
His heart's blood froze around the ice,
Colder than the snow.

"BALLAD OF THE FAITHLESS BARD," ANONYMOUS: POSSIBLY BY A
STUDENT OF DECLAN'S

A nd so death was the seed planted in Declan's mind that split and sent up a shoot that leafed and branched and finally flowered into the first bardic competition held in the Kingdom of Belden.

Before he announced it, even to his own students, he gathered the few who had been struggling over his twig-scratches and finally allowed them to see one another's faces.

They met in one of the rooms that Declan occupied midway up the tower, in which he kept his instruments and counseled his students. The students, grateful for rugs and fur underfoot, huddled close to the fire and eyed one another with dour surprise. None in the mangy, winter-bitten lot seemed to emit any kind of particular brilliance; they all worked hard, played well, sang well, and seemed to have no inkling of what in any of the others had persuaded Declan that they should be included in his secret circle.

There were five: the handsome, arrogant, ivory-haired Blayse, son of a Grishold nobleman; the plump and earnest Drue, whose father was a wealthy merchant in Estmere; the lovely, lanky Shea, with her hard violet eyes and a horse's tail of chestnut hair, whose father owned the village brewery; the angular scarecrow Osprey, whose father was steward in one of the great houses of what was once the southern kingdom of Waverlea; and Nairn the crofter's son.

They encountered one another daily; none were particularly close, not even Nairn and Shea, who had shared a summer's eve in passing, once, on a flowery riverbank. It seemed a very long time ago, Nairn thought, and in a green, warm, sweetly scented world long vanished from the plain. Shea, dripping with a cold, cast a brief, bleary glance in his direction and sniffed, maybe a comment, maybe not.

"My father taught me how to write," she said, "to do accounts. But nothing ever like this."

"Nobody taught me," Nairn said. "I thought that this is how everyone writes."

Blayse made a faint, rude noise. The pedantic Drue said solemnly, "I can understand how you could make such a mistake if you had never tried to write before. But you would have realized soon enough that you had run out of words. For instance, there would be, I think, no word for 'innkeeper,' or even 'garden,' such concepts being unimaginable to primitive people who did not differentiate between—"

"Or for 'tavern,'" Osprey interrupted irreverently. "Or, for that matter, 'beer.'"

"There have been hops grown on the plain for centuries, my father says," Shea argued. "My father says—"

"Hops," intoned Drue, "first came from the fields of Estmere. The art of growing them and making beer was brought to Stirl Plain long after the stones were raised."

"My father—" Shea persisted stubbornly.

"The earliest people on the plain had no word for 'beer.'"

"Well, they must have drunk something," Osprey said. He appealed to the bard, who was at his table, rapidly writing twigs. "Master Declan—"

"I have in my company the most gifted and promising of all my students, and all you can find to talk about is beer?"

They looked at him, surprised: what else better in that bleak world?

He gave them his rare, faint smile and rose. "Here," he said, passing lines of twigs written on parchment to each of them. "When you finish translating this, come and tell me what it means. It is the keystone of your art. Go," he urged them gently, as they stared blankly at the lines, turned the papers helplessly on their heads and back again.

"But, Master Declan, there are over two dozen lines," Shea protested.

"Then you'd best get started. Oh," he added, as they turned reluctantly from the fire, "you may ask one another for help."

Not likely, their faces said, as the students headed for the door. Not a chance. Declan's smile deepened, Nairn saw, at the scent of competition.

Curious, he spent his hours after supper matching the patterns on the page to the patterns on his list. "Plain," he found easily, and "circle," "stone," "bone," and others as simple and fundamental. Some patterns eluded him. Words he had not learned yet? Words newer in the world than the early, prosaic words of daily life?

On a plain of bone,
In a circle of stone . . .

He pored over the unknown words so long that he nearly fell asleep. They blurred in front of his eyes, swam together, made new patterns. He shook himself awake, translated all he could. Unable to write his own familiar language, he simply added them to memory, words making images in his head, as stark and elemental as the words themselves.

Three . . .
The speaking stone
The full cauldron
The spiral tower . . .

Mesmerized, he gazed at the mute patterns until they entered his head as well, filling the spaces in his poem he could not render. His tiny room was soundless; the school might well have vanished around him. Only his candle made a sound now and then, a sizzle of wick into melted wax, a flutter at an errant draft that shifted light into shadow for a blink of time on his page.

Three . . .

Three what? A bird's nest of twigs followed, then another "three," followed by two pair of crossed twigs. He stared at them stubbornly, willing them to speak, say what they meant, reveal what lay within the patterns.

And suddenly they did.

He felt his heart melt and his hair stiffen at the same time, at a vision of riches, at a vision of an enormity that came at him out of the shadows like a swipe of a vicious claw. His blood pounded; his eyes filled with gold, crowns, jewels, all tossed carelessly into a glittering pile that grew as its image filled his mind. Treasure. Terror. Treasure.

He blinked incredulously at the twigs, and they spoke again. He whispered, echoing them.

Three terrors ...
Three treasures ...

Sometime later—hours, days, another night—he stumbled through the dreaming school, the paper in his hand, the words burning in his mind. He ran up the tower steps to Declan's private chamber door and pounded on it.

Declan opened it. He was still dressed, his expression unruffled by sleep; he might have been waiting for someone, and he seemed completely unsurprised that it was Nairn. Nairn lifted the parchment; it shook in his hand.

"What is this?" he asked. "What is it?"

"Perhaps the oldest poem in Belden. I found it on a standing stone during King Oroh's first battle on Stirl Plain."

"But what does it mean?"

"I think it means exactly what it says. Come to the fire. You're trembling." He opened the door wider; Nairn crossed Declan's bedchamber to the hearth, tried to breathe in the warmth, pull it into his embrace.

"They spoke to me," he said finally, huskily. "They told me what they meant. I saw into them." He closed his eyes; the bright words burned in his head, waiting for his need of them.

"Tell me what they said."

"'On a plain of bone, in a ring of stone ...'" He went through it effortlessly, his eyes still shut, seeing again image after image guiding him to the strange, bitter end. "'. . . No end of days nor memory.'" He opened his eyes, finally beginning to feel the heat, and looked at Declan. "What was that? What did I do?"

The bard looked as strangely pleased as he had when Nairn had coaxed the jewels from his harp. "You found the magic in the words; they spoke to the magic in you. That's the beginning of power. You were born with the great gift for it, but you had no use for it until you met me. No one here could explain it to you. The bards of the land forgot their magic long ago."

Nairn was silent, still gazing at him. He had no idea what such words meant before that night; now, he knew enough to begin to feel his way into them, as into unknown waters, find their depths, their hidden currents, their dangers.

"It was always in you," Declan added. "Born in you. You just had no use for it before. In this land, the bards have forgotten their magic."

"It's not that obvious," Nairn commented, still clinging like a lover to the warmth, as close as he could get to the boundary between desire and danger. "Looking for magic in the simple language of your Circle of Days. 'Fish,' 'Thread,' 'Eye.'" He heard the words he spoke and shivered suddenly despite the flames. "What made you look there?"

"The poem itself. It promises such marvels to the bard who understands its riddles, its trials, and such sorrow beyond measure to those who fail to understand."

Nairn was silent. He turned away from the fire to ask the bard with wonder, "How could you read it? You were a stranger, faced with an ancient language carved in stone that no one else spoke."

He glimpsed the ghost of the bard's smile, the flick of fire in his eyes. "I saw the power within the words before I even knew what they meant. The way you did, tonight. They made me feel them before they revealed themselves as the simple, ordinary language of daily life. I searched, as King Oroh moved across the five kingdoms, for those who understood that language. I found no one. Until I met you in the Marches, I thought the ancient knowledge had vanished completely from this land."

"The Circle of Days," Nairn whispered, seeing such days on the plain, the simplicity of stone, root, spear. "I wonder how they used their power, the ones who spoke the words."

"I wonder, too," Declan said softly. "We can only keep studying them; perhaps they'll tell us that. They are your doorway into King Oroh's court. Learn them. Work with them. Test them and yourself. But you must also face another test before you can be called Royal Bard of Belden. There is also the matter of music." Nairn looked at him puzzledly. "The Royal Bard must also be the greatest musician in the realm. How would you fare against the court bards of Belden?"

"I have no idea," he answered, startled. "I never met one. Will I?"

"By tradition, in my land, the king's bard is chosen from a great meeting of bards who compete with both their music and their powers to win the position. I cannot do less for King Oroh in Belden. I have heard the music in courts throughout this land. Will you let me teach you?"

Nairn could only stare at him, stunned by the thought of such a contest. One thing to be best at what no one else knew, he thought; another for the master of the bladder-pipe and the marching drum to challenge the court bards of the five kingdoms. Declan came to stand beside him at the hearth. He lifted a hand; poised above Nairn's shoulder, it hesitated, finally settled. Nairn, looking down at the flames again, did not shake it off. The bard was offering him more than he had ever dreamed, he realized dazedly; he had only to accept it.

"Yes," he said finally. "Teach me. How else can I learn what else I don't know?"

Declan smiled, a true smile for once, with neither bitterness nor reserve in it. "The court music will be the easy part," he promised. "I have all the instruments they use."

"When—"

"Soon, but not before you are ready." His hand tightened briefly, then turned Nairn gently toward the door. "Get some sleep."

Nairn stopped at the threshold, looked at him again. "Were you waiting for me tonight?"

"You kept me awake. Of course I was waiting."

Thus began Nairn's brief and disastrous exploration of the most ancient bardic arts.

The circle of his own days lost their boundaries then, became fluid, unpredictable. When he wasn't learning exacting courtly music from Declan, he drifted like a dreamer or a drunkard, enchanted by every spoken word, every silent named thing around him, without paying attention to who had spoken, or what responsibility he might take for the things he saw: the dwindling pile of wood beside the fire, the candle guttering, drowning its wick in its wax, drawing the sudden dark behind it. He saw "wood," "fire," "dark" as separate, powerful entities; what they meant to him changed with every glimpse of them. He had no idea how the other students in the circle had fared with the task

Declan had given them. They spoke around him; he might have been hearing their voices underwater, so intently did he separate their words from any human origin. Only that mattered: the word, spoken, and the image, the burning rose of power that blossomed at the sound.

He heard Muire's voice occasionally; it held another kind of power.

"I miss you in the kitchen," she said one morning when he came down for breakfast. "You used to scatter words like little gifts in odd places. You used to see what I needed done almost before I did."

He mumbled something absently around a bite of bread and butter, swallowed, and saw her face with unexpected clarity, instead of an indistinguishable blur in the background of his thoughts. It looked wistful, uncertain, words he hadn't learned yet from the "Circle of Days."

"I'm finding my way into something," he said a trifle incoherently. "I'll come back one of these days, I think."

She nodded. "That's what Salix told me. She asked about you."

Salix. She had words, he remembered, all over her jars and boxes, sewn into cloth bags full of dried things. Already Muire's face was fading; the unknown words glowing in his head, brighter than all the old, familiar words surrounding him.

"Salix." He tore another piece from the loaf, shambled off with it. "I'll go and see her."

He did so, wandering out the door with his breakfast in one hand, his cloak in the other. He hardly noticed the steady fall of snow the clouds were sifting out of themselves, and how he slid on the fresh layers as he walked down the hill. He entered Salix's cottage without knocking, prowled silently around, examining the collection of twigs she left like a secret path he was compelled to follow, all the while a tall, white-haired figure stood just beyond his attention, stirring and stirring her cauldron over the fire.

"What are you doing?" he heard, and then himself, just as distantly:

"Taking your words."

"Nairn," she said, and he blinked. Another world fell into place around him: the old healer's cottage, with her weavings on the floor, across the backs of chairs, her tidy shelves full of all her makings, neatly stored and labeled.

He looked at her and blinked again, feeling as though she had shaken him awake. So she had, he realized; she had said the word that meant him.

She gave him a smile that was somewhere between exasperated and amused. "Muire said you had become entirely impossible. 'Distracted' was the word she used. 'Witless' was maybe what she thought. Do you need a potion?"

"A potion?"

"Is there anything," she said slowly and clearly, "I can make for you?"

"Oh." He shook his head. "I think there's no cure for what I've got."

"Is there a name for it?"

"I think—" He hesitated, looking at it, this ravening monster in him that ate words like fire ate twigs. "I think its name is magic. It goes where it goes. I follow." He added, pulling up a useful word that he'd all but forgotten: "Sorry."

"Ah, well," she said ruefully. "I wish I had been able to understand it better. Is it a good thing or a bad thing? Do you know that yet?"

"No." Already the warm cottage walls were wavering, blurring behind all the words he had learned within them. "Not yet. I'll tell you when I know."

The snow had stopped falling; the world around him, as he walked back up the hill, seemed mute as midnight. Even the river, narrowed to a slit of dark water between encroaching boundaries of ice, ran silently under the pallid sky. The school on the hill seemed shrunken, huddled against the cold. The narrow tower windows, the tiny, thick panes in the students' chambers, were barred with frozen tears of ice. The tower's battlements were a thick, upside-down crown of ice, from which jagged, fist-thick shards hung down like barbaric jewels. Nairn, busy patterning everything he saw with ancient letters, forgot, for a brief moment, the shape of the word for ice. He stopped, gazing up at the massive icicles hanging high on the battlements and saw the patterns of the twigs in the way the icicles fell: long and short, long and long and short, randomly, the way the world sometimes made things. Or was it only the tiniest fragment of a pattern so vast, so intricate, that it would take a different kind of vision to see the whole?

The sun came out then, unexpectedly, slipping a sudden, astonishing shaft of light between the sullen clouds. It struck the tower, ignited the crown of ice to golden fire, and Nairn's breath caught in his throat. The word in his head kindled as well, light running along the ancient pattern like a finger across harp strings, as the sun was doing, making a music of its own on a winter's morning. The word in Nairn's head leaped up to meet the fire within the ice.

There was a sudden crack just as, below, the scholarly Drue, bundled like a sausage, opened the door and stepped out.

The icicle struck him with all the force of a spear thrown from the battlements. Nairn, the breath turned to ice in his mouth, watched him spin and crumple, heard the ice shatter against the threshold stone. The sunlight faded. A swath of blood, the only color in the world, melted the snow around Drue's head. Nairn, frozen in that slow, amber moment of time, saw a flicker at the tower window above the door: Declan, disturbed in his music room, looking down, then across the yard at Nairn.

He vanished. A student, come to shut the open front door, stared out instead, and shouted. Others crowded behind him, pushed him out as Declan's own voice, still calm but louder than usual, bade them make way.

Nairn began to shake. He had cried so rarely in his life that he barely recognized the word, but he felt something like melted ice slide and chill on his face. The students came out, made a ring around the fallen Drue; Declan knelt in the snow beside him. Nairn moved finally, unsteadily, feeling vast mountains of snow shift at every step.

"Poor Drue," Shea said, her peremptory voice trembling. "Master Declan, is he dead?"

"Yes," Declan said briefly. He looked up as Nairn finally crossed some vast chasm of time and reached the edge of the circle.

"Nairn," Blayse said abruptly, noticing from which direction he had come. "Were you out here? You must have seen what happened."

Nairn opened his mouth. No words came out. There seemed none he knew for what had happened. How could he say sunlight, ice, the mystery within the word for ice, the sudden beauty that echoed so powerfully, so disastrously in his heart?

They were all looking at him then, their faces turned away

from Declan, who held Nairn's eyes, waiting, it seemed, like the others, for his answer.

Declan lifted his hand, held one finger briefly to his lips: another ancient word. Then he dropped his hand and his eyes, and Nairn heard himself speak.

"The ice broke from the top of the tower, fell on him just as he came out."

Their eyes loosed him, too, drifted back to the unfortunate Drue, silent for once, and gazing with interest, it seemed, at the splinter of bone whiter than the snow that protruded down from his eyebrow.

"His father will be rabid," Osprey murmured, awed.

"His father will be grieved," Declan said, shifting Drue's arm from behind his back. "He'll understand that it was an accident. Help me get him inside. Shea, go and get Salix."

"For what?" she asked bewilderedly. "He's dead as a doornail." He glanced at her, a quick flash of metal under his red brows, and she backed a step reluctantly. "Oh, all right."

"We want to be able to tell his family that we did everything we could for him."

Nairn helped lift the body, heard, as they brought him indoors, soft, moist, swollen noises of shock and sorrow following in the wake.

"Nairn," Declan said, as they let the body fall on Drue's tousled, fur-covered pallet. "Go up to the battlements and take an ax to the hanging ice. Blayse, you guard the door so that we don't lose another student."

"Watch out for Shea coming back," someone said anxiously. "And Salix."

"Yes," Nairn said tightly.

Declan looked at him again; his eyes withheld expression. "When you're done, come and let me know."

"Yes," he said again, hearing the implicit message within the request. "I'll tell you."

He realized, as he swung the ax and sent ice flying into the air to thump harmlessly into the snow, that even then, between the loveliness of the singing light and the sudden monstrosity of Drue's death, he still had no answer to Salix's question.

As the long winter finally ebbed and wild lilies bloomed in the melting snow, Declan sent out his message to all the bards of Belden, high and low, near and far, inviting them to the school for a great competition, on Midsummer Day, for the position of Royal Bard at King Oroh's court.

Chapter Eleven

*Z*oe sat with the old bard as he lay in his chambers. She watched him silently. His eyes were closed, but he was awake, she guessed from the hard lines converging just above the bridge of his nose. He was silent as well. The king's physician had examined him; he had let fall a miserly word or two then, grudging even those. He had choked on an errant salmon bone, he was told. Master Cle's flailing arm had accidentally caught him where it did the most good; he had some bruises from his fall, but nothing sprained or broken. He would be fit as the proverbial fiddle tomorrow, the physician promised, and left him something that would put him to sleep when he drank it.

He did not drink it.

His servants had undressed him and put him to bed, while Zoe returned to the hall to ask Phelan to sing in her place. He was surprised, but he didn't care. He had a fine, sinewy voice; he could perform the ancient Grishold love ballad as easily as pull on a boot. She went to give her excuses to the musicians in the gallery and to ask them to do what they could to replace Quennel, so that Lord Grishold's bard would not be pressed to entertain the entire long evening. Lord Grishold's bard was already there, tuning his harp and watching the guests below take their places for supper in the great hall.

She studied his absorbed face a moment and realized she would not want him to examine too closely the expression on hers. She turned away quickly without speaking and went back to Quennel's chambers. He didn't look at her or speak, even after she sent his servants away. She waited. He drifted a little at first, she thought, until she felt the deep focus of his thoughts, worrying at some kernel of truth within a husk held in the beak of some dark bird that held him fixed in the reflection of its black, black eye.

"Zoe."

She opened her own eyes, blinked the sumptuous room around her, the bright tapestries and carpets, the ancient, legendary instruments that Quennel had collected through the decades, each in its special place. She struggled between dreams and memory, straightening in the armchair, and remembered the bard tucked into silk and fur and glowing damask, safe in his bed beside her. She turned to him, smiling; the smile smacked like a fledgling against hard glass, dropped.

He had finally opened his own eyes, but the grooves of the frown between them had only dug deeper.

"Master Quennel. Are you in pain?"

"Did you sing?"

"Without you? Of course not."

"Then that bard from Grishold who wants my life is in the great hall playing for the king."

She felt her own brows draw together, but answered gently, "Many bards in this kingdom want your position. This bard will be gone like a spell of nasty weather in a few days, and you will be playing for the king again tomorrow."

He sought her eyes finally. "You don't like him, either."

"Not for a moment." She hesitated, feeling him want more, his weary gaze drawing at her. "I'm not sure why," she added finally. "Except that what we see—what he tells us to see—seems false. He is simply not convincing as a country innocent from the lonely tors of Grishold."

"Have you heard him play tonight?"

"No. I've been mostly here with you."

"Go and listen to him."

She hesitated, reluctant to leave him. "He must have stopped by now."

"No. I can hear him." How, in that ancient wing of the castle, through walls thick with history, Zoe could not imagine. She listened, heard only the endless silence of stone. "Go and come back and tell me if he's any good."

Quennel must have been playing the bard's music in his own head, Zoe guessed as she hurried down the stairways and quiet corridors, passing from rough-hewn walls and flagstones to marble floors and oak wainscoting before she heard the distant, muted din from the hall. As she drew closer, the noise ebbed oddly, like a tide withdrawing, into absolute, astonishing silence.

A harp note broke the silence.

She entered the great hall from the back and found the guests motionless in their chairs, as though some enchantment had been flung over them. The enchanter loosed a mournful cascade of notes, and she stopped, stood unobtrusively in the shadows between the wall sconces. Kelda sat at the Royal Bard's customary place, on a gilded stool in the center of the broad square formed by the tables. He faced the dais table, where the royal family and the visitors from Grishold seemed to have forgotten the food on their plates. A single wine cup flashed among the statues; as it fell again, clinking against cutlery, Zoe saw Jonah Cle behind it. Nobody else moved.

The bard struck a chord, and she recognized the ancient Grishold ballad he began.

It was a simple, powerful tale of a knight returning to his home in the western mountains after battle and imprisonment to find that all he remembered and loved had vanished. Only the birds in the rafters of his ruined hall were left to give him a message from his wife, to tell him what had happened in a language, like the harping, best understood by the heart.

Zoe felt her eyes burn at the sinuous, melting voice. She blinked away the tears, astonished at herself. On the dais, a couple of the young women were weeping openly, smiling through their tears at the bard. One of the household guards standing behind the king raised a hand to flick away something at the corner of his eye. The knight wandered away finally, exiled to his memories, riding forever into his past.

There was dead silence while the last chord flared like an ember and slowly died.

Then a sloppy, unwieldy wave of noise flooded the hall. Cups flashed, thumped; porcelain and cutlery collided; servants moved again, proffering dishes that had, for a time, been forgotten. It was as though the entire court had been spellbound, Zoe thought. Kelda put down his harp, then everyone could speak again. He accepted their accolades with a smile, enjoying the warmth flowing to him from all over the hall. Finally, he picked up his harp again, began a light, familiar dance that the musicians in the gallery above him knew, and one by one they leaped in after him.

Someone came down from the gallery stairs near Zoe and saw her. She recognized Phelan's pale head under the lamplight and realized then how tensely she stood, hands gripping her elbows, her whole body harp-string taut, waiting, it seemed, for the descent of the harper's hand. Phelan came over, leaned against the wall beside her.

"How is Master Quennel?"

"Physically fine, the physician said. Mentally—" She hesitated. "He's in a powerful stew. About what, I'm not sure. Death, maybe." She searched Phelan's eyes, found him unsurprised. "I've never seen him so dark. He sent me down here to listen to Kelda. I think—though it makes no sense—that Quennel blames him for the accident."

Phelan loosed the ghost of a laugh. "So does my father. I have no idea why, either. Have you eaten? There's a supper laid out in the gallery for the musicians."

She nodded, her eyes moving again to Kelda. "Maybe I'll go up there, while he's down here."

Phelan regarded her curiously. "You're avoiding him? He seems harmless enough. Very gifted, as well as very ambitious. A bit crude, suggesting that Quennel might like to retire."

"I suspect that Quennel thought Kelda was trying to help him retire."

"Forcing him to choke on a swallow of salmon mousse?"

"A salmon bone."

"Well." His mouth crooked. "There is poetic precedence in that. Taste the salmon and understand all things."

"Including your own death," she said somberly. "No wonder Quennel is frothing."

She went up to the gallery, where the musicians were rollicking happily along with whatever Kelda tossed to them. She made a hasty meal of roast beef studded with garlic, leeks braised in cream, strawberry tart. Then she hurried back through the castle, the noisy party receding again behind her, to the bard's chamber.

He was still awake, still brooding, still not inclined to share his thoughts. He watched as she came to settle in the chair beside him.

"Do you want me to send for some supper?" she asked. "Are you hungry?"

"I've swallowed enough for one night," he said grimly. "Is he good?"

"Yes. He's beyond good. Some of the things he's playing are more suitable to a country court than for a formal supper given by the king. But he brought the entire hall to silence—and much of it to tears—with his playing of 'The Knight Returned to Grenewell Hall.' His voice could charm a fish into a frying pan."

He stirred peevishly. "Don't talk about fish." Then he was silent for so long that Zoe thought he had fallen asleep. He sighed finally, and spoke, his voice hoarse; she could hear the weariness in it. "I'll take that sleeping draught now. I'm finished."

She poured it quickly into his cup, added water and a little wine as the physician had instructed, and watched him drink.

"Shall I stay with you until you fall asleep?"

"No." He put the cup down and reached for her hand, smiling finally. "Thank you, my dear, for staying with me. Come and see me tomorrow. I want to talk to you then."

"I will," she promised, mystified, and sent his servant in to turn down the lamps.

She sensed Kelda at the school before she saw him the next day. Rumors of his playing had wasted no time getting up the hill. The masters' refectory was full of the invisible bard when Zoe came up for breakfast. His name had somehow melted into the butter for the breakfast toast, insinuated itself under the shells and into the yolks of coddled eggs, so that a single bite transformed itself and fell as "Kelda" from everyone's lips. The masters were preoccupied with him, their expressions complex as they spoke softly together; wonder vied with envy, even a touch of wariness, in their faces. Small knots of students chirped and twittered together in hallways, and under the oak trees when Zoe passed to teach her singing class. Exclamations, moans, and fervid sighs escaped them with all the mindless, irresistible force of steam spewing out of a kettle spout. He was to visit this class, she heard, and then that, and then at noon, he would play for everyone.

She was pacing around her very young students, enjoying their high sweet voices and adding her own to keep them in time, when she came face-to-face with the bard in her doorway.

He nearly dislodged the note in her throat. Years of discipline kept it tuned, though it came out with more emphasis than she intended. His impeccable ear picked out what, from anyone else, would have been a startled squeak. The glint of a smile in his eye teased her. He waited, his face impassive, until the children finished their song; and then he came into the room, clapping for them.

Some of the masters followed in his wake, and a dozen students, Frazer among them, looking dazed.

"How wonderful all of this is," the bard marveled. "Declan's school, the standing stones, the oak—the perfect background for passing on the ancient bardic heritage. I envy you." He spoke so simply that for the moment she believed him. "I plucked my own skills from bush and bramble, from rutted back roads and the echoes within the empty ruins. I tuned my harp to the icy whine out of the back teeth of the wind, and to the oldest voices—"

"Of the standing stones plucked by the fingers of the moon," Frazer finished breathlessly, and was rewarded by Kelda's sudden, flashing smile.

"Yes! You astonish me. You know those hoary lines?"

"They teach us everything here," the boy said diffidently, deeply flushed.

"How wonderful," the bard breathed again, and turned his warmth upon Zoe. "I didn't see you in the hall last night. I was sorry you didn't sing."

"I was sitting at Master Quennel's bedside."

"Yes. I'm in awe of the little I heard from you just now. Will you come and listen to me play later?"

"I heard you play last night. 'Grenewell Hall.' You nearly brought me to tears."

"Nearly?"

"It seemed magical," she answered slowly. "For a moment. Whatever brambles and hedgerows taught you to play like that must have been enchanted themselves. Master Quennel, since you didn't ask, was resting quietly when I left him."

"I didn't need to ask since I was told this morning." Again his faint smile teased, mocked, challenged. "Will you come and listen anyway? It's an easy matter to raise a tear when emotions are already raw with the sudden illness of a friend. Not so easy in the clear and genial light of day."

That made her smile, which annoyed her almost as much as her tears had. He saw that, too. There was no hiding from him, she realized, when he held her fixed within his sights.

"I'll come," she said abruptly, both her curiosity and her hackles raised, but by what exactly she had no clue. He nodded and left her to her transfixed students; she watched Frazer turn into his wake, drift after him as helplessly as a feather on the flood.

At noon, students and masters, their paths braiding along the garden paths as they sought their classes or the libraries or refectories, stopped midpace when harping, strong and mysterious, rippled out of the still, shadowy trees. Zoe, walking out of the tower door, watched absorbed and purposeful moving bodies suddenly forget where they were headed and why. Their heads turned toward the trees. They veered from their chosen paths, seemed to float along the grass as though the music they heard had pulled them beyond time and gravity as well as memory. It seemed to come from the memory of trees, the singing voices of the ghosts of the first oak as they taught the first bard to play.

Zoe followed as mindlessly and as single-mindedly as any around her. They knew secrets, she realized for the first time. Those old oaks sang mysteries. If only she could get close enough, begin to understand their language of sun, rain, wind, night. They knew something she wanted. They knew the first songs of the world, the first word forged out of the lightning trapped in their boughs, shirred free of the fire and glowing among their roots like a fallen star. If she could get close enough to see . . . She was scarcely aware of the crowd around her, students and masters emptying the buildings to gather in the grove, all mute, as though they had not yet begun to learn this new language.

She stopped at the edge of the great circle around the singing tree and saw the face of the music.

She blinked, shaken out of a dream, she felt, and waking to a conundrum.

The bard was singing, not the trees. The bard was Kelda, who had watched an old man choke on a bite of salmon. All around her, entranced faces still seemed caught in the dream; transfixed bodies scarcely breathed. The bard, engrossed in his expert playing, dreamed as well, drawing his listeners ever more deeply into his wonderful vision.

"He's good," someone murmured beside her. "I'll give him that. Zoe, do you know where I can find your father?"

She closed her eyes, opened them again, finally shaken fully awake and astonished at herself. She turned her head, met Phelan's preoccupied eyes.

"Didn't you hear that?" she whispered.

"Of course I did. I followed you out here."

"I mean—the trees singing. Didn't you hear the oak sing?"

He shook his head. "I must have missed that part." He was silent a moment, peering at her; then he smiled. "You look bewitched. Even your hair seems full of elflocks. He's been having that effect. Frazer looks even more spell-raddled than you. Do you know where—"

"No." Then she pulled her thoughts together. "My father's not in the tower? He's usually still there at noon." Phelan shook his head. "Then I don't know where—Why? Is it important?"

"Yes, but only to me. He suggested I search some of the old stewards' records for my paper."

She shrugged, her mind straying again to the peculiarity in the oak grove. "Just take them," she suggested. "He wouldn't care. Most of them are covered with cobwebs and dust."

"Are you sure?"

The bard, she saw suddenly, was looking at them across the crowd spilling out from under the grove. She couldn't read his expression, but she could guess at it. He had unraveled his heart for them, spun it into gold and woven gold into a web. The two flies buzzing obliviously on the outermost strand of it would cause the bard dissatisfaction greater than his pleasure in all the trapped and motionless morsels within the shining threads.

"Yes," she whispered quickly, and turned her back on the bard, followed Phelan into the clear and genial light of day. "I'm going to see Quennel," she told him when they were out of earshot. "He asked me to visit him today. I'll let my father know you've borrowed his books. If he even notices."

"Thank you."

She mused equally over Kelda and Phelan on her way to the castle. About what she had heard, and what Phelan had not. She had been as transfixed, as spellbound as anyone, she admitted. Anyone except Phelan, who had blundered through such beauty as though his ears were corked like kegs. He had heard the notes, but he had missed the music. Why?

She had neglected to change her clothes, so determined she had been to get out of the broad range of Kelda's attention. Something was askew with him, brilliant as he was, something amiss. Her student's robe and her familiar face eased her way into the castle; she was escorted to Quennel's chambers and promptly admitted.

His color was better, she saw immediately. Not so his mood.

He smiled when he saw her; his pleasure was genuine but brief, before the frown turned the smile upside down. He was still in bed, she saw with surprise, covered with silk and eyelet lace, with a cap on his willful hair.

"My throat is raw," he said disgruntledly. "I can't sing tonight."

"You could play," she urged him, inspired. "I'll sing for you."

The thought brought out his smile again. It faded more slowly as he looked at her silently, his reddened eyes unblinking, an expression in them she couldn't fathom.

"I need you to do something for me," he said finally, when she thought he might be drifting off to sleep again.

"Yes," she said quickly. "Anything."

"I have been thinking about this yesterday evening, and most of the night, and this morning. You understand that I've given it my most careful attention."

"Yes."

"So don't argue with me. I am going to relinquish my position as Royal Bard of King Lucien's court." She opened her mouth; nothing came out but a rush of air. "I would wait until Lord Grishold leaves," he added distastefully, "if I had any hope that his bard would actually leave with him."

"You're going to retire? Because of a mouthful of salmon?"

"So why wait?"

"But—" She started to sit on air, looked around hastily to pull a chair into place. She sat, leaned forward, her hands folded tightly among the bed linens, her eyes wide, studying his face as though the answer lurked within his bones. "But why? There's no need. You are still vigorous, your voice as tuned and resonant as ever, your ear as fine, your fingers—"

"My ear, my voice, my fingers are all telling me that as well," he said so dryly his voice rasped. "But I saw my fate in that mouthful of fish. This is what I must do. I will announce my impending retirement but continue to play as Royal Bard until the moment a new bard is chosen."

"There will be a competition," she whispered, feeling even her lips go cold. "Between bards from all over the realm for the highest position. They will come to Caerau to compete, and I will be here to see it."

"You will compete in it," he told her grimly, and she felt the full weight of his determination, anger, and despair. "And you will win." She stared at him, breathless, mute. "You will win," he said again, harshly. "You will find the roots and wellsprings of this land within you, and sing them until the moon herself weeps. Because if you don't, that bard from Grishold, who is no bard but something ancient, dark, and dangerous, will sing in my place to the king, and I don't know what will befall this land when he has finished his song."

Chapter Twelve

It's here, around the time of Declan's competition, that the boundaries of history begin to blur into the fluid realm of poetry, much as a well-delineated borderline might falter into and become overwhelmed by the marsh it crosses. Where, the historian might ask bewilderedly, did the border go? Nothing but this soggy expanse of uncertain territory in front of us, where we were stringently following the clear and charted path of truth.

That Declan called the gathering of the bards is recorded in many places. Oroh's court chronicles mention it: "At last Declan gave the king hope that he would have a bard once again at his side, for counsel and for diversion, for the king loved his music greatly and would hear none but the best." We might pause here and give King Oroh a measure of sympathy, for no bard in his new court, however gifted, would know the cherished ballads and poetry of his native land; Declan and death had taken them away.

Evidence in other chronicles, in letters, in household records indicating the absence of a family member "who rode to Stirl Plain *for the gathering of bards": all give us proof beyond poetry of the event. And indeed the bards came from high and low, from near and far, from the wealthiest court, the meanest tavern, from the northern fishing villages, the crags of the west, the salt marshes of the south. From every part of Belden, bards, musicians, minstrels, anyone with an instrument or a voice to sing with, converged upon Stirl Plain.*

Fortunately, Declan allowed the villagers the few brief months between winter and midsummer to prepare for them. Before the bards came the builders and the traders, the barges carrying lumber from the northern forests, wagons carrying a wealth of other things, followed by people hoping for work after the terrible winter. One can imagine buildings sprouting like mushrooms up and down the riverbanks, crowding along the road leading up the hill to the school. Inns, taverns, shops flew up as both the wealthy and the poor began to make their way across the plain.

It was, as we can guess, the beginnings of the great city that later became the official residence of the rulers of Belden.

At the same time, it must have seemed a magical place, in which all the music of the five kingdoms might be heard, and, along with the bards, came their audience to listen and marvel at the best that Belden had to offer.

But before that, the fading shadow of winter left a stranger in its wake, an elusive, ambiguous figure sighted only briefly, at a tangent, in the poetry of the time, and in history only between the lines.

The oldest bard came, even he,
From the beginning of the world.
Old as poetry he was,
Old as memory.

The music on Stirl Plain
Woke the stones on Bone Plain,
And he came out from under
To play the first songs of the world,
That no one else remembers.

FRAGMENT FROM "THE GATHERING OF THE BARDS," ANONYMOUS

The stranger came at the forefront of the flow of musicians on the plain, so soon after Declan had sent out word of the competition that it seemed only the trees and stones of Stirl Plain could have gotten the word any earlier. Sometime afterwards, Nairn realized that was exactly so; earlier, he was simply surprised at the efficiency of Declan's methods. The bard spoke; the harper appeared almost before the moon had decided to change the expression on her face.

The students of the Circle of Days had grown oddly closer since Drue's death. With all their spiky differences and sharp opinions, they were bound not only by an ancient, secret language, but by a vision of the breathtaking randomness of life: not even they, possessing the oldest name for death, could see it coming. Sometime during the ebb of the endless winter, they had begun to meet, in the evening once or twice a week, at the tavern Shea's father the brewer had built on the other side of the river. They drank his ale, drew runes with burned twigs on his rackety tables and in the ashes sifting out of the grate, and challenged one another obliquely, in one language, to answer with the patterns of another.

Nairn, still struggling with the power and deadly potential of the ancient words, played their tavern games cautiously and ventured few opinions about what value Master Declan's list of words might have when the students finally learned them all. They had no clue, Nairn learned with wonder. The thought that he had flung his heart into a burning icicle and sent it plunging down onto Drue's oblivious head would never have crossed their minds.

"Do you think they would have believed you if you had blamed yourself?" Declan asked succinctly when Nairn had come to explain to him how Drue died. "You're the crofter's son who sang his first songs to the pigs in the sty, and who can barely write his own name. You couldn't claim such power without having to prove it, and how would you do that with all the fear that festers in you now? Drue's death was an accident. Let it lie."

"And lie and lie," Nairn retorted bitterly, white with horror and pacing circles around the bard in his work chamber. The golden eyes flashed at him, but Declan stayed silent. "And you're right. I am afraid, now. I don't know enough to know how to be careful. It was like killing someone with a love song you were playing to someone else entirely. Death was the last thing on my mind. Then it was all."

"Accept it. It happened. Learn from it so that it never happens again."

"I could just stop. Just. Stop. I don't need magic. Only my harp and the road—"

"You have gone too far, learned too much, to return to innocence," Declan said evenly. "Better to learn to control your great power than to carry such potential for disaster around with you and always be afraid of it." Nairn opened his mouth; the bard, reading his expression or his mind, interrupted. "Think," he urged. "You can live in ignorance and uncertainty, or with the knowledge and the certainty that you will never kill again without intent. Either way, you must live with the power. With yourself. Think. Then tell me what you want."

The bard was right, Nairn realized as days passed. About that, and about the other thing: his fellow students of the Circle of Days would have fallen out of their chairs laughing over Nairn's pretensions and arrogance if he had tried to claim Drue's death.

None of them, not even Nairn, noticed the stranger in the tavern when he first appeared. Nairn's eyes wandered toward a dark mass at a table in the shadows that was farthest from the fire. Something about it, or within it, made his glance glide over it as though it were a bench or a floorboard, a thing too familiar to bother naming. They were all nearing the bottom of their first beers, and wildly guessing, since Shea's father was back in the brewery and they seemed the only company, what mysteries lay hidden within the twig-words, when out of nowhere came the unmistakable sound of a harp being tuned.

They all jumped. Osprey knocked over the last of his beer. The man in the shadows, his craggy face oddly visible now above the harp in his broad, blunt hands, spoke first as they stared.

"You're students of his, then? Master Declan? The one who called the competition?"

Shea swallowed audibly, then cleared her throat of any remnants of twig language. "Yes," she said, and, unwontedly flustered, she got to her feet and barked for her father. "Da! Company!"

"Coming!" her father bellowed back briskly.

"You got here fast," Osprey remarked, righting his mug.

"I was passing across the plain." His voice was deep and gravelly, a sough of stones dragged in the undertow. "Am I first, then?"

"But for us," Blayse answered pointedly, and a smile, or a sudden flare of light from the fire, glided over the man's face.

"But for you. You were here first." He thumbed a string, then raised his brows uncertainly. "I doubt you'll want to spare a coin for my harping, being bards yourselves, then. But I'm all out, and as dry as any stone."

"Play if you want," Shea answered, shrugging. "Others might come in and think you're worth—"

"Play," Nairn said abruptly, interrupting her. "I'll buy you a beer."

"Me, too," the genial Osprey echoed, and the man's smile was more than illusion, this time.

"That's good of you," he murmured.

His fingers seemed a trifle stiff on the strings, as though he had not played in some time. But his notes were sweet and true. Nairn, listening intently as was his habit, heard the familiar phrase now and then, but always it wandered off in an unexpected direction. Wherever he had learned his music, it was not in the Marches, nor in any kingdom Nairn had passed through, including Stirl Plain. It sounded old to him: simple and lovely and haunted with ghosts of music he knew.

"Where are you from?" he asked, when the brewer had brought the harper his beer. He waited while the man drank half of it. Somewhere past young, he looked, hale and brawny as a blacksmith; his leather boots and trousers were old and stained with travel. His dark hair and the stubble on his chin were streaked with white. His harp seemed worn as well, plain and scarred with time, like the harper. He had strange eyes, both blue, but one pale and one dark, as though he saw out of one by day and the other by twilight. Both held the same narrowed, curious expression; both seemed always on the verge of smiling.

The man set his tankard down finally. "Upriver."

"Upriver. The Stirl?"

He nodded. "At the northernmost edge of the plain. My name is Welkin."

"You walked a ways. I don't suppose you're hungry as well?"

The man, riffling over the harp strings, stilled his fingers and gave Nairn an unfathomable look. "Depends," he said finally, doubtfully. "How do you like my harping?"

Nairn smiled. "Very much. You play songs I've never heard."

"Ah, it's all old. You're a kind young man."

"I've done my share of walking. I know how the road goes." He glanced at Shea, who huffed an exasperated sigh and got to her feet.

"Da! Food!"

"Coming!"

She threw her cloak around her, added tersely to Nairn, "I'm going back up, now we're finished talking. Coming?" she demanded of Blayse, and he shifted reluctantly, finished his beer on the way up. "Well, I'm not walking up in the dark by myself. Not after what happened to Drue."

"I'll stay to walk with you," Osprey said gravely to Nairn. "Fend off the slavering icicles."

"It's not funny," Shea snapped, and flounced out with Blayse in her wake. "Da! Night!"

"Good night, girl!"

Nairn and Osprey stayed to drink beer and listen, after Welkin emptied another tankard and a bowl of root vegetables and mutton stewed in beer. When Osprey laid his face on the table and began to snore, Nairn woke him with a scatter of moldy coins from the Marches and stood up. The brewer, a big, beefy man with florid cheeks, heard the sound of money through the music and appeared to bid them farewell. Welkin finished his song and moved to warm himself before he, too, wandered out into the night.

"Where will you stay?" Nairn asked him.

"I'll find a place," the harper answered vaguely. "That's never a problem." He set his harp on the table, opened his hands to the fire.

"You might find a bed at the school."

"Maybe. One of these nights."

Nairn wrapped himself against the brittle cold, taking a closer look at Welkin's harp. The scores on it were deliberate, he saw, made with a knife. Then the lines arranged themselves into some very familiar patterns, and his thoughts froze.

The harper took one hand away from the warmth, as though he had heard the sound of Nairn's brain stumbling over itself, and reached back to pick up his harp. "I'm grateful for the beer and food," he said. Nairn shifted his eyes to follow the path of the harp, saw it disappear into its matted sheepskin case. He met the harper's eyes then; the faint, enigmatic smile had deepened. "Good night to you, young masters."

"Stay," the brewer said abruptly. "Sleep by the fire there. It's brutal out tonight."

The harper shook his head. "I'll find my own way, but thank you, master brewer."

He opened the door. Osprey, yawning hugely, followed. Nairn

bumped into him as the door closed; he was stopped dead and peering bewilderedly here and there at the tangled moon shadows of tree limbs.

"He just vanished, the harper did. Just—" His teeth had already begun to chatter.

"Never mind," Nairn said, pulling him into motion again. "You heard him."

"But—"

"He can take care of himself."

By the time Nairn saw the harper again, the cruel winter had finally melted away into spring. Grass flowed over the plain again, green to the farthest horizons; its gentle hillocks melted into vivid blue. The Stirl melted and surged, bringing musicians, workers and wood for building, farm animals to feed the visitors. The plain buried its stillness deep in the earth; what went on above it was now a constant clatter of hammering, wagons coming and going, people camping on it, keeping a wild, colorful motley of music going that reminded Nairn of a barnyard before breakfast. Rich pavilions went up next to small tents that had mushroomed into circles on the grass overnight. Stalls selling anything imaginable rose on their ramshackle frames; fires burned from dawn to midnight as food was cooked and sold to the arriving bards. The village, so sparse and coldly gray during the winter, became, half a season later, unrecognizable, buildings flying up like magic, some for the few months before the competition, others to last past a lifetime.

Nairn searched constantly among the strangers for the mysterious harper who knew the language of the standing stones and had carved it onto his harp. What the harp said, he didn't know; the twig-letters, vanishing so swiftly into the harp case, were a complete jumble in his head.

What Declan said when Nairn told him about the harper, he remembered very clearly, once the bard had finally retrieved his voice.

"Find him," he said sharply. "Bring him to me." He was silent again, pacing a circle around his chamber in the spiraling tower. Then he added tersely, "It's one thing to take on the magic of another land that everyone there has forgotten. It's another to meet the one who has not forgotten. Be careful."

Nairn wondered at that: the eccentric harper seemed harmless and reasonably civilized. He kept looking for Welkin, enormously curious about this man who had discomposed the imperturbable Declan, and who could hide himself in wood smoke and shadows, and leave no footprints in the snow. But not even the brewer, whose tavern swarmed with musicians by the beginning of summer, had seen him after that winter evening.

The noise had driven the harper away, Nairn decided. Or maybe his competition had. Bards were coming from courts all over the realm, playing music far more intricate than Welkin's on instruments adorned with a filigree of gold rather than a fretwork of scars from a knife. When the bell beside the main door sounded one morning as Nairn passed, he pulled the door open absently, expecting yet another musician, newly arrived on the plain and anticipating Declan's immediate interest and attention.

"I heard Declan wants to see me," the musician said, and the sound of the deep, rumbling, rough-hewn voice left Nairn speechless. He reached out, grasped Welkin's brawny arm, and drew him across the threshold before he could vanish again.

"Yes," he said, guiding the harper through the empty hall to a side entry to the tower that bypassed the kitchen where, from the sound of the clanging and splashes below, Muire was scouring pots in the cauldron. "He does. I've been looking for you for months. Did you leave the plain?"

"After a fashion," Welkin agreed, and added, to make himself entirely clear, "I'm back now."

"'After a fashion,'" Nairn breathed. "What fashion?" He didn't expect an answer. Welkin, climbing up the winding steps, only glanced out the slitted windows without offering him one.

"Strange place for a tower," he commented. "What was it for, when it was built?"

"A signal tower, I suppose. A watchtower. I don't know. No one does. It's older than anyone's memory, around here. How did you know that Declan wants to see you?"

Welkin shrugged. "Word travels, in a crowd like this."

Nairn gave up. "It took long enough," he said dryly, wondering in what language that particular word had traveled. He rounded a curve, found the door open and Declan waiting for them: word had, in whatever fashion, preceded them up the stairs.

The two took a measure of one another briefly, silently, there on the threshold. Then Welkin smiled a tight smile framed by fanning lines, and Declan shifted so that he could enter.

Nairn asked uncertainly, "Do you want me to—"

"Stay," both said at once, so he came into Declan's work chamber. Welkin prowled a moment, looking at the small collection of rare and ancient instruments kept there, while Declan watched him. Then Welkin turned, said something guttural and incomprehensible, and Nairn, struggling to understand, felt the silent bolt of Declan's shock across the room.

"You speak it," Declan whispered. "You know how it sounds."

Welkin tossed him a smile again. "I am grateful to you," he said. "I haven't heard that language, even in anyone's thoughts, for—oh, longer than you'd care to know."

"Who are you?"

Welkin touched a ram's horn with holes whittled down the curve, its openings ringed with gold. He said softly, "On a plain of bone, in a ring of stone . . ."

"Is that what you said just now?" Declan asked hoarsely.

"It is." He opened his harp case, took out the instrument to show Declan the twig-words carved over every possible space. Nairn recognized them, then. "I cut them there to remind myself." He touched a letter, then looked up to hold Declan's gaze with his mismatched eyes. "It's all I've got, this battered old harp, to play against the fine, complex instruments of the court bards out there. It might do. I'm hoping it will. So you see, I have everything to lose all over again, and I will do what I can to win." He loosed Declan's eyes finally, gave a glance out the broader window the bard had built into the stones. "That's a pleasant sight, the river there. Well. If there's nothing else, I'll see you on the day, then." He nodded to the completely bewildered Nairn and to the bard just opening his mouth to speak.

Then, like a shaft of sunlight melting into cloud, he was gone.

Nairn felt the breath rush out of him. Declan closed his mouth, looking astonished, and so grim Nairn scarcely recognized him.

"Who is he?" Nairn demanded, his voice shaking. "Who in the world is he?"

Declan tried to answer; answers tangled, apparently; he could not speak. He went to Nairn, put a hand on his shoulder; his hold grew so tight he might have been falling headlong out of his window and struggling to hold on.

"You must win this competition," he said tightly, and shook Nairn a little to rattle the notion into his head and settle it there. "Win it. Or he will, and I have no idea what I will be loosing into King Oroh's court."

"But—"

"Just win it." The owl's eyes caught Nairn's fiercely, held them. "Any way you can."

Chapter Thirteen

Phelan sat on the floor of the broken tower, surrounded by dusty tomes. There was a threadbare carpet across the stones, almost as ancient as the record books, the first of which had been started during Declan's time. The forgotten history Phelan held in his hands made him reluctant to abscond with them; he would wait, he decided, for Bayley Wren's permission. There were over three dozen of them, all fat, every page meticulously lined with precise and mundane detail of the school's long past: "To Trey Sims, woodcutter, for two wagonloads of wood from the north, and for the labor of it, and the journey... To Haley Coe for nine casks of ale and five bottles of elderberry wine... To Gar Holm for six fat salmon from the Stirl and twice as many eel... Accounts received for room and board of student Ansel Tige from his father, late again... Accounts received for one night's lodging from Master Gremmell, and two servants, on their way across the plain..."

Why Bayley kept his office and his bedchamber within the chill walls of the tower instead of in the comfortably renovated portion of the ancient building, Phelan understood easily. The stewards charted and guarded the history of the school, and the silent walls were steeped in it. Declan himself had lived there, and had left the echoes of the music of the first Royal Bard of Belden. Phelan and Zoe had explored the place thoroughly when they were children. Worn stairs spiraled up and up the curved walls, where apertures scarcely wider than a knife blade eked out miserly glimpses of the city and the Stirl. The steps debouched now and then into a small chamber where the curious leavings of centuries, like remnants from a flood, gathered dust and owl droppings. The steward's office was as high as it could be without using the sky for a roof. Above it, the walls were jagged with the mysterious violence that had torn through the top of the tower, left the chamber they circled open to the seasons. There, as high as they could climb up the broken steps, the young Zoe and Phelan had sat, singing to the sun and the moon rising over the plain, watching in wonder as the oldest words in the world moved to their stately rhythms by day and by night, oblivious to the busy city crusting the shores of the ancient water.

There, once, he and Zoe had made love under the moonlight on the top of the broken tower. Phelan remembered that with a smile. But they knew each other far too well, which is why the experiment had been both success and failure. They had been grateful for the knowledge but too curious to be content with one another.

"This day by my hand: Lyle Renne, Steward . . ."

Phelan considered that. He closed the book, reached for another.

"This day by my hand, Farrel Renn . . ."

Intrigued, he put down that book, opened another. And then

another. Days flowed through months, years, centuries of detail: a new washtub for the kitchen, half a dozen student robes made by Mistress Cassell, a scullery maid promoted to cook, three bags of flour, a new master hired, a coffin for the death of an elderly master, accounts rendered to a midwife for the birth of the child of a student whose parents refused to take her back. All accounts signed for that day by some variant of Wren. Back and back Phelan looked, amazed, while the writing became awkward; letters changed shape; spelling grew fluid, arbitrary. Ren became Wren, became Renne, became Renn, and then, leaping forward through time, again Wren.

"Wren," he murmured, and there Bayley Wren was, opening the office door, crossing the room. Phelan gazed at him, this relic of history. With his gray-gold hair and the hollows in his strong face, he did seem balanced on the cusp of forever.

"What?" the steward inquired mildly of Phelan's expression.

"You're in here," Phelan marveled. "All the way back to the beginning of Belden. Like the Peverell kings."

"There has been a Wren at the school for as long as the school has existed. One in each generation was born with a taste for detail, for order, and for paying bills. It does seem an inherited position."

Phelan got to his feet, brushing at the dust of centuries and frowning as he contemplated the present generation. "I can't see Zoe entering accounts rendered in the records."

Bayley gave his rare, dry chuckle. "Nor can I. I wonder myself how history will find its way around her." He glanced at the untidy pile at Phelan's feet. "Something in particular?"

"Yes. Nairn."

"Ah," Bayley said softly.

"Also, a certain Circle of Days."

The steward shook his head over that one. "I haven't read all of the account books. I do remember Argot Ren's reference to Nairn. I have no idea what he meant by the Circle of Days. If it involved accounts rendered or received, it will show up in the records somewhere."

Phelan brooded a moment. "I have to start somewhere. It might as well be at the beginning. May I take the earliest books home with me?"

Master Wren hesitated at that, looking as though Phelan had asked to make off with his fingers. "Those books have never left this tower. If you can persuade them to cross the threshold . . ."

Phelan left with the three oldest, pledging his father's fortune as collateral if he left them on a tram or dropped them into the Stirl. The house was quiet when he came in. Sophy and Jonah were both out, he suspected on wildly different errands on opposite sides of the city. He settled himself on the sofa, opened the first account book, and, within a dozen pages, fell headlong into it.

He surfaced sometime later, at a query from Sagan as to whether he might like a lamp turned on, and would he be dining at home that evening?

"No," he said dazedly, rolling off the sofa. He collected the books, feeling off-balance in that world, two vastly different centuries clamoring for precedence in his brain. "I'm going out, thanks."

"Shall I take those books for you?"

"No," he said again, quickly, having a vision of his drunken father finding them, riffling through his bookmarks and snorting with laughter at the latest moldy turn of Phelan's paper. "I'll hide them myself."

He walked along the river, vaguely aware of the lights flickering on in the twilight, from streetlamps and buildings, streaking the water with their colorful reflections. The evening was warm; market skiffs still plied the waters among the gilded, lantern-lit barges that had rowed out for a meal or a party on the water. He wondered if his mother was on one of them. Jonah was probably sitting on top of a standing stone with a bottle in hand, trying to pick an argument with the moon. Phelan had little idea where he was going; he let his feet lead him. When, a mile or two later, they turned into the city's oldest tavern on the waterfront, the Merry Rampion, he was not surprised.

The crowd was a noisy mix of students and masters, dockers and fishers on their way home, and well-dressed patrons out on the town. He glanced around for Jonah, was relieved not to find him there. Chase Rampion greeted him genially, brought him beer, and left him alone in the crush, gazing out of the grimy, whorled window at the gulls wheeling above the darkening water.

Something portentous had happened between the time Nairn had first appeared in the records and when his name was no longer mentioned. Exactly what lay between the lines. The first school steward, Dower Ren, must have written his entries with his teeth clenched, so terse were they: "This day accounts rendered to Wil Homely, stonemason, for repairs to what is now the tower roof, and for removing the fallen stones from the school grounds." A day or two earlier, accounts had been rendered "to Salix, for tending to the minor wounds of the school steward, and to Brixton Mar, carpenter, for a new desk and bed frame for same. Ink and a new pot procured with thanks rendered to Salix, and to the school kitchen."

The old school tower had apparently fallen in, or blown itself

up, or cracked in two, right in the middle of the first bardic competition. Struck by age, by an errant wind, by an earthquake, by
an oak tree falling on it? The steward did not say. Whatever happened was beyond the pale of accounts rendered and received.

"Phelan."

He started. Someone had slipped into the empty chair at his
tiny table. Zoe, he saw with relief; at least he would not have to
make inane noises.

She had an odd expression on her face. A new one, he realized with surprise, after all those years of knowing her. The tavern keeper came to greet her, carrying a glass of her favorite
wine.

"Thank you, Chase," she said, kissing him; he lingered a moment, puzzling, like Phelan, over the distraction in her eyes and
the deep frown between them.

Then someone called him away, and she took a deep breath.

"Phelan," she said again, very softly, touching his wrist; her
fingers were cold.

"What?" he asked abruptly. "Is it your father? Mine?"

"No—it's Quennel."

"Is he dead?"

She shook her head quickly, leaned even closer to him. "No.
He's—he's going to call a bardic competition. He wants to retire."

Phelan sat back in his creaky chair, astonished. "Now? I thought
he'd die on the job in a decade or two, with his harp strings breaking along with his heart."

"No." She hesitated; he waited, riveted. "He—he said things—
I don't know if he's imagining them or not. He wants—Phelan,
are you going to compete?"

He stared at her, appalled. "Of course not."

"Oh, good. I didn't want to compete against you. Quennel said— Well, he asked me to."

"Of course he would want you to replace him."

"I tried to persuade him not to retire, but he seems to have lost heart." She took a swallow of wine, her frown deepening. Phelan watched her.

"What," he wondered, "are you not telling me?"

"Just something Quennel said." She put her glass down, dipped a finger absently, and ran it along the rim of the glass, brooding again, as the glass sang. "I want to be sure he's right, before . . . So don't ask. I'll tell you when I need to."

"All right," he said, mystified. Her eyes shifted beyond him, widened, and he turned, hearing a roil of boots and voices flowing through the open door, breaking across the room. Someone cried Zoe's name; she closed her eyes briefly. Then she put a smile on her face as Frazer reached her, with Kelda so close behind him they might have been racing, Phelan thought dourly, though if he had placed a bet, it wouldn't have been on Frazer.

"Come with us," the young man pleaded. He added, belatedly, "And you, too, Phelan."

"No, thanks. I'm leaving."

Frazer lowered his voice a trifle. "There's a group in the back waiting for Kelda. He's going to teach us an ancient language. He says the letters are magical. We hoped to find you—you must join us, Zoe. We're going to form a secret society—" He stopped, reddening, as Kelda chuckled. "Well, not secret now, I suppose, after my babbling." Zoe's eyes moved from his ardent face to Lord Grishold's bard, her expression complex again, reserved and oddly wary, despite her vivid smile.

"Magical?" she echoed.

"Grishold folklore," Kelda explained easily. "Something I picked up in my wanderings. It probably evolved from an ancient bardic exercise. Frazer brought up the subject—"

Phelan laughed; the bard's dark eyes queried him. "It's Frazer's constant question, these days. I'm glad someone can finally give him an answer. I'm tone-deaf when it comes to the subject of magic."

"Yes, so I thought," the bard said cheerfully without bothering to explain himself.

"Please join us," Frazer urged Zoe. "Kelda says that your voice alone is sorcery, and you understood, that day, what I was asking you. You know you did—I felt it."

For a moment, her smile became genuine. "Well, I would like to know what Kelda said that took the scowl off your face." She drew breath, held it, then stood up recklessly. "Why not? I'll come and listen, at least."

"Good!" Kelda dropped a hand on Phelan's shoulder, effectively keeping him in his seat. "You are welcome, too, of course. But since you seem to have someplace to be . . ."

"Yes," Phelan said without moving, watching Zoe's hand tremble as she brought her wineglass to her lips. She finished half of it in a couple of swallows and smiled brightly without meeting Phelan's eyes.

"Where are we going?"

"Back out the door," Kelda said, gesturing to the group waiting for him along the far wall, "to a much quieter place. Only as far as that, this evening. How far later, who knows?"

"I do," a sinewy, drunken voice said from behind Phelan as they moved away, and he closed his eyes, stifling a groan. Kelda, his back to the voice, halted almost imperceptively midstep, then changed his mind and kept going toward the door. Frazer flung a startled glance behind them, but Zoe, her backbone rigid, relegated the problem to Phelan and drew Frazer along in her wake.

Phelan rose quickly; Jonah, who hadn't noticed him, blinked befuddledly at the apparition.

"What are you doing here?"

"Drinking a beer," Phelan answered. "Join me?"

"No, thank you. I intend to join the party that just left."

"I don't believe you were invited. Anyway, there's something I want to ask you."

"Ask me later. I have a bone to pick with that bard. A salmon bone."

"Pick it later," Phelan pleaded, not wanting to chase his father down the street to forestall a brawl. "I need to know what caused the top of the school's tower to blow apart during the first bardic competition and rain down all over the grounds and nearly kill the school steward."

Jonah stared at him. Forgetting his query for the moment, he sat down slowly on the only vacant chair left in the place. "What have you been reading, boy?"

"The school steward's records."

"Dower Ren wrote all that down?"

"Accounts were rendered for a new roof, for someone to clean up the grounds, and to Salish for healing—"

"Salix."

"Whoever he was, for taking care of the steward's scrapes when the roof fell into his chamber."

"She."

"Dower Ren was a woman?"

"No, Salix."

"If it cost money, he wrote it down. Dower Ren did." He paused, eyeing his father. "You've read this, then?"

"No. I had no idea . . . It couldn't possibly have been . . . What exactly did he say about the broken tower?"

"Nothing much more. Only accounts rendered for three coffins for the remains of two students who were killed by the stones to be sent home in—"

"Two students."

"The third was never found. Blown up like the tower, most likely, though the steward doesn't speculate. He only wrote that since Nairn's family was unknown, and there was no body to put into the third coffin, said coffin went back to the maker, and accounts already rendered for it were returned." He paused, studying Jonah speculatively, while a waiter flourished his bar towel at a splash of Zoe's wine and set a foaming mug down in front of Jonah. "Odd," Phelan murmured finally. "That's one thing I did notice." Jonah, frowning down at his beer without tasting it, raised a brow at his son absently. "He never wrote that Salix was a woman. I had an image of a kindly, crusty village doctor in my head, with a huge hoary beard and hair in his ears. What have you read about those early years?"

"I haven't."

"Then how did you know—"

"I don't. Leave it—"

"I can't," Phelan told him recklessly. "I've decided to do my paper on Nairn and the mysterious Circle of Days. Do you know anything about that?"

Jonah glowered at him for no particular reason that Phelan could see. He raised his beer finally, downed half of it. "It's been translated a dozen times," he answered testily, coming up for air. "Mostly badly."

"How would you know?" Phelan asked curiously, and his father lurched up, beer dripping over his fingers.

"You are foul company tonight," he complained. "Not even your mother pesters me with questions like this. I have business with that bard."

Phelan sighed. "I'll come with you."

"No, you won't." Again Phelan was weighed into his seat, this time by Jonah's far heavier hand. "I don't want you anywhere near him. I'll deal with him. Somehow."

"Fine," Phelan said wearily, hoping that Kelda and his band of disciples had vanished by now into the back streets of Caerau. "You do that. Let me know where you end up when I have to bail you out."

"Fine."

"Fine."

What was it with everyone that evening? he wondered, watching Jonah wind his way through the merry company, gulping the last of his beer and pushing the mug into an outstretched hand raised in greeting. Kelda at his most annoying, Zoe trailing impulsively after him despite all her reservations, Jonah prickly as a hedgehog and threatening mayhem, everyone hinting of mysteries they particularly did not want Phelan to know ... The night revolved around Lord Grishold's bard, it seemed, and Phelan stood abruptly, finishing his beer on the way up, yielding to the pull of Kelda's oddly powerful orbit, into which his father seemed in imminent danger of falling facedown.

He hovered on the top step outside the tavern door, peering over heads to find his father, shifting this way and that at the flow around him. He glimpsed the back of Jonah's head finally, moving downriver along the road. Then a blur of purple coming up the steps hid Jonah again.

"What are we looking for?"

Phelan blinked. Princess Beatrice, in purple silks trimmed with blue the color of her eyes, her tawny hair in a tumble of curls down her back, had stopped on the step beside him to peer down the street.

"My father," Phelan explained tersely. "He's out looking for trouble, in the shape of Lord Grishold's bard." He realized he was effectively blocking a very well dressed group of her friends, and shifted quickly. "I'm sorry, Princess."

She didn't move. "Kelda. Yes, they seemed to know each other, didn't they, last night?"

"Did they?" he said, surprised.

"Maybe it was my imagination."

He gazed at her silently, struck by her perception. "No. You're right," he said slowly. "Either they've met before, or my father feels a mystifying animosity toward a complete stranger."

"I'm coming with you," she said abruptly.

"Princess Beatrice—"

"I like working for your father, and I don't want to lose my job because of some scandal to which my mother is forced to pay attention." She turned for a word to her listening friends, who laughed and began to disappear into the Merry Rampion. "Which way did he go?" she asked, following Phelan into the street.

"Downriver. But, Princess, surely you have more diverting plans for the evening than watching my father try to brain someone with a tavern sign—"

"No," she said with a suck of breath. "Has he really—"

"Yes."

"Anyway, we were only going on to a breathtakingly boring party where my sister-in-law-to-be will chatter endlessly about swatches and ruches."

"Is that some weird new kind of hairstyle?"

"You don't want to know. Isn't that your father? Just passing the fish-market stalls?"

"Yes," he said, tautly. "Thank you, Princess. Your presence might actually check some of his more lunatic impulses. But his brain is such a morass when he's like this, you might find it tedious listening to him."

"He can't be more tedious than my brother's betrothed," she murmured, hurrying beside him effortlessly it seemed, her high violet heels tapping briskly along the worn cobbles. "He's going into the fish market . . . Would Kelda likely be there?"

"Empty stalls are far quieter than the Merry Rampion . . . Kelda was trailing a horde of disciples when he left, whom he promised to instruct in ancient magical arts."

She slowed, turning a wide-eyed gaze at him. "Magic. How strange . . . so that's what's in his eyes."

"Whose?"

"Kelda's." Then she flushed quickly, vividly, under a streetlight. Phelan, watching, opened his mouth; she shook her head quickly. "It's hard to explain."

"Try," Phelan suggested softly. "Please, Princess. If you saw something in him, then it might explain what my father sees, or thinks he does."

"I'm sorry." She met his eyes again, patting her curls to order, it seemed, in lieu of her thoughts. "He confuses me, Kelda does."

"You aren't alone, there," he breathed grimly, thinking of the wine trembling in Zoe's glass, his father's incomprehensible obsession. "What is it about this bard that sets everyone on edge? He's coming back out of the stalls."

She turned her head quickly. "Kelda?"

"My father."

"He's crossing the street."

"He's going into—"

"The Wharf Rat." Her long fingers closed briefly on his wrist, surprisingly strong. "Phelan—"

"I'm not taking you in there," he said adamantly. "It's full of—"

"Wharf rats? I suppose that would be high on the list of things that would cause my mother to pack me off to the country. No matter—he's coming back out."

Windmilling back out, more precisely, Phelan thought, watching his father, on the next block, grappling at the air for balance as though he had been pushed out the door.

Luck held him upright, though a couple of passing dockers Jonah careened against were not so fortunate. They hauled themselves off the cobbles, cursing Jonah loudly. But he had already rounded the corner into a side street, and Phelan picked up his pace.

"There," Princess Beatrice said quickly, as they took the turn onto the narrower, shadowy street in time to see Jonah walk through the gate of a low white picket fence without bothering to open it. "Well. There goes that herbaceous border. Is it an inn, or someone's house?"

Phelan sighed, recognizing the bowed front windows fashioned from ovals of warped glass, the picturesque walls covered with neatly pruned ivy. "The Stonedancer Inn. They know my father. The last time I found him in there, he was sitting on the floor surrounded by the contents of an entire tea trolley, with potsherds on his shoulders and the lid on his head."

"He's going in—" The princess's voice wobbled, steadied. "No. He's going around the back."

"Then we'll go in the front. Meet him halfway."

"But what would make him think that Kelda might be here?" the princess wondered, hurrying down the brick walkway after Phelan. "Kelda hardly knows his way around the castle, let alone the back streets of the Caerau waterfront. And why this prim little inn?"

Phelan opened the door. The proprietor had abandoned the quaint reception desk. Doors along the creaky hallway were closed. Painted hands on signs pointed the directions of The Breakfast Room, The Library, The Lounge. Phelan turned to follow that finger.

"Wait for me in the library?" he suggested to Princess Beatrice, who ignored him.

He opened the door to the lounge abruptly, glimpsed a round table full of shadowy people next to a huge old hearth, whose fire provided the only light in the room. Then he heard a familiar sound that grew too loud, too fast, filling his ears, then the room, like the formless bellow of something as old as the world that had erupted from its sleep to rage at him.

The sound flooded into him; he felt it vibrate through every bone in his body from skull to toe, and in that brief moment, he listened for the sound that his thrumming bones might make, astonished that there could be so many. Then he heard his father's voice. The string that he had become keened and snapped, and he rattled down like a limp marionette onto the floor.

He opened his eyes a moment or a night later. From that

angle, under the table, he saw the lounge's back door hanging open on broken hinges. A pair of strange boots seemed to be arguing vehemently with a pair of familiar boots that were cracked with misadventure and old enough to have attracted a crust of barnacles. A third pair of shoes, pretty violet heels, came toward him, slowed, stood motionlessly for a moment at the table. He remembered them, and lifted his head dizzily to see the princess's face.

She was staring at something on the table. Phelan heard her voice very clearly, somehow, beneath the escalating battle of voices belonging to the boots.

"The Circle of Days."

Then her shoes spoke, coming toward him again, and he recognized the overwhelming sound that had driven into the marrow of his bones.

A single harp note.

Chapter Fourteen

The steward's records indicate none of the problems that Declan surely faced as he tried to fashion a fair and organized competition with the unwieldy number of musicians at every level of ability on the plain. This was not, beyond the occasional request for lodging, a matter of accounts rendered or received. For such detail we must explore other chronicles, letters, and court records, and even the ballads that took root in those scant days. The bard of the Duke of Grishold complained to the duke's chronicler of having, on that first day, to compete with "minstrels, street pipers, and others of such ilk," along with several bards well educated in the courtly traditions. He is happier on the second day, after the rigors of the first pared away novices, dilettantes, street and tavern players, and those without the hope of a chance, who could play a cheerful tune or two, and mostly had just come to listen.

It is difficult for the city dweller to imagine what Stirl Plain must have looked like to those used to the lonely silent stretches of grass and standing stones. From "sunrise to moonset," as one writer put it, the plain was covered with tents, wagons, campfires, pavilions, horses, oxen, dogs, with all the attendant noises, smells, colors. The school steward does list several of King Oroh's nobles whom Declan invited to stay at the school. In various chronicles and private letters, they comment on the vivid crowd, the motley of musicians, and though, in the opinion of Lord Cleaver, King Oroh's general and himself a musician, there are those "of great talent with their instruments, none seem trained in the necessary arts which King Oroh will expect of his bard, and which Declan brought with him to this benighted land."

None except, perhaps, for an unusual harper.

This musician, of little charm, no wealth, and vague background, summons such art out of his simple harp that even the rich instruments of the high-court bards grow mute as he plays. Whence he comes he does not say, and his only name is Welkin.

FROM "ON STIRL PLAIN" VIRUH STAID, CHRONICLER TO THE DUKE OF GRISHOLD

By the end of the first day of the first bardic competition on Stirl Plain, one word fell from everyone's lips like an enchanted jewel that contained the entire range of human feeling. Awe, disgust, envy, perplexity, suspicion, adoration, longing, curiosity, delight, and chagrin infused that single word; it changed every time it was spoken. That a craggy, threadbare, unknown musician with a battered harp, no family name or history, and only a vague direction as a place of origin, could render experienced court bards incoherent with his playing stunned everyone. On that first day, his name was most often followed by a more familiar word: Who?

Who was Welkin? Out of what nowhere had he come? Where had he learned to play like that? As though his harp were strung with the sinews of the heart, with sounds from the deep, shifting bones of the earth, with all the memories of music in the world before day ever opened its eye and night and time began?

Declan, moving through the crowds with his usual composure, confessed himself as ignorant as anyone of the harper's past. Nairn, who had spent his life listening for such wonders, was transfixed by the harper's skill until a skewed vision of Welkin dressed in leather and silk, riding at King Oroh's side, counseling the king and using his magic at Oroh's whim, bumped up against the homespun harper with the mysterious past, the glint in his eyes, and powers even Declan could only guess at.

Declan, only in private and only to Nairn, betrayed the one word that Welkin's harping truly inspired in him.

"Do something," he demanded of Nairn, when the contenders stopped to eat before they played the sun down.

"What exactly?" Nairn asked, disconcerted by Declan's fear. "He plays better than I do."

"Listen to him."

"I do. I have been, all day. How could I not? He plays—he plays music the standing stones must have heard when they were new."

"Listen to the magic," Declan insisted. "He uses those words I taught you in his music."

"How—"

"Learn that from him. You know the words; you have the

power. Learn to use it. I can't teach you that. You must find it in yourself. You were born with it. I breathe the air of this land, I walk on its earth, but I was not born out of it, rooted in it, the way you and Welkin are. I carry the powers, the music I was born with; there are overtones, undertones I will never hear in yours. You must learn from him, now. He knows the language of your power."

"I don't understand," Nairn said, genuinely bewildered. "He wants to be King Oroh's bard. He has what the king needs. He's why you called this competition. Why are you so afraid he'll win?"

Declan, pacing restlessly through his private chamber like an empty vessel pushed back and forth on a roil of tide, swung impatiently. "Use your head. You saw those words on his harp. He's something ancient pulled out of this plain by words I've wakened and by the hope of another chance."

"A chance."

"A chance to die, if we are fortunate. That could be all he wants. But I doubt it. This time, I think he wants everything he failed to get the first time. He wants all the powers within the Three Great Treasures. All that, he will take to the court of this foreign invader, and he will bring it down with a single plucked string."

Nairn swallowed something like an old, dry twist of rootwork in his throat. He backed a step or two until he felt the solid stones, and leaned against them.

"What are you saying?" His voice gyrated wildly around his question. "Are you saying that it's true? That old poem you gave us?"

"What do you think poetry is?" Declan demanded. "Something decorative? A pretty tapestry of words instead of threads? Tales that old stay alive for a reason. I think that, who knows how long ago, this harper challenged himself against the Three Trials of Bone Plain. He lost all three. The poem is very clear about what happens to the failed bard."

"No song," Nairn whispered numbly. "No peace. No poetry."

"No end of days."

"He has—he—you heard him play. He did not lose that power."

"Didn't he?" Declan stopped pacing finally, amid a rumpled froth of sheepskin. "I think it's in his harp, that power. Maybe he stole it; maybe he found it somewhere; it was given to him out of pity by a dying bard. I think if he tried to play any other instrument, even a simple pipe, his notes would wither into breath. Harp strings would warp out of tune; reeds would dry and split."

"But he can still—you saw him vanish into air!"

"He's been around a very long time. Who knows what he's been able to learn through the centuries?" He shook his head. "Maybe we did not translate the words precisely—they mean other things as well—Who knows?" He paused, gazing heavily at the shaken Nairn. "Suppose he does open the way back to that plain, that tower? What would you do to possess such gifts? If the heart of this land opened itself up and showed you what you could be, offered you all the songs it holds, would you refuse? Or would you do exactly what you've done since the day you ran away from that pigsty? You have followed the music. To this plain. To this challenge." He turned abruptly again, without waiting for Nairn's answer. "Go down, listen again to that harper, and think about this: What would you do to play like him? If you can't answer that, he will take everything that I chose for you."

Nairn took himself wordlessly out of the tower and down the hill to the plain, which glowed back at the stars with its own constellations of fires. He picked Welkin's music easily out of the merry confusion of sounds. He circled it warily, again and again, pacing as Declan had, listening from a distance until gradually he came to realize that his circles spiraled more and more into themselves. He orbited the last around the great crowd sitting and listening to Welkin and one of the court bards, who were exchanging songs. There he came to a halt behind the gathering.

Welkin played a complex accompaniment to a courtly love ballad. Even in the firelight, he seemed something imprecise: a smudge, a shadow, nothing to snag the eye or linger in the memory. The court bard, a tall, sinewy, gold-haired man from one of the richer houses in Waverlea, wore a robe of many colors trimmed with whorls of gold thread that matched the pattern of gold inlay over his harp. He had other instruments with him: a long ebony pipe, a small drum, a triple-mouthed horn. He shifted from one to another easily as he sang: he did not carry all his music in his harp. He played songs Nairn had barely learned, on instruments as pure as any he had ever heard.

All that the court bard had, he himself could possess, Nairn knew. Wealth and dignity, fine instruments, so much talent he could afford to wear that expression of geniality and encouragement toward stray harpers out of the forgotten corners of the land. He only had to win the competition as well as whatever ancient, dormant challenges Welkin seemed determined to bring to life with his playing.

A tower, a cauldron, a stone . . . What could be so difficult about figuring out what they wanted? They were words in a poem; such words never meant exactly what they seemed. If there were rewards, then the Trials must not be impossible. If they were possible, then why not for Nairn, the Pig-Singer, who had come as far as possible from his past and needed a place to go next?

The lovely ballad ended to much clapping and inarticulate cries. The court bard smiled, gestured to Welkin, and exchanged his harp for his pipe. Welkin paused, pulling a song out of the ancient barrow of his mind. He seemed to notice, then, the solitary figure standing beyond the crowd. He shifted; a reflection of fire glanced through his eyes like a smile.

His first note melted through Nairn's heart with all the sweetness of a love he had never felt; his second brushed Nairn's lips like a kiss; his third ran down the stubborn sinews at the backs of Nairn's knees and he sank like a stone to the grass, helpless as a child before such beauty, and as grateful for the gift.

Words echoed through his memory, then: Declan's voice.

It's in the harp. His power.

In the harp.

Nairn blinked, found himself hunched over, nose to petal with a wildflower folded up under the moonlight. He straightened slowly, feeling foolish and still entirely helpless against such art. When he could stand again, he slunk away, went downriver, far from the harper and his wily, dangerous harp, to see what enchantments he could get out of his own instrument. Beyond waking a few toads and causing sundry rustles in the underbrush, he couldn't claim much.

The next day, the harper sent him a clearer challenge.

The first day had whittled away at the contenders: minstrels who sang bawdy ballads on street corners, in taverns, for what coins they could get, novices in the art with lofty ideas of their talents, bards from the manses of wealthy merchants and farmers, where the same songs had been played for decades on instruments handed down through generations. These yielded to the great court bards, to a handful of Declan's students, and to skilled wanderers like Welkin. Of those who had been winnowed out of the competition, none left; they all stayed on the plain to listen.

Nairn, Shea, Osprey were still among the contenders on the second day. Other students had played at Declan's insistence on the first day, for the experience, he told them. He had divided the unwieldy number of would-be bards into three groups on the first day; none of the students had had to play against Welkin.

On the second day, the three groups had pared themselves, by general consent and Declan's judgment, into two. Nairn performed in one, Welkin in the other. Competition was fierce; court bards pulled out every instrument they had, challenged others with well-honed skills and intricate songs that ranged through the entire history of the five kingdoms. Nairn countered with songs grown out of the mists and seas and rugged valleys of the Marches that no court had ever heard. Still, he was surprised at the end of the day to find himself standing among the competitors, along with Osprey, a dozen court bards, and Welkin.

The sun lowered over the plain, filled it with light, and shadows stark as the standing stones, then with its absence. The gathering splintered into its smallest fragments to build fires and eat. Later, as evening deepened, one would begin to play again, then another, and listeners would merge again, eddy around the players, then flow away into another pool. Nairn, reluctant to face the unnerved Declan with his own certainty that Welkin would rout even the court bards, wended his way among the colorful camps, wagons, and pavilions toward the brewer's tavern.

Passing a lovely ivory pavilion hung with bright tapestries

and crowned with a flowing pennant, he saw what seemed to be the face of memory, and then again not. He slowed uncertainly. The memory, a tall, graceful young woman dressed in airy silks, her pale hair a mass of curls braided with gold thread and glittering with tiny jewels, looked back at him as she stood at the fire outside the pavilion door.

Again her face stopped his heart. Then she smiled, and it started up again, a bit erratically, like a flutter of wings in his chest. She moved around the fire quickly, leaving the cluster of well-dressed ladies behind her watching curiously, and came eagerly to Nairn's side.

He whispered, "Odelet."

She laughed at his expression. "You almost didn't recognize me. Am I changed so much since you saw me chopping up chickens in the kitchens?"

"Yes," he said, still breathless. "No. You look— You— What are you doing here?"

"How could I not come? To hear the finest musicians in all the realm. I had to—" She paused, her full lips quirked, her eyes flicking beyond him at her own memories. "I had to make promises to my father, and take my brother Berwin with me before he would give me permission. But nothing too binding ... We heard you play this afternoon. You melted my brother's heart. I could tell. You played that court ballad of Estmere, and Berwin had tears in his eyes. I didn't know you learned such music. He wagered money on you. It is extraordinary how gold finds its way into everything, isn't it? Even love and music."

"Yes," he said again, resisting the urge to touch her cool ivory cheek, trace her smile with his fingertips. "Declan has been training me," he explained. "He wants me to win."

"Ah." Her eyes darkened in sudden comprehension. "He wants to send you to King Oroh."

"Yes."

"How wonderful. Then you might indeed come to play in my father's court." She laughed again, a peal of lovely notes, a little breathless herself, suddenly. "Oh. I hope so. I do hope so."

He nodded, swallowing. "It is my greatest wish."

"I miss those evenings when we talked and played. I miss the smell of the plain, the sounds of the wind blowing the long, long way across it." Her eyes clung to his a moment, the tender green of new leaves, then flicked over his shoulder. She smiled wryly. "There is Berwin wondering where I've gone."

"Will I see you again?"

"Yes. Oh, yes. Listening to every song you play tomorrow." He felt her fingertips, light and warm, an instant on his wrist. "Look for me."

"I will," he promised dazedly. "I will."

He watched her rejoin her company. The fire billowed between them, and he moved away slowly, still hearing the music of her voice, her clear thoughts, and he realized that nothing Declan might have said would have rendered the complex, improbable matter suddenly so simple: he would win for her.

The tavern was full of people, but the only one he saw, as he walked through the doorway, was Welkin.

He sat on a stool beside the hearth, playing softly, big, callused hands wandering dreamily over the strings. His strange, mismatched, smiling eyes followed Nairn across the room, where a chair waited for him between Osprey and Shea.

The deep voice, rattling shards of shale, stopped Nairn before he reached it.

"Play with me."

Nairn looked at him silently a moment. Then he laughed. "Why? So you can bring me to my knees again with that harp?"

Welkin's eyes narrowed slightly, still smiling. "Best the harp then, as well as the harper," he suggested. "Break my strings and bring me to my knees."

There were whistles from the onlookers, tankards drummed against wood, a cheerful cry from Osprey.

"I'll buy the beer."

Nairn shrugged, preparing for any humiliation; at least, on the final day, he would know what to expect.

He took out his harp, sat down on the bench at the other side of the fire, over which a cauldron of bean and pork and onion stew bubbled richly.

"Supper's on me," the brewer told them, pleased at the crowd around his tables, which included several of the court bards, who had no doubt followed Welkin in.

"Kind of you," Welkin murmured and touched a string. Then he launched into a song so old and rarely played that Nairn barely remembered it had come out of the Marches: "The Riddle of Cornith and Corneath."

Around and around
The circle of days
Go sun and moon
And my twin eyes:
Guess my name, and you shall take the music of my heart.

Nairn's fingers were riffling down the strings; he heard his own voice answering before he had begun to think.

Beyond, beneath the world I live
Between the words I lie:
Find my name in wind and light
And you shall hold the secrets of my heart.

"Who are you?" he heard in every lilting line. The one question everyone was asking about Welkin, he was giving back to them in his teasing fashion. He was also revealing something, Nairn realized. The question was there, the answer was there, between the beginning and the end of the ancient lines. All that Nairn needed to win was there. The old doggerel sparked to life. Words said what they meant when they were heeded, which was, in the case of hoary verses older than the standing stones, precisely when they were needed.

He settled into the music, passing verses flawlessly back at Welkin, who told him something else before the interminable song came to an end, and even the court bards shouted with amazement.

The fact that they were still playing together after that hour or two or five, that Welkin and his enchanted harp had not blown Nairn out the door and left him too disheartened to bother finishing the competition meant one mysterious thing.

Nairn had something Welkin needed.

Chapter Fifteen

Princess Beatrice heard about the Royal Bard's decision from her mother, who summoned her before she could flee the castle in her dungarees. The tide had turned in the river; the work crew would be waiting near Dockers Bridge for her to pick them up. She had hoped for a word with Master Burley before she left about the hen scratches she had seen the evening before, drawn with charcoal on the lounge table at the inn. But no: work crew, hen scratches, and any thought about Phelan had to wait while she attended the queen in her mauve-appointed morning room.

As usual, the sight of her daughter in pants and grubby boots caused Queen Harriet to close her eyes and delicately pinch the bridge of her nose. That, as usual, caused her daughter to wonder why, after so many digs, her mother was not inured by now. It was as though she thought she had two daughters named Beatrice and a vague hope that one of them would disappear entirely.

"Yes, Mother?"

The queen opened her eyes again and frowned. "You never appeared at Lady Phillipa's party for Damen and Daphne's engagement yesterday. It was noticed. You were missed."

"They have had so many engagement parties. I didn't think they'd care."

"I was told you went off somewhere with Phelan Cle. And yet no one can tell me where. No one we know, that is. You vanish into dank holes during the day; I feel very strongly, and so does your father, that you should not begin to disappear at night as well."

"I'm sorry," Beatrice said penitently, alarmed for her freedom. "It's only—Phelan Cle had a slight accident and—"

"I know. The bill for that 'slight accident' arrived on Grishold's breakfast tray earlier this morning." Beatrice's eyes widened; her lips tightened over a startled laugh. Her mother's voice thinned. "The back door and doorframe of an inn, historical though it might be and with period door hinges, in a not entirely reputable quarter of the docks. And his bard blamed for the damage. Your uncle was nearly incoherent. Such details should never have come to his attention. Nor mine. Apparently Jonah Cle offered recompense for all damages, but the innkeeper felt that, in his dissolute state, he wouldn't remember a thing the next morning, and so he sent his claim to my brother. Why were you anywhere near this sordid little scene? Explain to me again?"

"It wasn't really— We were— How did you know I was there?"

"The innkeeper recognized you and named you as a witness."

"Oh."

Queen Harriet closed her eyes again, briefly. "I will assume he has seen you on certain public occasions. Beyond that, I don't want to know."

"Yes, Mother." She glanced at the antique water clock on the mantelpiece and thought despairingly of the tide. "I really am sorry. Phelan was worried about his father, so I—I went with him to help."

"Worried with good reason, apparently. Really, Beatrice. You abandoned your friends and went trailing off after the soused Master Cle, who has left a litter of broken things across the entire city of Caerau."

"He didn't break the door. It was Kelda, escaping out the back—"

"I really don't want to know," her mother said adamantly. "Bards should make music, not scenes, and now we have another incident, so soon after Quennel's accident with the salmon mousse, and I'm told that the city will very shortly be overrun with bards."

Beatrice raised her hand, dropped it, resisting a childhood urge to chew on a lock of hair when confused. "It will?"

"It most certainly will if your father can't persuade Quennel not to retire. It's absurd of him, of course—Quennel, I mean—he's perfectly fine now, except for a slight sore throat, and there's no reason for him to inflict such a competition on us all now."

The hen scratches, the glint in the young bard's eye, the powerful flash of light that had come out of the charcoal scribbles on the table merged suddenly in Beatrice's head. She breathed, illumined, "Kelda."

The queen regarded her frostily. "Kelda?"

Beatrice wished she could inhale the name back out of the air. "I'm sorry, Mother," she said yet again. "I didn't mean to interrupt you. I really will try not to be so impulsive."

"I was going to say—" Queen Harriet paused, inspired by the

sight of her daughter's outfit, to bring up another subject now that Beatrice was in a placatory mood. "I think," she began slowly, "that you should give some serious thought to your own future. Your father allows you to indulge your whims because you have similar interests. With him it's a hobby; with you it's becoming a career. A rather undignified and completely unnecessary one. You've played in the dirt long enough. It's time you followed the example of your sister, Charlotte. Yes, Lucien, I'm just speaking to your daughter. What is it?"

The king, who had appeared in the doorway, said perplexedly, "I've just been handed the most amazing message from your brother." He broke off, noticing his daughter. "Beatrice! Why are you still here? You'll miss the ebb tide."

She escaped with relief, before she accidentally committed herself to children, dogs, and endless country garden parties.

Down in the site, helping Campion coax the line of stones out of the wall of dirt into daylight, she was so absent that Ida, sifting through the earth at her feet, asked sympathetically, "Is it getting worse?"

"Is what?"

"Being in love."

Beatrice stared down at her. "In love. Oh—" She remembered some distant time, when she had met Kelda's gaze and had felt it everywhere, all over her body. She flushed, wondering how she could have ever misread the power in his eyes.

"When love is gone, how little of love—" Campion intoned sonorously.

"I was never in love," Beatrice said crossly. "It was an accident." Even she had to smile, reluctantly, as they hooted. "A very silly mistake."

His face was still on her mind, as she had seen it the previous evening. Phelan had opened the lounge door, and Kelda, standing at the table with students watching him, drawing a pattern on the pale wood with a burned splinter of kindling, had raised his head at the interruption. His eyes had seemed scarcely human then. The eyes of a raven, a wild horse, a toad, they seemed to recognize nothing human. He hadn't touched his harp. The sound had come out of him, or the word he had drawn: a deep string, vibrating until it seemed to shake the floor. And then the streak of light . . . When she could see again, the back door hung on its hinges, Phelan lay on the floor, and Jonah Cle had appeared out of nowhere. Everyone else had vanished.

A shadow blocked the sunlight overhead; she started, peered upward, and found Jonah leaning over the site edge, peering back at them.

"Ah, you are here, after all, Princess."

"Barely," she told him ruefully, aware of the tools growing quiet around her as everyone listened. "My mother was not happy with me. How is Phelan?"

"I don't know. I haven't been home. Come up a moment?"

She mused a bit darkly, as she climbed the ladder, about the carelessness of parents. Jonah added, as though he read her mind, "You could ask him." He helped her off the ladder. He smelled like a brewery, and his eyes squinted painfully at the cheerful sunlight. But he seemed sober enough.

"Then how do you know that Phelan made it home?" she asked patiently, stifling an unaccustomed urge to raise her voice. Jonah had put them together into a cab; Phelan was coherent by then, though he kept his eyes shut. Yes, he promised, he would call a physician; no, the princess should not see him home since the cab would pass the castle first. Yes, he would be fine if he could just fall into bed, only he had something extremely important to tell her if he could remember what it was . . . He couldn't, not before the cab left her at the castle gates. She watched it roll away with a hiss of steam; that was the last she had seen of Phelan.

"Where else would he have gone?" Jonah asked with annoying unconcern, and added, "I searched all night for Kelda. Did you see him this morning at the castle?"

She shook her head. "No. I wasn't looking, though. Speaking of bards, my mother said something about Quennel wanting to retire, and that the city would soon be overrun by bards. Have you heard anything about that?"

"The bardic competition," Jonah said grimly. "That's what brought Kelda here."

"But he didn't—Kelda had no idea Quennel would—" She faltered, staring at him. "Are you suggesting that he planned this? He—he used his magic against Quennel?"

"Quennel choked on a word," Jonah said harshly, and she blinked, as stray, wordlike objects in her head fit together like broken shards.

"The Circle of Days."

His eyes narrowed at her; she had managed to astonish the jaded Master Cle. "You know about that?"

"Master Burley told me, when I remembered where I had seen the hooded face on the disk. He said it's an ancient language in which very common words hold enormous powers. So the theory goes. Nobody has ever been able to read into the words, beneath them. I saw the pattern Kelda drew on the table. It was also on the disk. What does it mean?"

"Bread."

"Bread."

"Look in any bakery. You see the pattern still used on cottage loaves."

"Really?" she said, amazed. "How fascinating. But what is its other meaning? Its secret?"

"You know that, too. You saw its power last night."

She stared at him again, wordlessly. Standing under the bright noon sun, she felt suddenly chilled and oddly helpless. "All that power," she whispered, "under my father's roof."

"Yes."

"How—how do you know all this? Where did you first meet Kelda?"

His eyes held hers. For a moment she thought he would answer; she could almost hear the words gather in the silence between them. Then he shifted abruptly, glancing at the city across the bridge. "Be careful of him," he only said. "Did he see you last night?"

"I couldn't tell."

"Don't let him find you alone."

"But what can we do?" she pleaded. "You know this language— Do you have its power?"

He started to answer that, then stopped, and gave her instead a wry, very genuine smile. "I wish I did. Whatever he wants, he'll wait to take it during the bardic competition. I might be able to change his path then. Just try to stay away from him. And look in on Phelan if you can."

"Yes," she said dazedly, and watched him pick his way across the barrens of the ruined city before she descended once again to the simpler mystery of stones.

"What was that about?" Campion asked curiously, as she picked up her brush. She answered with a vague tale of Phelan having an accident while trying to keep his father out of trouble, and his father having to rescue him instead. It sounded solid, she thought, until she glanced up and found Campion's disconcerting gaze upon her.

"And you had nothing better to do with your evening than rattle around the Caerau waterfront chasing Jonah Cle?"

"You sound like my mother," she complained, her mouth sliding into a smile in spite of herself. "It didn't seem odd at the time."

She found it difficult, after her conversation with Jonah, to keep her mind on her work. The meticulous task of coaxing what was most likely an old brick mantelpiece out of a wall of earth with the equivalent of artists' brushes and dental tools seemed mildly absurd. It strained her patience, which she had always thought was considerable. Now she wanted to toss her brush on the floor and groan. She gritted her teeth, watched the sunlight shift with painstaking slowness across one bit of grit on the floor, then another. She only realized how the strain of her silence had spread through the site when Curran finally broke it.

"Go," he told her gently. "Just go where you need to. You're already out of here and away; you just haven't caught up with yourself yet."

She drove the steam car over the bridge, debated about changing her clothes, passed the castle without deciding, and parked along the old, quiet streets where Phelan lived. For a moment, when the ageless Sagan opened the door, she regretted her dungarees and her dusty hair.

He only murmured at a query behind him, "Princess Beatrice,

Lady Sophy. Come from the archaeological digs, would be my guess."

"Sorry," the princess said to Sophy, wondering how many times she had overworked that word in one morning. But Sophy, who after all had married the mercurial Jonah, only saw what she chose to: the princess on her doorstep.

"How lovely of you to pay us a visit! Jonah is away, but Phelan is here, resting."

"Yes. How is he?"

"A slight fever. I gave him some meadowsweet tea and took away his inkpots. Please, sit down."

"I'm a bit untidy."

"Nonsense. Sagan, please tell Phelan that Princess Beatrice is here." Beatrice perched herself on the edge of a chair. Sophy fluttered down onto the sofa, adding, with her charming smile, "I'm not at all certain what happened last night. Phelan is vague and Jonah is—well, his usual self. Do you know?"

"Something—" Beatrice managed guardedly. "Only a little."

The gray eyes, so like Phelan's, regarded her temperately. There was, Beatrice realized for the first time, a great deal of focus beneath the disarming flightiness Sophy scattered around her as a distraction. It kept her from having to answer questions about her impossible husband. It didn't keep her from wondering. And now she was asking.

"Yes," Beatrice blurted. "I know some of it. I don't understand it all. It's complex."

"Well, it would be, wouldn't it, considering Jonah. Nothing trivial, nothing predictable . . . And now, Phelan. I must go out in a few moments. A women's party: we have secured a barge for

Lady Petris, to row her upriver and picnic along the water at a place with a very fine view of the plain. You would be entirely welcome to join us."

"I'm hardly dressed—"

"And you have come to talk to Phelan. Straight from your dig, and wearing the dust of antiquity in your hair."

Beatrice brushed at it. "I think it's barely a couple of centuries old."

"Not likely to be of great interest, then."

"Some kind of common brickwork. No. I came rather impulsively." She hesitated, added as impulsively, "I am sorry to be so mysterious. I simply don't know exactly what I'm looking at."

"Jonah does have that effect . . . Yes, Sagan?"

"Phelan seems to have gone out," the butler said apologetically. "Sometime ago, and by way of the kitchen, so he could take his breakfast with him. The cook said he was carrying books; perhaps he's at the school."

Sophy ticked her tongue. "My fault entirely: I should have let him work."

Beatrice stood up. "I'll look there, then."

"I have the perfect skirt, Princess Beatrice."

"I beg—"

"Yes, I'm sure it would fit you, though a bit shorter than you're used to, since so am I."

Beatrice smiled. "I'm glad you reminded me. Yes, I would be grateful; I won't have to stop at home, then." And sneak around hiding behind pots and doors to elude both my mother and the bard, she did not say. "Thank you, Sophy."

Her scruffy boots partially hidden under Sophy's skirt, and most of the dust out of her hair, she drove back down the river road. She turned up the hill to the school, startling a matched pair of skittish grays when she changed gears, and the car let out one of its goose-honks. Halfway up the hill, she braked abruptly, with another clamor of gears and a snort, beside the pale-haired man with an armload of books trudging toward the school.

"Phelan! Get in."

He cast his brooding glance in her direction, then the thoughts startled out of his eyes. He pulled the door open; he and his books tumbled into the seat beside her. "Princess Beatrice." He was sweating like a candle and about as pale; his eyes glittered a bit like Jonah's did after a wild night. "What are you doing up above ground in broad daylight?"

"I came looking for you. Your father couldn't tell me whether or not you had gotten home safely, and you successfully eluded me when I stopped at your house. Couldn't you have taken the tram up?"

He shrugged, a smile flickering suddenly into his pained eyes. "I was waiting for you to come by, I suppose. I need more books for my research. And I completely missed my morning class. My students are probably still languishing hopelessly under the oak."

"No doubt. Surely your father's library—"

The smile faded. "My father doesn't keep what I want to know," Phelan answered restively. "He gets it out of the house, buries it in someone else's shelves. Last night in the cab—"

"Yes."

"Things kept fragmenting in my head. I wanted to tell you something, but I couldn't sustain a coherent thought. Now they're piecing themselves back together."

"What thoughts?"

He frowned, concentrating. "When I was with my father in

the Merry Rampion, he told me details about these books that he said he had never read." He shook his head abruptly, then closed his eyes tightly a moment as though to quiet a sudden welter of pain. "He must be mistaken; his brain must be a sieve by now—"

"Last night you said it is a morass. You can't have it both ways."

He smiled, and pleaded, "Please don't interrupt, Princess. My own brain is a rotting fishing net; things keep getting away from me. But I can't stop thinking about that moment in the Merry Rampion when I tried to distract my father to keep him from chasing after Kelda. I went back and forth through these books with a jeweler's eyepiece, and—"

"Very weighty tomes," she said, impressed. "What are they?"

"The school's household records. They go back to the very first year that Declan built his school. Nobody ever reads them. They aren't even kept in the archives. Bayley Wren hides them up in the tower. Wren. That's another thing—"

"Try," she begged, "to keep to one thought at a time. That's all I'm used to in my line of work."

"This is the same thought, I promise. My father knew the name of the first school steward though he said he hadn't read the records."

"Surely that's not uncommon knowledge, with everybody doing papers about everything."

"And he knew about the tower falling then, in that first year. And that Salix was a woman—"

Beatrice closed her eyes, opened them again, hastily, as the steam tram chugged past. "Salix."

"I thought she was a man; my father said I was wrong. The

school steward never says one way or the other. How would my father have known that?" Beatrice opened her mouth. "And there's the third coffin—"

"Coffin?"

"That Nairn would have been buried in after he was killed by the falling tower stones. But nobody ever found his body. So the coffin became accounts returned."

Beatrice turned onto the school grounds, pulled into the paved area where the steam trams turned around, and parked. "I'm not," she said apologetically, "entirely understanding this, though I know it is very important to you."

"Well, it would certainly explain a few things."

"I'm sure it would. I couldn't with any degree of certainty tell you what those things might be. Perhaps your father read different books about the first year of the school? Got his facts somewhere else?" She waited. He had turned to gaze at the oak grove, pursuing his own perplexing vision. "Phelan? What's on your mind?"

"Always," he breathed. "Always my father . . . It's impossible. But it would explain . . . I need to know what happened at that first bardic competition. And I need to know where Kelda came from."

"Grishold," she said, but again without any degree of certainty. "He speaks the language of the Circle of Days . . . Is that common knowledge in Grishold?"

Phelan turned his head abruptly, his eyes, heavy and feverish, clinging to her. "You recognized it last night."

"So did your father." Her voice sounded faint, distant; she felt the imperative intensity of his gaze, searching, waiting. "Master Burley said no one had ever been able to translate it beyond—

beyond—what the words say into the secrets they conceal. Phelan, what exactly are you thinking?"

"That I need to finish my research on Nairn as soon as possible. Look." He loosed her eyes finally, nodded toward the trees, where a circle of students sat around the dark-haired harper, in the shadows of the ancient oak.

"Kelda," the princess breathed.

Phelan looked at her again, his face colorless, harrowed with light, his mouth clamped tight. She saw what he was not saying: Zoe in the transfixed circle around Kelda, listening to him play.

Chapter Sixteen

On the third day of the bardic competition, the tower blew apart, and Nairn disappeared again from history.

Both events are transformed into accounts rendered or received in the steward's records. Dower Ren himself makes an appearance as an account rendered for the wounds he suffered when the roof and the battlement stones crashed down into his chambers; he gives his shattered inkpot more mention than he does himself. Two students were killed by the broken tower; one vanished. The names of the two sent home in their coffins appear in their own families' household records, and in chronicles of the period. They had both heard Declan play during King Oroh's visits to his nobles and had left their comfortable homes to meet their fates in the school on the hill.

The third student, Nairn, seems to have been missed by no one, at least for a couple of centuries, except for some sharp-eyed bards and minstrels, who had glimpsed something more on the plain than is anywhere recorded outside of poetry.

The foremost question the historian must ask, in attempting to understand the events of the third day within the rigorous boundaries of the field is: What did those on the plain actually see?

The household records of Dower Ren deal only with the aftermath of the day, and they are terse to the extreme. Before then, when the two bards, Welkin and Nairn, were the only ones left to compete for the highest honor in the realm, we must explore other sources. Like the steward, Declan himself was mute about that last, intense struggle between musicians. His comments come later, in a letter to King Oroh:

". . . we send you the best the land has left to offer, with my hope that, in the following year or two, I might again find one of such gifts to which you are accustomed in your bard, and so proceed with the training." That's all. He makes no reference either to his student, in whom he had placed such hope, or in the harper out of nowhere who challenged him. What happened to Welkin, at the end of the day? Why did one or the other not claim victory? Who knows?

Declan, of all, might have, but he will not say.

When we look through the records of the court chroniclers, busily taking notes on the plain, we find odd, conflicting comments about the end of the competition. Lord Grishold's chronicler, Viruh Staid, confesses to a peculiar lapse of attention. He flirts with a bard's wife; he wanders down to the river to relieve himself among the trees—whatever he found to do, it seems astonishing and highly suspicious that he chooses to do it in the middle of the final songs of the competition.

His disclaimer makes more sense in light of King Oroh's own chronicler's mind-boggling description: "It seemed to me that the wind itself grew very old as the harpers played. The moon grew full, though it was scarce past half when it rose. My heart overspilled itself like a seething cauldron with wonder. The very stones within them turned and turned and the stones sang ... Such was my dream ... Then the dream blew into fragments. I woke, and the competition was at an end."

Others, writing letters or descriptions later in the calm of their own chambers, were equally nebulous about how the great event ended. They barely comment about the broken tower, as though that was the least of their memories. One remembers following the scent of an enormous cauldron, and how he craved the "heady broth" so much that he forgot to listen to the music, but no one offered him any. Another complains that an ill-chosen mushroom must have clouded his memory, for what he does remember of the final song could never have happened. And so on.

At the end of the day, we have the results set down very succinctly by the king's chronicler:

"I watched the bard of the Duke of Waverlea given the title, by Declan himself, of Royal Bard of Belden."

> *... No song, no peace, no poetry,*
> *no end of days, and no forgetting.*
>
> "BONE PLAIN," ANONYMOUS: TRANSLATED FROM THE RUNIC BY J. CLE

They had never stopped playing. At sunrise, only Osprey and a couple of court bards were left in the tavern. Osprey's head lay on the table in a ring of beer mugs. The court bards caught at melodies they knew with harp and pipe and small drum; otherwise, they listened silently, their faces stunned with weariness and wonder, to songs from all over the five kingdoms that had never been permitted to pass the thick stone walls surrounding court music.

The brewer, who had gone to bed hours before, woke up and gave them all breakfast. Welkin and Nairn, drunk on music, chewed intermittently on bread and bacon as they tested one another, Nairn pulling music out of his back teeth, songs from his Pig-Singer days that he must have learned by listening to the grass grow, or to a blackbird's passing whistle, for all he was taught back then. Welkin had the same teachers, it seemed; all his music sounded eldritch, haunted. Finally, they left their benches, accompanied by a ringing wake of gold tossed on the tables by the court bards, and moved up the hill.

They barely noticed the gathering of musicians for the final day, so engrossed they were in their own competition. The two court bards left to play, then came back again, followed by others. Through the noon and afternoon, it became clear that the true contest pitted the young, charming student from the Marches with the scruffy, odd-eyed wanderer out of nowhere discernible. Their struggle was congenial and absolute. They matched song for song, took them back through their various changes, so far back sometimes that word and wind seemed to veer close enough to overlap, borne on the rilling notes of a brook or a bird cry.

They were moving very close to the language of the Circle of Days. Nairn felt it like a tidal pull, a whirling exuberance that tugged, lured, tempted into its roil of beauty and danger. His craft sheered closer and closer to its wildness. Welkin heard it; the smile in his eyes grew deep, honed. The listeners, more and more of them drifting from the circle around the final competitors to this private battle, heard it as well. They stood, wordless and motionless as the stones on the hill, while court bard vied with court bard in some other world, until even they yielded to the irresistible and astonishing engagement that overwhelmed even their great gifts.

By then the sun had crossed the plain to lower itself into the western forests, drawing long shadows of stone and tree and bard across the grass. Nairn, helpless in the crosscurrents around the vortex of power he and Welkin had opened between them, saw Declan's face one last time: his gray eyes fixed on Nairn, his fierce, triumphant smile.

The sun went down.

The crowd around them seemed to melt into the twilight. They might have been alone, he and Welkin, with the simplest and oldest words: wind, earth, stone, tree. The sky, in that misty realm neither day nor night, ringed the plain as gray as slate. For the first time, Nairn felt tired. Not in his fingers, or his voice, or his churning brain, but of the competition itself, which never ended, but drew and drew at him, forced him to reach ever deeper into memory and experience, farther than he thought even he had traveled in his life. The power in the ancient songs fed his hands, his harp, possessed him; he felt as though he were the instrument, sounding every note out of blood and bone marrow. Still it never ended, and still he would stand there until his feet took root in the ground and birds built nests in his hair before he would yield to Welkin.

The first breath of evening breeze wafted over the plain. He nearly fell to his knees at the smell in it: tender salmon, onions, celery, peas, rosemary, lavender, pepper. The savory scents threatened to cloud his mind like errant fog, overwhelming even the forces that drove him until he yielded and followed his nose across the grass, where a great cauldron reflected the fires under it, turning copper to gold.

Welkin smelled it, too; he spoke through their flurry of notes. "Could stop a moment."

"No."

"A swallow of cold water? Or ale? A mouthful of that?"

"Help yourself," Nairn said tersely.

"I'm parched as a pebble in a desert. You may not be the better bard, but you're the younger. Have mercy on an old worn harper. Call it a truce? We'll go back to playing after—"

"No. You may not be the better bard, but you're the craftier. You make yourself comfortable inside a blizzard. I'm not stopping. I'll stop, and you won't, and you'll claim victory."

Welkin gave one of his shard-shifting laughs. He was silent for a bit, while one tune ended, and he pulled another out of his inexhaustible memory that Nairn clawed out of his own by a thumbnail and a thread. They settled into it.

Welkin spoke again, softly. "Ah, look."

Someone—Muire?—had come down the hill to add an apronful of something to the stew. She emptied it into the cauldron, gave it a stir. Smoke billowed, blurring her. She seemed taller, as it frayed around her again: willowy and graceful, with long, frothy hair of the palest gold. Nairn's eyes widened; he nearly missed a note. Odelet? Doing what she had always done at the school: chopping, stirring, cooking, feeding the hungry?

"I'd stop for such as that," Welkin grunted, and showed Nairn the teasing smile in his twilight eye. An expected fury shot through Nairn that the old battered boot sole of a bard had riffled through his thoughts; he nicked a note so sharply, he nearly broke the string. He heard Welkin's sudden, indrawn breath; a note under his thumb wavered weakly. Then he turned himself back into a solid slab of stone with hands. Nairn stared down at his own fingers, rage transformed to wonder. He had hurt the impervious Welkin with an errant harp note.

What else might he do?

He was so engrossed in possibilities that he barely noticed the figure standing in front of him sometime later, smiling, stirring a richly fragrant and steaming bowl.

"Nairn. Shall I give you a bite?"

It was darker now; the fire under the cauldron and the moon glowed brightly in the vast, tidal flow of night, but little else on the plain did. Her face was still blurred, shadowed with twilight; her sweet, clear voice sounded as distant as memory. A dream, a wish, his weary, hungry brain had conjured, he suspected. Or she was something Welkin had picked out of Nairn's head and shaped with his harp string. Nothing that could possibly be real.

He answered her tersely, "No."

She was gone so abruptly, in the blink of an eye, he knew she must have been an enchantment, until Welkin complained, "You might have been more polite about it. She would have offered me a bite, too, then, before you drove her off."

"Who?"

"Who?" He snorted like a horse, then roused his harp and his voice into a long rollicking ballad. Nairn pulled his thoughts out of the mysterious realms of power and caught up with him within a beat or two. The moon ascended, flooding the plain with silver. It was strangely full, as though more time had passed during their private battle than he realized. The ballad seemed to last forever, Nairn picking verses out of his head so old he must have been born knowing them, for all he remembered where he had learned them.

"We could walk down together," Welkin suggested, when they had finished that and Nairn had challenged him with a dance he had only ever heard played on the bladder-pipe. Welkin only chuckled and leaped into it. "Charm her a bit, and she'll feed us both."

"Right. You'll wait until my mouth is full and I can't sing a note and you'll call victory while I'm trying to swallow."

Welkin shrugged. "Who's to notice? No one's paying attention but him."

That seemed true enough. Everyone had wandered off to listen to the last of the court bards, maybe, but for the tall old man standing with his back to the moon. He was cloaked from head to heel. Nairn saw a flutter of hair white as moonlight out of the hood he wore, but nothing of his face.

Then his vision shifted, became clearer in the deceptive light.

"That's not a man," he said. "Just one of the standing stones."

"You're in poor shape if you can't tell stone from man. We've been playing for a night and a day and about to begin another night. How much longer can you keep up with me? I've a long, long road behind me that crisscrossed all over this land. You've gone a mile or so from your pigsty."

"Farther than that," Nairn retorted. "I'm still standing. And you're the one who brought up the words. Food. Ale. You're the one who needs them." He nodded at the stone. "Maybe he'll fetch them for you, if you ask."

Nairn gave his gravelly laugh. "I could make him dance. I could make him sing."

"He's stone."

"I could make him tell our fortunes, which of us is still on his feet and playing by the dawn. I'll make you a wager: whichever of us makes him speak goes down and charms her back up here with her bowl of stew."

"He's stone. And you'll cheat."

"You're just afraid of facing her."

"What 'her'? She's just something you've conjured up with your harp strings. I'm not wasting my fingers or my breath trying to make a stone speak. I intend to be standing right here, come the dawn, and you'll be wondering where the magic in your harp went."

"Is that so."

"Yes, old man," he said between his teeth. "I'll find the way to make it so."

Welkin laughed.

The sky darkened; stars gathered thick as the crowd on the plain, more and more of them pushing out to listen. Nairn played and sang to them, for they were all he saw. Even the night fires across the plain had been neglected, except for the one still burning beneath the great cauldron. No one else seemed to be eating from it either. They were all gathered somewhere in the dark, he guessed, somewhere beyond time, silent and entranced, waiting to see which of them would come to the end of songs and put down his harp, and finally feel the exhaustion, the torn fingers, the throat so raw and swollen nothing but a toad-croak would ever come creeping out of it again.

Even then, as the wheel of stars turned above them, he heard Welkin's playing strengthen, gather energy from the night, at once so unfalteringly wild and so precise that the question nobody could answer welled again through Nairn:

Who are you?

The old harper's eyes caught starlight, glinted at him. He heard Declan's voice again, his only answer:

The magic is in the harp.

The strings played themselves, maybe; Welkin had only to stay on his feet and remember the verses. It didn't make a great deal of sense, but nothing did, not the cauldron full of food that no one ate, the crowd that never danced or sang with the bards, or even spoke, the only one visible even in the dark either a hooded man or a stone, either way as silent as the rest.

Something prickled over Nairn then, like a chill breath from the midsummer moon. His fingers went cold; his eyes grew swollen and dry, too dry even to blink, look away from what he recognized, must have known long before, in some part of his mind that was not busy trying to overwhelm the bard beside him with his brilliance.

I know this song, he thought, but not of the one under his fingers. The one in the plain in front of him. The cauldron. The stone. The tower of night around him, stars endlessly turning, turning. The ancient plain itself, everyone on it as mute and ephemeral as ghosts.

Bone Plain.

He felt a sudden, fierce shock of exultation and dread. It was what he wanted, he knew then: an end to the never-ending competition. The tower appeared first in his memory's eye: rooted close to where he and Welkin stood, its stones coiling endlessly upward into the stars. He had watched it appear once before in all his innocence and ignorance, before he knew it had a name. Now he knew it. He named it, gazing at it with his heart's knowing eye, willing it to appear, build itself note by note, stone by stone, spiraling out of him, a stone for every note, a swirl of stars crowning its ascent into the night. It was what they both wanted, he and Welkin: the only place where they could finally be judged.

The Turning Tower.

He dreamed it as he played. In another world, a harper with sweat dripping onto his harp strings, his muscles burning, fingers cracked and bleeding, wrenched yet one more song out of himself. In his dream, the massive tower grew to engulf the plain, the campfires burning on it scarcely bigger than the flickering stars within the stones. Grave and kindly voices filled it, stopped the interminable competition. The Trials and the Terrors were simple matters compared to the song he was dragging out of his anklebones, his ear bones. The voices commanded; he did as he was told; he accepted the justice demanded in the ancient lines of poetry; at last he could rest.

He only had to open the tower door . . .

He could see it: a paler oblong of stone in the dark wall, the color of the standing stones. Twig-words ran across the lintel stone; a single word glowed in the middle of the door: a circle containing an endless spiral that started in the center and whorled around itself to merge with the outer ring and begin its backward spiral. The word teased at Nairn. He knew it; he did not know it. Declan had not taught it to him, but his fingers knew it. They kept trying to play it like a song, pull it out of the strings, shape it, say it in ways his weary brain could not begin to form. He felt Welkin's eyes on him, as though he heard the changes in Nairn's music, the odd patterns, the unexpected rhythms that drove him. It was the door latch, that word. It was the lock and the bar and the turning key. Sweat stung his eyes, blinding him; he shook it away, felt the limp, wet strands of his hair. They had played for a night and a day, and now began another night, and little had passed his lips except his own sweat. It didn't matter. Not even Welkin mattered anymore. Only that word, drawn by fire, it seemed, on the face of the door.

He closed his eyes, let it fill his mind, whatever it was, and let his fingers speak. He felt it before he heard it: a wild, jarring sound like a string breaking, or a small animal crying out in sudden pain. He opened his eyes again, startled.

He heard his own voice, then, loosed in a ragged shout of pure terror. His fingers froze.

Death, the word on the door said, and it surrounded him: ghost after ghost pulling themselves out of their bones laid to rest on slabs of creamy yellow stone and long picked clean by time. The wraiths wore their memories of wealth and honor, fine robes and mantels of many colors, adorned with soft fur, intricate embroidery, buttons of carved bone. Their armbands and collars and hairpins were fashioned of silver and gold. Precious stones gleamed on the instruments they carried; other instruments encased in fine leather leaned against the burial pallets. The ghosts were the oldest bards of the plain, Nairn guessed, looking much as they might have the day before they died, except for their eyes. All were empty and black as skull sockets, swimming with the reflections of fire from the single torch beside the open door.

"Welcome."

He was greeted in the language he had heard Welkin speak. This time he understood it. He backed a step, not wanting, in any language, to be welcomed into the company of the dead. But he was, he reminded himself, where he had wished to be: inside the lines of the oldest poem in the realm.

Welkin answered, and Nairn started, remembering that he

was not alone, that the bard had his own very powerful reasons to be there, and they had a contest to finish.

"What must we do?" Nairn's voice came out as a poor, shredded phantom of itself, splintered between fear and wonder and the endless songs he had sung to get where he stood.

"Play," Welkin answered grimly. "Play your heart out. That's the only true door out of here."

"Play," a wraith echoed, a woman robed in orange and purple, her gray-gold braids wound with golden thread. "The 'Ballad of Enek and Krital.' You, Pig-Singer. Play it the way I sang it."

Nairn's mind went instantly blank. These were all court bards, he knew, no matter how forgotten the courts, and he doubted that even Declan's knowledge had reached as far back as they went. But his fingers were moving again, suddenly, along the path of a teasing little phrase that had danced out of nowhere into his head. The wraith was smiling by the end of it, the rich threads in her hair spiraling with reflections of fire as she nodded. She said nothing. Another bard, an old man in white, with long hair and a longer beard, broke the brief silence after Nairn finished.

"Play 'The Gathering of Crows,' Welkin."

A song Nairn had never heard, the ballad of a dying young warrior, melted through his heart. The old bard sang out of the harsh beginnings of time and song, both stripped to their essences. It sounded eerie, haunting, as though a stone on the plain were singing to itself. Nairn's skin prickled again with sudden, cold terror. He was going to lose this contest. The scruffy wanderer with the mismatched eyes and a voice like a collision of old bones and shards, knew the songs that had been buried with these wraiths. Where Welkin had heard them, what graves he had sat on, listening to the singing of the brambles growing out of hollow skulls, Nairn could not imagine. But somewhere in his travels, Welkin had learned the songs of the dead.

He would walk out of this tomb triumphant and alive and take his place as Royal Bard in King Oroh's court. Wealth, honor, and all the music of the realm would be his. And there Nairn would be, as ever, outside the walls, outside the windows, looking in at what he could not have.

At that unlikely moment, as he stood within the heart of the oldest secret of the plain, Nairn heard Declan's voice.

The magic is in the harp . . .

The young lover died; the crows descended. There was not a word, not so much as a flash of fire lit silver or running thread of gold from the motionless listeners.

Then a third wraith spoke. "Pig-Singer. 'The Journey of the Wheel.'"

Nairn raised his harp, hoping against hope that his fingers would know the song that he was certain, in all his rambles, he had never encountered. They hovered, silent. The wraiths stood as silently, waiting.

Then his fingers moved to the deepest string on the harp, played that one string all at once, echoing the deep, fierce longings, despair, and certainty strung along Nairn's sinews, reverberating in his bones, that Welkin cheated, that Welkin had no great gifts, that all the ancient power belonged to his harp, and Nairn could break those strings with a wish and prove it.

One string in Welkin's harp did snap, before the old bard himself gave an anguished, untuned cry. The harp dropped first, then the harper, following it to earth.

From out of the suddenly starry sky, stones began to fall.

Chapter Seventeen

Quennel sent his message to the school before the day ended: a formal request, brilliant with colored ink and the king's seal, that a search for a new Royal Bard should be called without delay across the land, and all musicians from village to high court be welcomed to compete on Stirl Plain on the first day of summer. Zoe was stunned by the date. It seemed scant breaths away, one final smile from the moon at spring before it turned its face toward summer. But, she realized, any day within the next century that pitted her against Kelda would be too soon.

"I can't do it," she whispered numbly as she stood staring at the parchment pinned to the board where all could see. Students and teachers jostled around her, exclaiming, laughing with excitement; she could almost feel the air tuned to their tension as they mentally tightened their strings and calculated their chances. "Quennel, I can't win this thing for you."

She could hear his answer, his aged, light eyes fierce and burning: Do it anyway.

"Zoe."

She started. It was Phelan beside her, whom she hadn't seen since the previous evening, when he had appeared so unexpectedly in the fussy little inn, his father blowing in the back door like a squall at the same time. Kelda had said something, or maybe Jonah had. Then she had found herself hurrying along the walkway between herbaceous borders, caught in a scurry of students fleeing the place as though they had been discovered stealing the tea service.

Phelan's fingers coaxed her out of the crowd; she looked at him silently, puzzled, when they stopped under the shadow of an oak tree. He seemed weary, oddly bruised around the edges. His father, she thought instantly. But that wasn't what came out first.

"What made you go off with Kelda last night?" he asked her bewilderedly.

She gazed at him a moment longer, not entirely sure herself. Then she gave him the simplest answer. "Something Quennel told me. I wanted to know if it's true."

"Is it?"

She paused, searching his face again. They had known one another so long and so well it seemed by now there would be nothing she couldn't read in his eyes. He looked unsettled, wary and strangely distant, as though half his mind had gone off on some wayward road she didn't know existed. They both had secrets, she realized then, from each other.

"I don't know," she answered, to her own surprise. "Maybe. I don't know yet. I have to find out. Phelan . . . I'm not really sure what happened at the inn. I heard a word spoken when you came in, and—"

He shook his head. "It was a harp note."

"No—One of them—Kelda or your father—said—"

"You think it was my father?" he asked incredulously. "He didn't have a harp."

"I didn't hear a harp note."

"That's what I heard. The power was in the harp. That's what—Well." He looked away from her briefly, at the memory. "Who did what is not so important at this moment. What's important is: you're doing this for Quennel?"

She nodded, and wasn't, in the next moment, entirely sure that was true. "He's afraid of Kelda," she told him. "I want to find out why."

Some of the confusion lifted; his eyes became familiar again, seeing what he thought he knew. But he was still frowning. "Be careful," he pleaded. "I'm not sure myself what happened, but Quennel may well be right to be afraid. My father would say so."

"Would you?" she asked quickly. "You seemed indifferent to Kelda yesterday."

"I'm not anymore. Not after last night. Somebody blew the back door of the inn off its hinges, and Kelda was the one with the harp." She stared at him; his mouth crooked. "Magic," he admitted, and she felt the word flow like water through cracked, parched earth.

"Yes." She shook her head, half-laughing suddenly, and stepped into light. She lifted her face to it, let it burn the edges of her vision, let the wind blow her hair like leaves. "Yes."

"You're bewitched," Phelan breathed, watching from the shadow.

"I'm fascinated," she amended. "That's better than being afraid."

"Zoe—"

"Don't worry. I promise I will be careful. You, too. Stay away from flying doors and strings that speak."

She left him with that, all she had to give him at the moment, for Kelda was crossing the lawn toward them, and suddenly the last thing she wanted was the two of them face-to-face. Fortunately, Phelan, after giving her a skewed glance, took himself off in the opposite direction, toward the library, with an inexplicable amount of energy and purpose. Zoe turned to meet the bard.

Time elongated as she watched him, slowed and lingered over each long stride, each ruffle of black silk tunic in the wind, each spark of light along the brass studs patterning his harp strap. He seemed to walk a long way across the grass and the intricate patterns of oak shadows, as though he moved out of some distant past, his expression blurred, unreadable. Then light drew his features clear, and time caught up with itself. He reached her in a step or two, speaking before he stopped. For once he was not smiling.

"Was that Phelan Cle? I wanted to apologize to him."

"For what? Exactly?" she asked, genuinely curious.

"For what happened last night. I seem to raise his father's hackles for some reason. Maybe my ancestors offended his. Or he is simply enraged at the sight of me for no particular reason. Did Phelan mention anything?"

"Only vaguely," she said carefully. "I couldn't make the incident any clearer to him. One moment we were sitting around the table in a perfectly ordinary lounge discussing eggs or clouds or cauliflower, the next we were all out skulking through the back garden as though we were trying to avoid the innkeeper's bill. What did happen?"

"A bit of carelessness," he answered ruefully, "between Jonah

Cle and me. It was unfortunate. I'll see that it doesn't happen again. There are far more private places where we can meet. Have you seen Quennel's announcement? I found it astonishing."

"Did you?"

"Well, of course. He told us all that he wanted to die midsong in the king's hall. I believed him. You didn't?"

He paused for an answer, one brow raised innocently; she felt her own hackles stir.

"Of course," she said, settling them ruthlessly. "And you? Are you going to compete?"

"I wouldn't miss this competition if it meant my death," he said complacently. "And I intend to win." He flashed his glowing smile finally. "But, please, don't let that make you hesitate to compete with me. I love hearing your voice. And Phelan? Will he compete?"

"He says no."

"Pity. Try to get him to change his mind, will you? The better the competition, the better I play. I feed on challenge. You may have noticed."

Indeed, you feed on something, she thought grimly, and saw his eyes narrow, glinting with amusement as though he had read her mind.

She backed a step. "I must go. My father will want his supper."

"You cook as well? Fortunate man. Tomorrow, then? The Circle of Days?" He waited, neither complacent nor challenging now, but as though, she felt, something important to him depended on her answer. She gave a short nod. "Good," he said softly. "I have some time in the late afternoon before Quennel plays at the king's supper, and I must go and be polite. I'll find a more suitable place to meet and let everyone else know."

He turned in time to greet a multitude of students just out of class, eager to share with him their excitement about Quennel's announcement. Zoe went her way, feeling buffeted within by inarticulate questions, and went to the tower kitchen to chop up a chicken while she tried to ignore them.

The bard walked in and out of her thoughts many times that day and the next, to her annoyance. He exuded ambiguities, she decided: that was his fascination. His mouth spoke; his eyes said something other; his smile belied everything. He was a crofter's son from Grishold; he had never been anywhere else. So he said, while he made his way easily through Caerau without a map. He dabbled, he said, in magic; he played with the language of the Circle of Days like a child with an arsenal of twigs. His music said otherwise; it seemed to echo through time out of a past as old as the stones on the hill. He lied with every note he played. Or, in his music, he finally told the truth.

What that truth was, Zoe glimpsed only fitfully: crazed, scattered notions that flitted like bats in the twilight around the edges of coherent thought, scarcely visible, gone when she tried to make sense of them. Lost in thought, she only noticed Phelan as something as familiar as furniture, when he appeared at the table reading some ancient book of her father's, or when she found him coming down the tower steps with his arms full of them. He was as preoccupied, as distracted as she; when she came out of her brooding enough to wonder and ask him, he only murmured something vague and got out of her way. He was possessed by his paper, she guessed, and about time. What was it about? Bone Plain? Apparently he had found something at last to say about it, that maybe had been said only a dozen times, not a hundred.

The place that Kelda chose for the next meeting of the Circle of Days took her breath away.

It was under the king's own roof, or at least under his courtyard.

"One of the queen's ladies showed it to me," he said disingenuously. "It's a very old passageway, connecting several inner chambers of the castle to the riverbank. No doubt it had many uses through the centuries, for trysts and spying, for escape under siege. Likely it was an ancient sewage channel; it's locked tight now against the curious and the malignant. I doubt that even Jonah Cle will find us there."

"It seems—it seems so clandestine. As though we are plotting under the king's very nose."

"Yes, doesn't it?" He gave her his kelpie's smile, all innocence and complicity. "At least it will be private. Lord Grishold requested no more inexplicable incidents involving door hinges and inn-keepers' bills. What could possibly happen in a place everybody has forgotten?"

What indeed? Zoe wondered, as the reckless, cheerful group of students gathered like conspirators at an iron grate sealing a vaulted stone channel that began under the shadow of the broad Royal Bridge near the castle. She would have sworn the grate was locked the moment Kelda opened it as easily as a nursery door. They filed inside quickly, followed the dry, musty sluice. When they left the lowering sun behind, Kelda produced fire from somewhere—out of his sleeve or a pocket—causing ripples of awe that echoed off the stones to drift against the murmuring tide behind them. Zoe, startled, felt eager fingers lock around her wrist, heard Frazer's indrawn breath.

"Did you see that? He kindles fire out of air—out of shadow—"

"I saw it."

"I was right! I knew there was magic in the words, and he knows it. Zoe, he can teach it to us!"

"Yes," she answered, chilled under the empty, secret path that led to the heart of the king's house. Frazer's fierce hold loosened, but his fingers brushed her now and then, cold with excitement, she guessed, and reassuring himself with her presence. She had no such reassurance: every step she took over the uneven ground led her closer to the enigmatic heart of the kelpie. She walked that pathway alone, she knew; there was no mistrust, only eagerness and wonder in the hushed voices around her.

For a man who had never been to Caerau before, the bard led them with astonishing certainty, ignoring or choosing passage-ways that shunted this way and that under the castle grounds, until he reached, to his own satisfaction, a place that looked like any other in the long vault, and stopped there.

He said nothing to the students gathered around him, just set his fire on the ground and motioned for them to sit around it. He pulled the case from his shoulder, took out the strange harp he had carried to the inn. It seemed very old, unadorned by metal or jewels, only by what looked to Zoe's perplexed eye like the random knife-whittlings of a very bored harper.

Kelda spoke then, holding the harp over the fire so they could see more clearly. "I was shown this harp by an old villager whose fingers had stiffened too badly for him to play it any longer. He liked my harping, and thought I'd find it interesting. He couldn't read the words on it, nor could his own father. He thought his great-grandmother might have learned them, so the family lore went. There was another bit of lore handed down as well: that the harp traveled its own path, went where it would, gave itself to whom it chose." He smiled. "I felt that it chose me, and so I took it. I learned to play it. I have learned to play it very well . . ." He touched a string lightly; the fire responded, a flame leaping upward, bright, coiling in currents that must have been stirred by the string. "You might have heard it the other night. If not, no matter. You will hear it tonight, I promise. And in a short time, all of Caerau will hear it."

"The Circle of Days," Frazer broke in abruptly, his eyes riveted to the harp. "Those are the words you're teaching us, carved all over the wood."

"The harp speaks that language," Kelda said simply, "if you know how to ask it."

Zoe felt a tremor deep within her, as though the harp had already sounded, and her heart's blood had answered in terror, in wonder, in desire. She closed her eyes briefly, tried to remember why, exactly, she had followed this harper underground, to such a secret place so far from anything she knew, so close to the oblivious royal court above their heads that if Kelda played a note wrong, the king himself might tumble into their circle along with the stones overhead.

She opened her eyes to meet Kelda's dark gaze, at once masked and illuminated with fire.

He said, "Listen."

He struck a note so pure and sweet that her heart melted with astonishment. She closed her eyes again, breathing in the notes that followed, taking them deep into bone and marrow, into the place where tears began.

Chapter Eighteen

So where are we now in the story of Nairn? He dies in history during the destruction of the school tower. But where his life goes blank in history, it springs to life again in poetry, generally in the kinds of ballads that are sung long before they are transcribed to paper. From bawdy street jingles to elegant court ballads, he appears again and again, without introductory comment, as though his name and his story have become so familiar across the centuries that he needs no explanation. He is "The Failed Bard," "The Wanderer," "The Lost," the beggar-minstrel whose harp is perpetually out of tune, who is more laughed at than shunned, or "The Cursed," the tragic figure of cautionary tales: the bard gifted enough to attempt the Three Trials of Bone Plain and foolish enough to fail them all.

He is "the Unforgiven."

As poetry, he is of no interest to the historian, in whose eyes the vanished become footnotes and the dead remain dead. But if the historian is in a mood to speculate and has an ear for the musical and symbolic footprints of the centuries, the nature of Nairn's disappearance takes a fascinating, albeit fantastic, turn.

He leaves no obvious path to follow between poetry and history. In the utterly prosaic accounts of the school steward, he is assumed dead at the end of the bardic competition, and is not mentioned again by Dower Ren or by any subsequent Renne or Wren for centuries. Declan himself, ever loyal to King Oroh, taught at the school for some years after the competition, trying, we must assume, to train a more suitable replacement for the Royal Bard. Blasson Purser of Waverley, the king's chronicler comments, "... pleases the king greatly with his music, but is deaf to any notion of other bardic powers the king so sorely covets."

The founder of the first bardic school in Belden died in his sleep twelve years after the competition. Accounts were duly rendered for "a coffin made of finest oak and ash, hinged and rimmed with gold, to contain the body of Belden's first Royal Bard," as well as for "the burial and the funeral feast." Those sums, as well as the cost of three days of lodging for nobles from the court, were subtracted from "accounts received from the king's envoys in the form of the king's most generous donation to the school."

An odd detail emerges from the king's chronicler, who notes that one of the envoys later complained to the king that "the jewels in Declan's harp were stolen out of it before it was buried with him." The king, the chronicler continued, "evinced great interest in this, though he forbade any inquiry or accusations against the school." Nothing ever came of that, at least to King Oroh's benefit. The jewels followed their own path, and the Royal Bard Blasson kept his position for nearly thirty years, until King Oroh himself breathed his last of the "foreign airs" so far from the land where he was born.

Two hundred and twenty-nine years after the fall of the school tower and the disappearance of Nairn, his name again surfaces in the school's accounts, and with it the words that at last open the pathway between history and poetry. In Argot Renne's meticulous records, we find this unexpected entry: "... considering the craggy agelessness of his face, the unremitting dark of his eyes, and that he knew my name, Renne, though he had been stone all our lives, and considering, above all, his astonishing question concerning the existence of the ancient Circle of Days, a secret conclave that existed briefly during Declan's time, I believe him to be the bard in search of his death: Nairn."

The Circle of Days is the link we seek.

He went in the front in his boots and trews
And out the back in her shift,
Vanished again amid cries and hues,
With a coin as her parting gift.

FROM "THE BALLAD OF THE WANDERING BARD," ANONYMOUS

For the second time in his life, Nairn, creeping in utter ignominy out of eyesight, felt as low as any earthworm. Lower: even the worms underfoot were good and useful creatures, leading unselfish and productive lives. He, by contrast, belonged nowhere, had nothing anyone could need or want. The poem, he thought grimly, tripping over rootwork and bouncing off trees in the dark, had left a few things out. Even the hero crushed beneath the dragon's claw could breathe his last knowing that his intentions were worthy, his courage unfaltering; he had done all he could. His failure was honorable. The bard on Bone Plain, failing every trial, had no such consolation. The list of his failures was precise; judgment was unrelenting. What the poem had left out was the taste in the back of his throat, as though he had eaten the charred, dry, bitter ashes of yesterday's fire. The poem had not mentioned that even his bones seemed to radiate shame. There was no comfortable place anywhere in his body that he could crawl into and hide. Unlike the hero, he could not even find release in the dragon's claw ripping apart his heart.

That was not the worst of it.

The worst he discovered slowly through days and weeks and months. His harp would not stay in tune; his ears could no longer distinguish the point at which the tightening string spoke true. His fingers might as well have been overstuffed sausages, for all the dexterity left in them. He forgot lines, verses, sometimes entire songs. He could earn a coin or two on a village street playing for pity: the fool pulling tatters of a dance or a ballad out of his pitiful mind. It was as though he had burned himself to the heartwood playing against Kelda, and there was nothing left of his music but a few feeble, slowly fading embers.

The poet had not mentioned those things.

Nor had the poem warned of the constant loneliness, the need to hide himself, to change his name, to move constantly, but with none of the earlier curiosity and joy he had taken in his wanderings. Now he moved to escape himself and always took himself along. All this he learned in the first seasons of his changed life: that cruelly sweet, golden summer from which he had exiled himself, the first bright fires of autumn. Other things he learned took much longer. Still others took centuries.

He dreamed incessantly during those first long months: the same terrible, fragmented visions of the tower. The idea that it might somehow return, and he could enter it again, remake his past and future, kept him hovering along the edges of the plain, in small farming villages near the forests, where he could find some mindless work, even a little money, move on, never any farther than where he could turn his head and see the wide, broad emptiness flowing green to the edges of the world, the gentle hillocks, the random, gnarled tree growing alone here and there in all that green, isolated and mysterious as a standing stone. Then he could almost hear the music within the wind, blown from the school, perhaps, or maybe from the memories of the plain itself. Then, he could almost remember what he had once loved.

At night, if there was a standing stone close by, he would sleep against it, taking cold comfort in its own agelessness and hoping against hope that it might somehow merge with his dreams to shape the endlessly spiraling stones around him again, the place where he had entangled himself inextricably within the image and the word and the power.

It took a few decades before he fully admitted the truth of the matter. Gradually, as years passed, he was almost able to forget the poem itself in the sheer ordinariness of his life. Crofter's son he was born, crofter he became, working for others at first, then on his own piece of land at the edge of the plain. He built his house, relegated his harp to a forgotten corner of it, took a wife who bore him children, all of which made it easier for him to expect for himself the predictable fate of every other living thing. It was with stark horror that he found himself outliving everyone he knew in his tiny world, including his children. He would outlive his grandchildren, who would begin to eye him warily, soon enough, and count backward on their fingers to find his true age. No one living knew exactly how old he had been when he first put down a root in that particular patch of earth, but still . . . It wasn't natural. Time didn't write his life on his face the way it did on others'; he seemed at once ageless and unfinished.

He finally took his harp out of the cobwebs, walked out the door, and admitted who he was: the Unforgiven. He had no idea how to live with himself, and with nothing else occurring to him beyond sheer despair, he made his way back to the school.

It was going through difficult times, as well. Towns were prospering all over Belden. The solitary village of Caerau, so promising that one summer, seemed to be withering away as the harsh winters drove out all but the hardiest and most stubborn. The school's reputation had spread far and wide, causing bardic schools to spring up everywhere to emulate it. It had become legendary, and as happens with legends, it was relegated mostly to the imagination. Worthy, gifted students, inspired by its existence, went to more comfortable schools that were closer to home; the poor and brilliant came to be taught and to teach at the school on the plain, drawn by tales of Declan and the first great competition. When the Wanderer returned and stood in the dark listening to the music coming out of it, nearly a century later, it didn't seem much different from the school in his memories.

He sat down on the hillside among the ring of standing stones, where he could see a scant handful of lights along the river, and the immense flow of icy stars above the plain. He had no idea what to do. He couldn't play the harp he carried; he could barely remember the glittering lengths of verse, long enough to unfold across the plain, which he had once carried so effortlessly in his head. He doubted that, if he revealed himself, anybody would remember him, or even much care. If anyone even believed him.

He worked some magic, then, which surprised him enormously, as he felt it overwhelm him. He made a wish, sitting there with an abandoned past and no future except forever. He gazed at the crown of stones on the hill and wished he were one of them, rooted and bound to the plain, an ordinary battered old boulder with no need to explain anything and none but the most primitive of memories. As he felt the unexpected, welcome change reworking his mind, his heart, his breath and bones, he must have left a path open for his own return, as he wondered, in the final instant, why he had not tried that before.

So, for a couple of centuries, Nairn became stone. Oddly enough, in his absence, he flourished. In ballad and poetry, his reputation grew like a hardy weed, scattering seed on the wind, blown into every corner of Belden. He lived many lives in spite of himself as he slept the still, slow-dreaming sleep of a hoary, lichen-covered boulder, only waking very slightly, somewhere deep inside himself, when students sat on him to practice their music.

It was a song that woke him completely, reached into stone and found the human heart of him. He opened an ear to listen to it, and then another. He opened his eyes finally to see the singer with that treasure of a voice as wild and pure as the wind on the plain. He found his feet out of long-forgotten habit and pulled himself out of the earth that the boulder had shifted around and settled into to make itself more comfortable. The singing stopped abruptly. He stood in a morning that smelled of spring, new grass, turned earth, a harp on his shoulder he'd forgotten he possessed, blinking stone out of his brain under the wide-eyed stare of a dark-haired young woman picking wild strawberries among the stones.

She was absolutely motionless for a breath, stunned with amazement. He cleared his throat. At the sound, all the bones in her tried to escape at once out of her body. Then she whirled and fled headfirst into a hawthorn hedge and out the other side, leaving an uproar of mating finches startling into the air behind her.

Nairn watched the birds settle. The hedge was new. He walked around it, testing his movements. The school grounds looked oddly civilized, broken into flower gardens and swaths of lawn. There was a road downhill, neatly lined with low stone walls that ran to a bridge across the river. The village had grown far down both sides of the river. New houses and barns had gone up since he'd closed his eyes. A bit of cobbled road divided the houses across the far side of the river. In the distance, a great massive thing was growing beside the water, the fieldstones mortared into walls, and spiraling upward into eerie unfinished towers that seemed to mirror the broken tower of the school.

All around Caerau, the flowing green had been divided, hedged, walled, in squares and fans and lozenges of black, tilled earth.

He wondered how long he had been stone.

Something intruded into his thoughts. He recognized it finally and went, out of habit, around to the back of the school, where he smelled food for the first time in a couple hundred years.

He had to open a gate in the wall that surrounded the substantial kitchen garden. The shadow of the broken tower loomed over him, and he reared back, staring up at it, as more memories wakened of the moment the stones had begun to fall. He wondered confusedly which tower he had brought down. The Turning Tower, he had thought. Maybe this one had gotten hit by the explosion of ghostly stones. Or was the Turning Tower truly the shadow of the ancient watchtower on the hill? It had never been rebuilt, which he found strange. Did anyone really remember the magic that had ripped through those stones? Or did it just stand like a question on the plain? A mystery out of the past: the place where something terrible or wonderful had once happened, but nobody remembered what.

He found the young woman again, inside the open kitchen door.

She gazed at him mutely, as she gave a stir to the stew bubbling in the cauldron over the fire. He felt his body come suddenly, painfully to life again, at the smells in the smoky air of leeks, mushrooms, lamb.

He heard her voice again, faint and shaking slightly. "You can go up those stairs. The students are eating now. Sit, and I'll bring you a bowl."

He nodded gratefully, remembered the words. "Thank you."

"If you—if you want to play for them, they'll listen. Most musicians pay that way, and the students are always glad to hear a stranger's song."

He turned to the familiar, worn stairs. "I have no new songs." His own voice sounded harsh with disuse, a stone's voice, weathered and hard. "Only the oldest in the world."

She brought him a great bowl of stew, bread and cheese, the strawberries she had picked. He ate every crumb, grateful for her perception that an old boulder that had been around since before she was born might be hungrier than most. No one spoke to him, although most threw curious glances at him and his harp. But he did not offer to play for his meal, and the students went off, leaving their empty cups and bowls scattered across the tables.

He could do that much, at least, he thought, and went back down to the kitchen. It was empty. He found a tray to stack the dirty dishes on and brought them down. He was in the middle of washing them when he heard steps on the tower stairs.

A man followed the young woman down; he carried their own emptied bowls. Nairn glanced up and saw him hesitate briefly between the bottom step and the floor, brought up by whatever was in Nairn's eyes. Even after so many years, he recognized that studious, attentive expression: that hadn't changed, though his face was older, grayer, than the one Nairn remembered.

"A Ren?" he guessed, taking the bowls. "School steward? You're still up in that tower, then."

The man nodded cautiously. "Argot Renne. This is my daughter Lynnet. And you?"

Nairn turned back to his wash water. "No one. Just a stranger who needed a meal."

"I told him," the girl murmured in her voice like a rippling stream, "he could play for his meal."

"That's the last thing you need around here, another harper. I'll finish this and leave."

"Where?" the steward asked abruptly. "Where will you go?"

Nairn looked at him. Argot Renne was staring again, his gray eyes wide, stunned with conjecture, as though he recognized the tale that pulled itself out of the earth and stone to walk into the tower kitchen and do the dishes.

"I don't know," Nairn said at last, scrubbing the bowl in his hands. "I haven't thought, yet."

"There's an empty chamber in the tower. You could stay awhile. Think here."

Nairn shook his head. "No," he said tersely. "Not here."

"Well." The steward paused; Nairn could sense him groping for coherence. "Is there—is there anything I can do for you? Before you go?"

Nairn rinsed the bowl; Lynnet reached out silently, took it from him to dry. He remembered the voice that had wakened him, brought him back to life, then his own magic that had laid him to earth.

"Maybe," he answered huskily, "you could tell me how long it's been since Declan died?"

The steward told him. He calculated, and was amazed.

"All that time . . . No wonder I was hungry." He scrubbed another bowl, a question flitting around his head like a butterfly until it finally lighted and he caught it. "Is there—is there anything like the Circle of Days still in existence?"

The steward opened his mouth, closed it. "The Circle of Days . . ." he repeated finally, very softly.

"Do you know what that is?"

"Yes. I've read the old—I read about it. No. Nothing I've ever heard of around here." He paused again, musing. "Maybe somewhere else, though. There are many bardic schools open now across Belden. You might ask at them."

Nairn considered the idea, handed a cup to Lynnet. "I might do that. Do some traveling." He handed another bowl to the girl and smiled at her, his face feeling its way into it slowly, creakily.

"You have the most beautiful voice I've ever heard," he told her, and surprised a tentative answering smile out of her. "You remind me of someone I knew once, a long time ago . . . She worked in the kitchen, too, and she sang like dawn breaking over the world."

He finished the dishes and left the tower to look for the Circle of Days.

Chapter Nineteen

Phelan began stalking his father.

He hadn't made a coherent decision to do so. Reason had nothing to do with it. Why he found himself in peculiar places at odd hours of day or night, hiding behind a trash bin or an elegant steam carriage and watching to see where Jonah went next, he didn't bother trying to explain even to himself. Some nuggets of research he'd tripped over, a conjunction of wildly disparate facts he could barely remember, had sparked against each other like flint against steel. The light had fallen upon Jonah. Once he saw what he saw in that light, Phelan couldn't stop looking. He could not have discussed it rationally with anyone else, least of all Jonah. He was looking for something he had glimpsed beyond language, between the lines, and it drove him, as nothing his father had ever done, to resolve the conundrum that was Jonah Cle.

So distracted, he rarely noticed the constant influx of musicians into the city, except when the streets and taverns were so full of strangers that they hindered his pursuit of Jonah. Sometimes, an unfamiliar song caught his ear, as a would-be bard from some far corner of Belden was moved by the ancient history and legends of the occasion to add to it on the sidewalk. Phelan, pausing in surprise, would remember why Caerau was filling with music and people. Then he would hear the phrase that had stopped him in his tracks echoing in his heart, and he would place it to memory, as he had been taught, music woven into the smell of fish chowder, the clamor of gulls on the docks, the glitter of light along the musician's instrument, for future reference, and move on.

When Jonah eluded him completely, left the house in the odd hours Phelan slept, fitfully and most often with a book over his face, he would find himself retracing his father's haunts: the museums, forgotten dig sites, standing stones along the Stirl, where the footprints, the bottles dropped into the mud, might well be Jonah's. He remembered to teach his class; he worked on his paper sporadically on the rare occasions when he and Jonah were in the house together. The pile of pages was slowly growing as he rummaged through the school library or the steward's records. Like his thoughts, the pages of his paper were homing toward something that could not yet emerge into the light of language; he could not finish it until he had found his own way through the labyrinth of fact, conjecture, and wild improbability that was Jonah's life.

Jonah was stalking the bard Kelda.

Phelan realized that after the third court occasion that Jonah had turned up at sober, on time, and without elaborate machinations on Sophy's part. He could, Phelan noted, pass intelligent and appropriate comments while seeming to absorb the young bard's music through the black, implacable gaze he trained on

Kelda during every note. Kelda was never at all discomposed by it. Meeting Jonah in a crush, he would exchange a genial remark, generally about the impending bardic contest, which would only render Jonah's expression even more bleak until, satisfied, Kelda wandered off with a smile to charm a fairer face.

I am watching you, Jonah's eyes said. I have my eye on you. But to what end, Phelan wasn't sure; Jonah's only response to the imminence of Kelda was to reach for the nearest passing drink. So Phelan thought, at any rate until he found himself following Jonah through an abandoned sewer.

It had already been a long day and seemed about to get a great deal longer. Officially, it had begun early enough, at breakfast with Zoe before his class. They found each other that morning in the masters' refectory, among a scattering of teachers and retired bards who still woke at the dawn song of the birds. Phelan, entering, saw Zoe sitting alone at a table, with the colors of the high stained-glass windows around the hall cascading over her. Red-eyed and disheveled, hunched over her teacup, she looked the way he felt. He pulled out a chair beside her, and she jumped, unaccustomedly nervy. The impending contest, he guessed. It would make anyone skittish as a cat. Unofficially, his day had never begun, just melted into light out of the previous night, when he had followed Jonah to an ancient tavern in south Caerau that stood in a ring of standing stones and had attracted, for most of the night, half the visiting musicians in Caerau.

Which was likely why she took one bleary look at him and burst into laughter.

"The Merry Rampion," she explained succinctly, reading his mind. "You?"

"I think it was called Dockers Haven," he answered through a yawn. "It smelled fishy enough." A server put coffee down in front of him; he dived down, took a deep breath of it. He added, after a scorching swallow, "It was up to the rafters with musicians."

She nodded. "It's like that everywhere. I was playing with them half the night."

"Sizing up the competition?"

She smiled without humor. "Yes. Exactly. Were you?"

"No."

"Kelda thinks you should compete."

He took another scalding sip, asked mildly, too tired for drama, "And I should care exactly why what Kelda thinks?"

She held her breath, gazing into her tea, then looked at him a little, genuine smile underscoring her eyes. "I wish you would. It might inspire me. It may not help me play better than Kelda— I'm not sure anything could do that—but you would make me play better than myself."

He gazed at her; the question that came out surprised him. "Are you afraid?"

She lowered her eyes, reading tea leaves again. "Yes. No. Why should I be? Why wouldn't I be?" She straightened, shifting her elbows for a plate the server, a student in his other life, put down between them. That morning's breakfast was thin herb omelets rolled around asparagus, strawberries in cream, biscuits studded with onion and chives. His brow cocked a question at Phelan.

"Please," Phelan said, and studied Zoe again while he waited. She ate hungrily, ignoring him or avoiding his eyes, he wasn't sure which. His own breakfast came up promptly, and he lost himself in it for a few bites until he heard her say,

"Will you?"

"What?"

"Play in the competition. To keep me company." She was watching him now, fork suspended over her plate, her eyes luminous, troubled. He shifted, murmuring inarticulately, reluctant and annoyed that the bard from Grishold could cast his shadow even over private decisions made between them. "If you do," she added, inspired, "you could write your paper on the competition instead. It will be brilliant—the first formal piece written from the point of view of a musician who played in it. You said you've been having trouble with your topic."

"Not anymore," he said, and felt her swift surprise. He forked in a mouthful to avert questions, aware of her attention as he chewed.

She only said, after a moment, "Good. Then you'll be that much less distracted by it. I understand why you're not interested in the competition. But there are reasons—" Her voice caught, making him stare. She ducked her face, hiding behind her hair, such an unusual impulse that he put his fork down, astonished. "Things," she went on finally, "that I'm not so certain about, and I want you to see them, too."

"What—"

She shook her head quickly; he saw her face again, her fine profile rising against the dark, and then her eyes, nearly black in their intensity. She said softly, her voice trembling, "I would be very grateful if you would play your heart beside me like the most magical instrument in the world. I'm not certain what to expect from this competition, but I think, that at the very least, it will be like nothing anyone could ever predict. Play to win. You'll need to, against Kelda. You'll need all that your heart can give."

A fragment of what he had glimpsed in his research slipped

into his mind. He went rigid, recognizing it in what she saw: the oldest competition in Belden, in the five kingdoms, and older even than that.

"I won't win," he warned her. "Most likely I'll get tossed out on the first day."

"It doesn't matter. Please. I need you with me."

He nodded finally, briefly, and felt her fingers brush the back of his hand, cold as any stone.

That had been the beginning of his day.

He taught his class, from which Frazer was markedly absent, probably recovering from a more compelling subject the night before. No one there focused very well on the rigors of memory; the students forgot their verses without compunction and only wanted to talk about the bardic competition, and whether or not Phelan thought there could possibly be a bard in the realm better than Kelda.

He dismissed them with relief and went in pursuit of his father.

He didn't expect to find Jonah at home asleep in his bed after tumbling into it at dawn. But he checked there first, anyway, and found his mother at the breakfast table, with a pair of half-moons balanced on her elegant nose, sipping her morning coffee and reading his unfinished paper.

He blinked incredulously at her. She didn't vanish, just tilted her head to look at him over her lenses.

"Oh, it's you, dear. I don't suppose you've seen your father?"

"What are you doing?"

"I'm reading."

"That's my paper."

"Yes, and it seems quite wonderful to me. I hope you don't

mind too much? Sometimes I actually do try to pay attention to your lives."

Phelan moved finally from his transfixed stance, joined her at the table. He was still in yesterday's clothes, he realized, which probably smelled pungently of Dockers Haven.

"It can't be easy," he commented, pouring himself coffee. "Reading that, I mean. I didn't even know you had spectacles."

"There, you see? The things we don't know about one another. For instance, where Jonah might be at this moment."

"I saw him a few hours ago—near dawn, actually—at a tavern along the south river, listening to the musicians play." He paused, added awkwardly, "He was alone."

"Except for you, of course," Sophy said imperturbably.

"Well."

"He does seem to have something on his mind, though, doesn't he?" She aimed the half-moons at him, her fair brows raised. "Do you think it's the bardic competition? You are going to compete, of course, aren't you?" He nodded wordlessly. "I wonder if he wishes he could. Do you think so? Yesterday—I think it was yesterday. Yes. We served up our annual fish-chowder luncheon on the royal docks for the Relief of Widows and Orphans of the Stirl. It was a great success. He sent me flowers."

"Who?" Phelan asked, startled.

"Your father."

"It's serious, then. Is he going to die?"

"Well, I'm wondering, too. Do you think you could find him again? He's been far too—well—civilized lately. It worries me."

Phelan realized that he was gawping at his mother. He closed his mouth, then opened it to ask, "Do you want me to give him a message? Is there someplace he should be?"

"That's exactly it, isn't it? He's always where he should be, these past days. Just keep an eye on him, will you? Discreetly, of course. You might let me know if he's in any kind of trouble. Beyond the usual, I mean. Do you mind?"

"No," he answered dazedly. "I believe I can work him into my schedule."

He took a steam tram down the river road, spent some time wandering through the streets, following the music that seeped out of doorways, blew down piers, drew crowds on street corners. The music gave him a place to look, at least, gave his meanderings a pattern. Mostly, he moved on the assumption that if he kept Jonah in the forefront of his thoughts, Jonah would appear. Which was not at all hard to do, considering his own crackbrained suspicions. Sometimes, though, Sophy tugged at his thoughts, the vision of his unpredictable mother reading his scholarly paper in her dressing gown. And Zoe. What had she persuaded him to do? The last thing in the world he wanted . . .

No Jonah in the cheerful morning light. On impulse, he walked across Dockers Bridge to look for his father down a hole. Or maybe asleep on a midden full of the previous century's rubbish. Perhaps the princess would know.

Beatrice came up to talk to him, already grimy and sweating in the warmth. She took her straw hat off, fanned herself. He watched curly tendrils of gold, escaped from her ruthless pins, flutter around her face.

"He was here earlier," she told Phelan. "He wanted to know if I'd seen Kelda before I left the castle this morning. Of course I hadn't—I try not to see anyone when I'm dressed like this. That's all your father said, really. He went off, and I went back down to dust my mantelpiece. I have no idea where he might have gone."

She paused, her cobalt eyes querying him through the mask of grit. "I've seen the way he looks at Kelda lately, during gatherings at court."

"Yes," Phelan answered tightly. "I think there's something between them in their past, despite everything Kelda says. I'm trying to keep an eye on my father. I'm trying to understand."

She put her hat back on, studied him under the shadow. "It makes no sense," she breathed. "None of it. Kelda—he shouldn't know what he knows. He couldn't be as young as he says if he has a past with Jonah in it."

"I don't think he is." Phelan slid one hand over his own face, to keep from telling her what he did think. He felt the sweat gathering at his hairline.

"If I see your father again, should I tell him that you're looking for him?"

"No. He'd only try to hide from me."

"Because you'd both be in danger, then." Her mouth pinched a moment, then she loosed a breath gustily. "I do so want to help you look. If I get into trouble again, my mother will send me to my sister Charlotte's home in the country to be influenced by children and apple orchards and cows. It would be maddening."

He smiled, envisioning her among the apple blossoms in sedate country clothes, moodily tossing sticks to the dogs.

"A terrifying prospect," he agreed. "But think how well you would learn to understand the Circle of Days."

She thought about that, clamping her hat on her head to keep it from flying into the Stirl. "I suppose that's where it began, isn't it . . . The language of endlessly repeating days . . . Was the magic there from the beginning? Have we just forgotten it?"

"Kelda didn't forget." He shivered suddenly, there under the full noonday sun, as he glimpsed again strands of an impossible tale. The princess in her dungarees, coated like a sweetmeat with the dusting of centuries, watched him gravely.

"Tell me if I can help," she said abruptly. "I can survive Charlotte and her circle of days."

Can you? he wondered. Can any of us? He nodded wordlessly and turned toward the bridge again. He looked back once, found her still watching him. She gave him a little sidelong smile and turned. He watched her disappear step by step down the ladder into the earth.

He went back across the bridge.

The crowds had grown thick with musicians carrying their instruments, visitors come to listen to the legendary contest, everyone drawn in the midday maelstrom toward food and drink and company. He heard his own name called from an open tavern door; friends waved him in. He joined them, wanting food and some cheerful, mindless conversation. The tavern was so packed that musicians ate standing with their instruments dangling out windows over the water. No one talked of anything but the competition: what they would play or sing first, what bards of which great courts had been seen already in Caerau, what odds were being given where and by whom on who might take Quennel's place. Kelda was the odds-on favorite, of course. But he was, after all, just a country bard out of Grishold, and who knew what amazements from other distant courts might be even now wending their ways to the city?

"Are you competing?" someone asked Phelan, and he remembered, with surprise, that he was. Pressed, he admitted to little preparation and less ambition to win; it would be something to tell his children when they started wondering if he had ever done anything remotely interesting with his life. He lingered there over his beer, listening to various musicians, caught again in the web of excitement, speculation, and song spun over the entire city.

When he walked back into the street finally, startled at the angle of light and shadow over the cobbles, he saw his father.

Jonah was walking upriver quickly and purposefully; he hadn't seen Phelan. Phelan followed his undeviating path a long way, trying not to trip over instrument cases lying open on the sidewalks, or careen into too many pedestrians. The crowds thinned past the docks. Jonah was easier to keep in sight, though if he glanced back, there were fewer bodies for Phelan to hide behind. He didn't. Closer to the castle, where there were still random knots around visiting minstrels, and he could feel the cooler edge of the late-afternoon breezes flowing off the water, he saw his father finally veer from his determinedly straight path, go over the embankment, and down out of view.

Phelan quickened his pace, eased cautiously across the tree-lined embankment, and peered upriver from behind a trunk. Jonah was down on the tidal mudflats, leaving footprints in the muck. He veered again, as Phelan watched, toward a large pipe half-overgrown with brush, left from a time before sluices, canals, and newer water systems had shifted the shape of the ancient riverbed.

He vanished into the pipe.

Phelan groaned softly and slogged down to follow his father into the dark.

Chapter Twenty

It's at this point that Nairn's footprints through history vanish again. What we can see, rising like tussocks across an indeterminate expanse of bog water, is the Circle of Days. The secret face, half-hidden within a hood, the three parallel lines, the middle one longer at both ends than the outer pair, in the ancient word for "bread" signals to those who recognize it from an astonishing array of unlikely places. Stamped into the hilt of a sword. An etching on the frontispiece of a book. Rosy cameos carved on both sides of a lady's locket. Painted on the sign of a tavern calling itself The Wanderer. Another such sign hanging over a bakery. The oldest, most recently unearthed: a metal disk with the hooded face on one side, the cryptic lines on the other.

Whose face is it?

Who wore the disk?

What did it signify to the wearer?

Did Nairn look for those solid tussocks of something familiar and constant through the centuries, rooted as they were in his own past, and as long-lived? It seems likely. Within his own endless circle of days, little else was as immutable as this signal out of his youth. The original face might have been his. He might have discovered such a conclave during his travels, after he spoke to Argot Renne. Perhaps he revealed his history to those in it, and, even better, told them what he had learned of the secret powers they sought. Perhaps he founded such a group, trying to revive whatever powers he might have had, that had exhausted themselves or been taken away from him on Bone Plain. Perhaps, for a while, members of that occult group wore the disks to identify themselves.

Or perhaps the face belonged to Declan, who died still searching for a bard with equal gifts in magic and music to send to King Oroh.

Perhaps Nairn himself left all such signals throughout history, in the various guises he might have taken—bookmaker, baker, warrior, lover, tavern keeper—like a cry across the timeless twilight in which he lived, where all that he knew, anything he loved, he must watch flow endlessly away from him toward night.

In the Circle of Days, we glimpse the path of the Wanderer, still unforgiven by the intractable powers of the land he roamed. And we begin to wonder, in pity and fear: unforgiven for what act that set him on his lonely trek through history?

What could possibly be that unforgivable?

What exactly happened in that tower?

Beyond the world he knew, he wandered,
The Unforgiven,
So far that he heard each word, each sound
Torn from its deep roots in history
Ratchet through the exacting grind of time,

Wear down to a new, fine gloss.
That long he wandered:
Through his dying and reviving language.

FROM "SONG FOR THE UNFORGIVEN" BY E. M. NIGHT

O n his first journey beyond Stirl Plain, where he had lived, in one shape or another, for over three hundred years, Nairn left his mark all over Belden.

As he had in his youth, he wandered, not in search of music this time, but in search of the Circle of Days. Within that source of power, he might revive his own shadowy, flickering powers that permitted him to mask his age and turn into a stone when he craved forgetfulness. But little else: he could not tune his harp to magic. He couldn't tune it to the simplest scale, either; he wondered if, rekindling his magic might fine-tune his ears again as well.

To that end, he sought out the burgeoning cities of Belden, put out a call to anyone who recognized it. He had all the time he needed to learn new professions, and many places in which to practice them. His seal, his sign, hung over different shop doors of all kinds; it marked jewelry, bread, weapons, books, anything that might attract the cognizant eye, the kindred mind. In each new place, he founded his own Circle of Days, following Declan's methods. Finding inquisitive minds, enthusiastic disciples with a penchant for mystery, ceremonial robes, and identifying disks wearing a convincing patina of age, was easy. Finding anybody with actual abilities in the prosaic kingdom seemed hopeless. It was as though the magic had died when the ancient words were relegated to the past, carved on stone that no one could pronounce anymore, even if they could, out of scholarly curiosity or dreams of sorcery, learn to decipher them.

He gave up finally, closed his last shop, bade farewell to friends, acolytes, and mistresses, and took the tide out of the sprawling city that the tiny village of Caerau had become, down the Stirl to the sea. The ship was bound for the land where King Oroh had been born.

The land was either lost in myth or prudently shrouded with magic against strangers. Maps were imprecise, sailors' information ambiguous; violent winds rose and blew them off course just when they finally seemed close. Nairn, recognizing the forces that hid the magic from him, wondered at such abilities even as the ship's mainmast snapped with a sound like a harp string breaking. He wondered with relief if he was finally going to die.

He woke on the tide line with his mouth full of sand and lifted his face groggily to the sight of birds with plumage of such rich hues that even he, with his jeweler's eye, could not precisely name the colors. They whistled cheerfully as they flew among great trees with massive trunks of dark, smooth wood streaked with tones of amber and ivory. He stared, then let his face fall back onto the sand, wearily recognizing the next turn in the tedious path of his life.

He took samples of the wood and the plumes back to Belden with him on the next passing ship, and, through the decades, despite his boredom and unending frustration, he became a staggeringly wealthy merchant. Later, he became a pirate and plundered his own ships; it only made him richer. He became a recluse for a while, a legend in Caerau, amassing books and allowing only traders with the most exotic rarities through his doorway. Then he closed up his mansion beside the Stirl and became a tavern keeper. Then a chef in a restaurant frequented by the nobles of the king's court. A thief, until he realized one day that most of what he stole he had owned at one time or another. A librarian. A museum curator. A traveler again, this time a professional forager into the debris and treasures of ancient history in other lands.

That made him wealthier still.

He had long lost track, by then, of how many wives and mistresses he had loved and mourned, how many children he had left to multiply all over Belden, how many different ways he had tried to die. He had forgotten the crimes he had committed that doomed him to hang or burn or lose his head: being a pirate, probably, or inciting treason against the Peverell kings, or trying to blow himself up in a public place, some such. Rain had doused the fire; the rope around his neck had broken, leaving him sprawled on the ground with a sorely strained knee, and the distinct plink, in his ears, of a harp string snapping. Even the executioner's ax had refused to touch him: its swooping blade flew off the handle and nearly decapitated an innocent bystander. In each case, according to murky tradition, the intent of the law was satisfied, and Nairn was freed on the grounds that he couldn't be killed twice for the same crime.

He gave up trying to die. Reinventing himself yet again, he became a young student in the bardic school on the hill, which was now completely surrounded by Caerau. As the only heir of deceased parents, his great wealth kept him at the school despite the fact that he was without a doubt the worst student ever to ignore all hints that he should leave. He couldn't distinguish one pitch from another; around him reeds split, harp strings broke, drums shrugged off any kind of rhythm. His voice, pleasant enough when he spoke, grew wavery, reedy, when he tried to sing. Great, gaping holes developed in whatever ballads or poetry he tried to memorize.

"You love music," one of his masters told him bluntly. "It does not love you."

"It's as though you are bewitched," another said as perceptively. "Or under a curse. Perhaps you'd be more successful in another course of study?"

But he persisted, failing pretty much everything, though not, his teachers saw, without a great deal of utterly wasted, very hard work. He chose, for his final research paper, the hoary mystery of the location of Bone Plain, and failed, despite all his research and the books and manuscripts he had amassed through the centuries, to solve that puzzle as well.

When the pretty, rich, and well-connected Sophy Waverley, dabbling in classes at the school to pass the time, took pity on him and married him, he felt extraordinarily grateful. She took him away from the school to live in the antique house her father had bought them, and encouraged his eccentricities so that she could pursue her own activities, which mostly involved good works done in congenial surroundings. She introduced him at court, where the young King Lucien encouraged him in his forays into Caerau's past and marveled at his grasp of nearly anything that did not involve music.

He and Sophy had a son.

Nairn began to roam, then, at night through the quiet city streets, the corridors of stone standing so high above him they blocked the stars instead of speaking to them, as the ancient stones did. He sought out the places where past and present merged, where ancient songs lingered among the abandoned hulks of worn-out buildings. He craved the company of the moon, of old winds that swept through burned-out windows, doorways that had lost their doors and long forgotten where they led. In such places, the lost winds spoke an ancient tongue; the moon seemed to have wandered overhead from a distant time. With its pale light sliding over ruins, making shadows out of nothing, it seemed to search for a past it remembered. This dreaming moon could not see the complex, modern city, with its engine-driven ships and snorting steam trams. Nairn could speak to this moon, and often did, settled on a pile of rubble with a bottle in hand and another one beside him.

"You must know where it is," he pleaded, demanded, shouted. "You must have seen it. Touched it. Tell me where it is."

Sometimes, he set his digging sites on places the ancient moon illuminated. Why not there, as well as any other place? He could afford the expense of his impulses, and he did not have to explain himself to anyone. Enough oddities and valuables were found in those sites to transform his lunacy to prescience. He donated the findings to the city museum, or to the private collection of the king. What he searched for seemed, in broad daylight, as ephemeral as that moon. But he existed; he was proof of it; he had lived every hour, every year, every century under its curse.

It was death he searched for in those sites.

A stone. A cauldron. A tower.

One hint of that plain where he had risked everything and lost, that's all he wanted from the moon. A chance to find it, to change his life. To make it ordinary. To tune a harp to true, to feel his singing voice. For once in his endless life to talk to his child without the stark, unbearable burden of foreseeing both their fates.

For that he pleaded with the moon, littered Caerau with holes, and found only more treasures, more of what he already had, never the arrow pointing the way to the doorposts, the lintel, the ancient threshold stone, the passage to Bone Plain.

That moon alone, of everyone in his life, had seen what happened there. He could talk about it to the pale, distant face that never judged him, just ignored him, as he sat among the charred bones of the past, and went her way like the hunched, mumbling old woman in a tale, collecting twigs on the forest floor for her fire. She alone knew his name.

He had read every paper ever written about Bone Plain. Nobody knew where it was. A poet's dream, they said. Or perhaps within this particular ring of stones, or that one. The burial mound where the great bards were interred along with their memories and instruments to swap songs for all eternity. Obviously a metaphor for death. For life. For the process of creativity. A mangled fragment from far older times, a jumble of mixed metaphors, images whose origins had grown obscure, shards of ancient tales, all tossed together and carved in stone to torment the brains of scholars for the next millennium or two.

What exactly had he done on Bone Plain?

He had killed an old harper. At least he thought he had. He seemed to have blown the roof off the school tower as well, according to his son. He thought he had shattered the Turning Tower with that last harp note, the one that had sung the depth of his longing, his latent magical powers, his dreams. The one he played to break Welkin's harp strings. As he had snapped the icicle on the tower roof and killed Drue, so his misbegotten magic had struck Welkin and silenced both him and his harp. Jonah remembered stones burning out of the sky like falling stars, thudding on the ground around him. Cries from those who had been as silent as the standing stones, who had vanished, it seemed, into the night. He remembered the plain suddenly coming to life again, with a hundred cooking fires, the smells of bubbling cauldrons. He remembered running. But then so was everyone else, under that onslaught of stones, smacking into one another, and tripping over tent pegs. Children wailing, dogs barking, birds startling out of the trees, sweeping over the plain.

Not a song, a note of music left anywhere on it. Just shouts and children howling like the dead as Nairn slunk through the chaos he had made, left it behind him, not realizing then exactly how much and how thoroughly he had lost.

He had killed the best harper in the kingdom and had indelibly engraved his own name into the unforgiving annals of poetry.

At least he thought he had, until he saw that ancient, knowing smile in Kelda's eyes.

Chapter Twenty-one

Princess Beatrice, finally uncovering stone under the dust and packed dirt of centuries, gazed at it blankly. The level line of outcropping she had freed with such painstaking care had become as firmly defined in her mind as it was entrenched in the earth: an old brick mantelpiece, maybe from a basement apartment that had succumbed to the silt and water of the Stirl swelling over its bed. Something chipped, hollowed, worn, but as recognizable and prosaic as that. She would find the rest of it farther down under the protruding ledge: the walls, the hearthstone between them, with probably some smoke staining it and bits of charcoal mingled with the river silt.

So she had thought.

Her silence slowed work around her; the others glanced up, vaguely aware of broken patterns of sound, the pause of predictable movements. Campion, working with her at the other end of the protrusion, broke off his brushing to see what had mesmerized her.

"It's stone," she told him. "Not brick."

He shrugged. "That's common, fieldstone used for chimneys, mantels."

"It's not fieldstone. It's yellow. Like the standing stones."

He dropped his brush. Behind her, Ida scrambled off her knees from where she was worrying at something on the floor of the dig. Curran, picking at a bump in the wall, straightened. They all came to look at it. What she had thought was bricks and mortar looked like a solid ledge indented with lines carved into the front of it.

Campion whistled. Curran brushed at the hair over his eyes, left a smudge.

"Looks like that disk I shoveled up," he grunted, peering. "Those lines. More runes. Princess, what on earth have you found?"

"I think," she breathed, "the Circle of Days."

Campion cocked a brow. "The what?"

"It's an ancient runic system." She started brushing again, violently enough that the others backed up behind her. "It was on the disk, too. Campion—"

He had his own brush working again by then, raising dust storms.

"I'll help," Curran said abruptly, and Ida nodded vigorously, her hat sliding over her eyes. Hadrian picked up his tools, shouldered in among them.

"Master Cle will definitely love this."

"I'm already in love with it," Campion murmured. "Looks like the oldest thing we've ever found."

"It looks like the oldest thing in the world," Ida sighed rapturously, and splashed a dusty sneeze across it.

They worked carefully but energetically, impelled by the mystery revealing itself under their brushes and picks. Hours passed. One by one, they climbed up the ladder to eat their sandwiches and came back quickly, before they had quite finished chewing. They managed, with more haste than method, to bare the long face of the ledge, with the pattern of lines running from one end to the other, and had begun to brush away the packed earth beneath it. They slowed, as the familiar daily shafts of light and shadow in the hole shifted until they stood in shade, and the line of light began above the ledge.

The floor was beginning to dampen. Beatrice sighed, stepping back reluctantly.

"It doesn't look like any kind of a fireplace," she commented, studying it. Curran moved back to join her.

"Looks more like a door, to me. That's the lintel stone we've been dusting off."

"Is that possible?" Hadrian wondered, unkinking his thin shoulders.

"Reminds me of things I see in the countryside. One flat stone balanced on two . . ."

"Can't be a door," Campion said. "No wood there."

"Well, there might not be, after all this time; might have rotted away."

"A door to what?" Ida wondered.

"I'm feeling stone where a door would be," Campion argued.

"Nobody makes a door out of stone," Ida scoffed. "What kind of a door would that be?"

They were all silent then, gazing at one another. They bent abruptly, gathering tools, hats, paraphernalia, before the floor got any wetter.

"How early can we get back tomorrow?" Ida asked.

Hadrian consulted his tide table; they scheduled a time to meet where the princess picked them up near the bridge. She dropped them there before she drove the crowded road upriver to the castle, puzzling over their find and scarcely hearing the music rising from one corner of the street and running into the next, played by musicians in every kind of antique costume.

She left the car in the chauffeur's hands and made her usual path through the back gardens toward the door nearest her chambers. The harping she heard then seemed so much a familiar part of the city those days that she only noticed it when she realized that she had stepped into a garden full of women in flowing silks and flowery hats. With an inner jolt of dismay, she remembered she had promised to be there among them two hours earlier.

Of all the faces turning to stare at the dust-plastered apparition wandering into the queen's garden party for Lady Petris, she saw her mother's first, rigid as an ice sculpture and as chilly. Her aunt Petris seemed equally frozen; only her eyelids moved, blinking rapidly above brows about to take flight. Beyond them, Kelda harped a love ballad, watching the princess gravely. Everybody else had gotten very quiet for a crowd of women carrying plates full of exquisite morsels and glasses of champagne. Only Sophy Cle, reaching for a salmon croquette at the table, missed being transfixed. She turned around, caught an eyeful of the walking disaster that was Beatrice, and smiled with pleasure, stepping immediately toward her.

But the queen got to her daughter first.

"I am so sorry," Beatrice said softly.

"Go and change, please."

"I forgot. We found something—something very old, I think, and wonderful—"

"Bea," Charlotte interrupted. "You look as though you've been buried alive. Marcus, stop patting the dust clouds from Bea's boots; they're unspeakable."

"We found—" the princess tried again, desperately. "Well, we hardly know what it is, but Father will be so intrigued, and Master Cle—"

The queen closed glacial blue eyes, opened them again. "Please."

"Yes, Mother."

"We'll talk when you are presentable."

She sounded dubious. The princess made her escape, found her lady-in-waiting patiently waiting, and was delivered in short order out of her clothes and into a bath, where the patina of centuries rained gently from her hair to float upon the water.

Neatly coiffed and disguised from collarbone to shin in flowers, she went back to the garden party, hoping that her mother would mistake this aspect of her for the good and dutiful Beatrice and forget she ever saw the other one. Suddenly ravenous, she lingered at the table, filling a plate with the odd bits still remaining of smoked trout, marinated vegetables in aspic, little pastries shaped like the suits of playing cards and filled with a bright concoction of sweet red peppers and hearts of palm. She could hear her mother's voice as she ate, reassuringly at a distance. Her brother's betrothed drifted up to talk to Beatrice about wedding-candle colors, so Beatrice could let her own thoughts flow underground again to puzzle at the mystery, while suitable noises came now and then out of her mouth.

"Beatrice," Charlotte interrupted, descending out of nowhere, it seemed, onto the tool-strewn floor of the dig with a jam-faced child in her arms. "Our mother and I have come up with the most perfect solution. Idea, I mean. You must come and spend the summer in the country with me and Great Marcus and Small Marcus and Tiny Thomasina." Beatrice, appalled, inhaled a crumb; while she coughed, Charlotte tumbled on, a glint in her eye alarmingly like their mother's. "Just think a moment about it. Small Marcus adores you, and it would get you out of a city swarming with ragtag musicians from every corner of Belden—"

"But—"

"But what about Damon's wedding, you mean? We'll all come back for that, of course. And I do so want you to meet one of our neighbors, so charming, connected to a distant branch of Peverell cousins, with a stableful of horses and running what he calls his hobby farm."

"I can't just—"

"Of course you can. We'd love to have you, wouldn't we, Marcus? Marcus. Where did that child run off to? Oh, Marcus, leave the bee alone!"

Marcus, poking at a rose on a bush nearby, opened his mouth suddenly, so hugely that he seemed about to devour the flower. Then came the wail, like a steam tram trying to break for a drunken sailor. Charlotte darted off to rescue him. Beatrice, watching, mute and horrified, absently crammed an entire diamond pastry into her mouth.

"Princess Beatrice."

She turned, chewing hastily and trying to smile at the same time. It was Sophy, she found to her relief, who chattered amiably about the lilies blooming in the fish pool, until Beatrice could swallow her bite.

"Of course, I really came over to ask you what you unearthed—besides yourself, I mean. You looked positively extraordinary, earlier, like a walking artifact. Your mantelpiece at last?"

Beatrice nodded, grateful for the chance to talk about it. "Yes," she said, and lowered her voice so that her mother wouldn't hear. "Only it's covered with runes, and we're thinking it's not part of a fireplace at all."

"Oh, how marvelous. Does Jonah know?"

"We haven't seen him yet. Please, tell him when you do. We're all so excited, and dying to know what it is." Out of the corner of her eye, she saw her mother on the move, looking purposeful, still chatting as she pulled Lady Petris and an entourage in her wake, a bouquet of hats, it looked like, on colorful, slowly swaying stalks. On the other side of her, Charlotte had pacified Marcus with another jam tart and was leading him to Beatrice's side.

"It sounds quite mystifying and exciting," Sophy said, seemingly oblivious to the gathering forces. "Along with something else I learned today. I wasn't sure he would actually do it, he's seemed so distracted lately with his paper—which is finally coming into being and so brilliant, I think—but he is, and I couldn't be more pleased."

"About what, Sophy?" the queen asked curiously, she and her bevy reaching them at the same moment that Beatrice felt Marcus sit on her feet to eat his tart.

"Phelan," Sophy said happily.

"What?" Charlotte demanded. "Is he engaged, too?"

"No, I don't think so. At least, I haven't heard. He is going to enter the bardic competition, compete for Quennel's place. I'm so thoroughly proud of him. Of course, you must stop your digging, Princess, long enough to listen to him play. I'm sure Jonah will understand even though he'll be so impatient for you to continue work on such an important find." She turned her candid gaze to the queen. "Of course, the king will be impatient as well, when he hears, Lady Harriet, don't you think? Our children are accomplishing such amazing things."

The queen looked slightly dazed for a moment. Charlotte said blankly, "Well. Beatrice can't, of course, do any of that. She's coming to spend summer in the country with us."

Sophy found nothing to say to that, only smiled pleasantly, rather bemusedly, into the sudden silence. Beatrice, eyeing the table helplessly, felt something already in her mouth, growing and clamoring for exit, like an irritated wasp.

She let it out finally. "No." She swallowed under Charlotte's stare, and said it again. "No. Thank you, Charlotte. I will be extremely busy this summer here in the city. And I would so very much appreciate it if you would stop Marcus from trying to stuff his tart into my shoe."

"Marcus!" Charlotte cried, glancing down without interest. "Stop that. But, Beatrice. We're already expecting you."

Beatrice slid off her heel, bent, and shook the crumbs out of it. Before she straightened, she realized what had put the edge in her voice, and that it had little to do with a hoary stone covered with incomprehensible words.

Her mother wanted her to go.

Phelan's mother wanted her to stay.

"We'll discuss this later," the queen said calmly, and with that the fascinated faces around them had to be satisfied.

The queen signaled an end to the harping soon after; Kelda packed up his instrument and slipped away. The guests began taking their leave of her and Lady Petris. Beatrice drifted with them unobtrusively back into the house, then angled down a quieter hallway toward her father's collection, where she could consult with Master Burley about the new find and hide from her mother for a while until the queen got distracted by more interesting matters than her dusty daughter.

A black back vanishing into a wall in an empty guest chamber caught her eye. A door in the wainscoting clicked shut and became invisible. She stopped, blinking. She knew that secret door: she had discovered it when she was a child exploring the ancient castle. It had been there for centuries and last used, according to chronicles shown to her by Master Burley, by King Severin to visit his mistress late at night when his queen, in her bed-cap, put down her book and her sherry glass and began to snore.

It wasn't the ghost of Severin Peverell blurring into the walls. He didn't have that black, glossy, engagingly disheveled hair, nor could he have played a note on the harp hanging from the broad, black-clad shoulder.

It was Kelda, sneaking around in her father's house. Kelda, who knew the language of the Circle of Days and had loosed its power at Phelan. Beatrice stepped out of her heels, picked them up, and stuffed them under the pillows on the bed as she passed it. She pressed the wainscoting until a panel gave under her hand, and the narrow door opened. Ahead, in the dark, she could see the light Kelda had kindled and carried on his palm as easily as a stolen jewel.

She followed him.

He had led her, she guessed from the cessation of random, distant noises on the other side of the walls, and the change under her stockinged feet from floorboards to flagstones and then to dirt, beyond the castle and underneath the main courtyard, when she lost him. The glow in his palm vanished, left her stranded in the dark, abruptly motionless, and breathing as quietly as possible. She strained her ears, listening for a shift of earth, a soft footfall too close to her. Her skin prickled, anticipating the harper's touch out of the blackness.

Nothing happened. Kelda had just gone his way without her. Perhaps he had sensed someone following. Maybe he had simply turned down a side path, an old sewage channel connected to a different part of the castle. They all merged into a main passage that went to the river, she knew. She could find her way back, if she didn't go wandering off perpetually down side paths. Her mouth crooked at a thought: what the queen would say if she caught her shoeless daughter coming back through the wrong door in the castle with filthy stockings and cobwebs in her hair.

It wouldn't just be summer in the country with Charlotte; it would be the rest of her life there.

She took a step forward and heard voices.

She froze again. They seemed to be coming toward her, and they weren't trying for secrecy. The students in Kelda's Circle of Days, meeting out of sight in the abandoned shaft? Was that where Kelda was headed, to teach his dangerous magic practically under her father's feet? The voices, both male, their words distorted slightly, bounding flatly off earth and stone, became suddenly, hauntingly familiar. Her brows, already quirked over the headstrong bard, leaped even higher. Phelan and Jonah Cle seemed to be arguing underground and in the dark somewhere ahead of her.

"What on earth are you doing down here?"

"What are you doing here?"

"I'm following you. You know who I am now; will you get that light out of my face?"

"What exactly are you researching, boy?" Jonah demanded, sounding intensely irritated. "The ancient sewage system of Caerau? Or that insidious bard?"

"What?"

Beatrice couldn't see so much as a glimmer of light; she blundered on helplessly, feeling her way along the stone-and-dirt walls, in the general direction of the argument.

"Do you have any idea what dangers you are tracking?"

"Don't tell me Kelda is down here, too," Phelan said incredulously.

"Beneath the castle of the Peverell kings," Jonah reminded him pointedly.

"What are you suggesting? That he's intending to blow the place up with his magic? If he's that powerful, he doesn't have to skulk around underground to do it, does he? Anyway—"

"Kelda—"

"Kelda has nothing to do with why I'm here. I saw you come in. I wanted to know why—I wanted to know—"

His voice veered suddenly off-balance. He stopped; so did Beatrice, struck by the strange uncertainty in him. She stood motionless, scarcely breathing, trying to hear in the silence what she could not see in the dark.

"What I do is my business," Jonah said finally, harshly. "You should not have followed me. Period."

"How was I supposed to know that you were sober at this hour of the day?" Phelan retorted weakly. "You could have gotten completely lost down here."

"And which of us is carrying the light?"

"How was I to know that until you switched it on? Why would I turn around then and walk out of here without the slightest curiosity about what my father might be doing wandering around underground? And why did you bring the light?"

"So that I could see what fumble-footed creature was stumbling after me, why else? Now that you're here, let me show you the way out."

Princess Beatrice moved forward again at that. She couldn't see their light yet; they must be down a side path, but there was no reason why Jonah, crotchety as he sounded, shouldn't rescue her as well. She wondered how he had figured out that the bard might be in this unlikely place. Finding Phelan on his heels explained his fit of temper. But Phelan seemed oddly shaken by something beyond his father's acerbity, and she wanted, deeply and irrationally, to know what.

"You're looking for Kelda," Phelan said, echoing her thoughts. There was that odd tone in his voice, that mingling of wonder, fear, and uncertainty that halted the princess again, midstep. "And I'm searching, through a thousand years of poetry, for you."

There was dead silence in the tunnel. Beatrice was overwhelmed with a sudden, urgent need to see their faces. She lifted one foot, set it down in a cautious, silent step, not wanting so much as the sound of a shifted pebble to distract them.

Phelan continued finally, to the wall of Jonah's silence. His voice shook again, badly. "On a plain of bone, in a ring of stone . . . That's when you last played your harp. You brought down the school tower. And then you vanished. You were supposed to be in that third coffin that Dower Ren wrote into the school records. But nobody found your body. Because. Because you hadn't died. You are Nairn. You are the bard who failed the Three Trials of Bone Plain, and now there is no end of days. And no forgetting."

Beatrice took a step, felt air beside her instead of earth. She turned toward it, saw them finally. Or at least she saw Phelan's face, completely illumined by the electric torch Jonah sent glaring into it. Jonah himself was hardly visible: only a sleeve, a hand that had begun to tremble, making the light waver on Phelan. Beatrice had no idea what Phelan was saying, but her own eyes welled as she saw the tear flare down his face, disappear into the dark.

The light bobbled so erratically then that Phelan's face blurred into shadow. Jonah lowered it finally, moved toward the tunnel wall, slumped wearily against it. Phelan followed after a moment, leaned beside him. The light illumined two boots now, one glossy black with polished buckles, the other earth-colored, battered and cracked.

"You can't possibly imagine," Jonah said at last, his own voice soft, frayed, "how many times I have wanted you to know me. You, of all people in the world, could understand the poetry. But I was terrified of my own hope—that's why I threw so many obstacles at you. I was terrified that even you might fail, might go through your life never saying my name." He paused, finished heavily, "Or that, knowing it, you might regard me, rightfully, with utter contempt."

Beatrice, hearing an inarticulate sound from Phelan, put her own hand over her mouth to stifle a sudden, indrawn breath.

A sharp exclamation bounced off the walls around her; the roving light caught her in the face. She stared into the dark beyond it, weeping without knowing exactly why yet but beginning to glimpse pieces of a tale as ancient as the runes above the door made of stone.

"Princess Beatrice," Jonah Cle said, astonished.

"I was—I was following Kelda," she whispered. "I lost him. Then I heard you."

Phelan pushed himself away from the wall abruptly, followed the path of the light Jonah had lowered to the ground between them. He found Beatrice's elbow, then her wrist, tugged her gently forward to join them. She leaned against the wall beside him, fumbling for the ineffectual scrap of monogrammed lace in her pocket.

"I don't even know why I'm crying," she said into it. "Except that you are. It sounds so desperately difficult. I'm sorry. I shouldn't even be here—"

Phelan said nothing, just put his arm around her shoulders, tightly. She felt his lips move across her cheek, tasting her tears, then find her mouth through the monogram.

He said huskily, his forehead tilted against hers, "You understand ancient things. You love them. Where else would I want you to be?" He raised his head then, turned toward Jonah. "Who is Kelda? I can't find him anywhere in your long life, and yet he must be far older. Old enough to know how to pronounce words that haven't been heard for a thousand years and more. He has all that power. Why all through history has he been so silent?"

Jonah flicked the light around them as though the bard might be standing quietly in the dark as well.

"Not here," he said tersely, and pulled himself away from the wall. Beatrice saw him put his hand on Phelan's shoulder, very gently, and her eyes burned again. "Thank you," he breathed. "Thank you for looking for me. I hoped you would, but it's a cruel thing to wish upon a child."

"You got used to yourself," Phelan said huskily. "So will I."

The light illumined Beatrice again: her flowery frock, her torn, soiled stockings. "Ah," Jonah said. "Sophy did mention some sort of garden party. That explains the dress. But why did you do away with your shoes?"

"Heels," Beatrice explained. "Far too noisy."

"You can't walk up into the world like that. We'd better take you back the way you came."

"No," she said adamantly, as her hand slid down Phelan's arm, groped for his fingers, and gripped them. "No. I'm coming with you. You know who you are, and Phelan knows who you are, and I don't even know for certain why you both just broke my heart. Tell me, Master Cle."

"It's a very long story," he warned her. "And possibly the oldest. I thought I knew it, until I met Kelda. He taught me what it really meant, and I have been sorry ever since."

She felt her fingers chill, even holding Phelan's, but she walked with them through the dark toward the light of day, which she saw, as though with Jonah's eyes, as something endlessly, tirelessly old as well, waiting patiently for yet another night.

Chapter Twenty-two

Zoe stood near the bar in the Merry Rampion, singing to a post. It was well past midnight; beyond an open window, the moon spangled the river with its slow descent. The place was packed with musicians, so tightly wound with the imminent competition that only liberal quantities of cold beer kept them from flaring and snapping where they stood. Zoe's voice had swept them all up into an enthusiastic fervor; they sang with her, banging pewter tankards if they had no other instruments. Even that couldn't overpower her; she sang, as Quennel had demanded, to crack the icy heart of the moon, which from what she saw of it, was as impervious as the court bard sipping wine in the shadows.

He was the fair-haired, hard-eyed bard of the Duke of Waverlea, and he bristled with a small arsenal of instruments: harp, pipe, flute, hand drums. He alone refused to rouse to her music, much as she tuned her voice to his ears alone, loosed all her skills to make him blink, smile, even tap the table with a fingernail. But he only watched her woodenly, raising his glass to his lips now and then, sometimes glancing at the moon as though he might hear the music it made floating through the night if only Zoe would stop making such a racket.

She gave up on him at last and let the music flow from other hands, turning thirstily to the chilled wine that Chase put in front of her. He, at least, looked vaguely stunned.

"You sent chills down my spine," he said. "It was like listening to the dead." She squinted at him; he laughed a little, running fingers through his sunflower hair. "How they might have sung it back then, before city lights and steam trams." He paused again, then took a kiss from her, gently. "What if you win? I'll never see you, then."

"What a thought," she said in a suck of breath.

"It hadn't occurred to you?"

"Not in this world."

"That you'd be all busy with courtly matters and never have a moment with me?"

She stared at him mutely, uncertainly for the briefest of moments, then shook her head adamantly. "Let's not think about it. We'll worry about it if and when and after."

She sang again later, playing someone else's harp. It was nothing much, just a lullaby as old as the night to bring the crowd back down and coax a few students to bed, where they belonged. No one sang with her then; they just listened to her, motionless, silent, their eyes heavy, as though she were lulling them to sleep on their feet. Her silence, as the song ended, woke them out of a dream; they looked around blankly, rubbing their faces, picking up their instruments. A few straggled out the door, still not talking. Others drifted to the bar for one last beer. The bard from

Waverlea played then, very softly, on his flute, echoing Zoe's lullaby. The sound wove among the crowd, his flute glinting silver like the moon-spangles. He cut it short before the ending and stood up.

He said to Zoe across the silent room, "Be careful. You'll wake the stones with that voice of yours, and you'll find yourself in the last place you expect to be." He smiled at her then, a thin, wry, marveling smile, slid his flute into its case on his belt, and left before she could even find her voice to answer.

She went to bed with Chase and got up again with the sun, bleary and worried about seven different things the moment she opened her eyes.

The first was getting home to wash and change before her class. That simple task was complicated, as she opened the tower door, by the sight of her father and Phelan sitting at the kitchen table with a pile of books between them. The table was otherwise bare; nothing but a teakettle stood on the stove, and even that was cold. They both glanced at her vaguely, breaking off a conversation, but expectantly, as though she had appeared at their wish expressly to cook them breakfast.

She felt a moment's annoyance and desperation, that they couldn't anticipate how harried she might be and figure out how to crack an egg for themselves. Phelan looked as hag-ridden as she was, his hair on end from raking it with his fingers, his eyes so remote, she couldn't begin to guess at his thoughts. Her father had a peculiar expression on his face as well. She wondered for a moment if one or the other had got somebody with child.

Then she summoned some rag end of patience, for she was hungry, too, and pulled a pan off its hook.

"Good morning to you, too."

Phelan stirred, finally, in his chair. "Sorry."

"Good morning, lass," Bayley said absently. "Phelan just brought back more record books."

"You didn't offer him coffee? Oh, you haven't made it yet. No, don't bother. I'll do it." She heard him subside back into his seat, and she sighed soundlessly. She put the kettle on for herself as well and rummaged for bread, eggs, fruit, listening, as a halting conversation started up again behind her.

"You've finished your paper, then?"

"Nearly. I'm very close to an ending. There's only one thing I need to understand. To research."

"Anything I might have?"

"I don't think so. I found the name in other sources: letters, court chronicles. A bard called Welkin. He's not listed as an account rendered or received."

"Welkin . . ." her father mused.

"Do you recognize the name?"

"I'm thinking. Tell me something about him."

Zoe's thoughts drifted to the competition, so close now her fingers seemed, even stirring eggs in the hot pan, perpetually chilled with anticipation. Quennel had summoned her to court for a final word of advice, maybe to encourage her to wile out of Kelda what he intended to play. Competing bards, she understood, had devastated one another's chances by stealing their songs and playing them first. Kelda would only laugh at that, and play whatever it was a dozen times better than anyone else. Nothing would discompose him, she knew by now. He was the bard who could melt the jewels out of Declan's harp and find the one true note that would break hearts and harp strings together.

"Zoe?"

She was burning the eggs, just thinking about him. She pulled them off the heat and turned to cut bread. Phelan's eyes caught at her, now disconcertingly attentive. She smiled at him, but he was not deceived.

"Are you in love?" he inquired baldly, and her father's chair rattled across flagstones as he rose abruptly to get cups down.

"No. Of course not. Who has time? Except for Chase, I mean. I'm just preoccupied. Have you decided what you'll play first?" He only gazed at her bemusedly, as though she had asked him what he planned to wear for his funeral. "The competition," she reminded him, astonished that he had forgotten about it, even for a moment.

"Oh."

"You are still going to—"

"Yes. I promised you. It's just—"

"You're distracted, too," she guessed, "by your paper." She buttered the bread, cast another glance at him, and was amazed again, by the sudden burn across his cheekbones. Whatever caused that, it wasn't his interminable paper. She turned away quickly, wrestled with the eggs in the pan, and gave up, gazing with despair at the speckled black-and-gold mess.

"Never mind," Bayley said gently.

"I never burn things."

"We'll eat them anyway."

"Sit down," Phelan said brusquely. "I know where the plates are. You'll wear yourself out until there's nothing left of you but your bones and the music coming out of them."

She smiled again, gratefully, and sank into a chair, slid her hands over her eyes. She smelled tea, opened one eye, and found the teapot and a cup in front of her. She raised the lid, watched the leaves steep, while Phelan and her father moved around her, rattling cutlery, opening cupboard doors.

"Have you found any reference to Welkin beyond those few days of the first competition?"

"No. I'm still searching. As far as I know now, he vanished like Nairn off the plain and out of history, though, from most accounts, he was expected to win."

"Who are you talking about?" Zoe asked, still gazing at the tea leaves.

"A mysterious stranger at the first bardic competition," Phelan told her. "Origins unknown, carried nothing but a battered harp, and he had all the court bards in awe of him by the end of the first day. By the end of the third day, he was pitted against Nairn for the title of Royal Bard of Belden. One of them should have won."

She raised her head, pot forgotten. "The winner was Blasson Purser of Waverlea."

"Yes."

"So what happened? Welkin sounds like someone in a story. Was it folklore? Ballad? About Nairn and Welkin?"

"No."

"They both just vanished? It's documented?"

He gave a faint laugh then, his face so pale it might have been his own bones she was looking at. "It will be."

Her eyes narrowed. "Phelan, what are you not telling me?"

"And what are you not telling me?" he challenged her.

She answered quickly, before he brought words to play like "magic" and "secret" and "abandoned sewers" that would have disconcerted her orderly father.

"I'll tell you when I can," she promised.

His eyes held hers a moment, gray as old iron; he nodded briefly. "So will I."

After they finished the unfortunate eggs, she tossed her robe over last night's outfit and taught her class. Then she finally had the time to wash and change into something suitable for visiting the Royal Bard. She pondered Phelan's odd paper as she rode the tram downhill and along the river road. It should have been as dry as dust; that had been his original intention, to write it as quickly and as painlessly as possible. Instead, it leached the blood from his face and gave him secrets to eat that he would not share even with her. Fair enough: she kept her own secrets from him. From the sound of it, neither of them even understood exactly what they were carrying around locked behind their teeth. It was an exhausting weight to bear, along with the demands of the competition, and having to hide it from Quennel that day was a burden she could have done without.

Fortunately, he was so preoccupied with his own passionate determination and ambitions for her that he didn't sense the turmoil in her own head. He was completely well by then, and his playing more skillful and vibrant than ever, fueled by the sudden glance death had given him and by the dire figure in the tale he forged daily for himself about Kelda. Zoe wished he would just change his mind, tell everyone to go back home, including Kelda, and keep harping through his waning years, as even the king had urged him to do. But no, he was adamant: Zoe must take his place, or the kingdom would fall.

"I have thought of what you should play and sing in the opening round of the competition," he said as they sat in private in the musician's gallery.

"But you told me to play—"

"Yes, I know, but I was wrong. This is the perfect ballad for you."

"But—"

"Hush," he said, hands poised on his strings. "Listen."

Choosing her song for her yet again reminded him of his own experiences during the last bardic competition. He cautioned her about this, offered practical suggestions about that, remembered a story, embellished like a formal ballad with details from years of retelling, about a pair of not very good but extremely competitive musicians, and the tricks—the split reed, the suddenly sagging drum, the missing harp string—with which they undermined one another.

Thus reminded, he turned grave again, warned her to guard against Kelda's meddling.

"Kelda doesn't need to play tricks," she told him bluntly. "All he has to do is play."

He shook his head, unconvinced; his Kelda was capable of anything. Which was exactly true, she knew, but not in ways that Quennel could imagine even at his bleakest.

He finally let her go. At the bottom of the gallery stairs, she found Kelda waiting for her.

He had probably heard every word, she thought wearily, judging by the amusement in his eyes.

"A final lesson?" he asked lightly, indifferent to his voice carrying up over the gallery balustrade. She walked out of the great hall without answering, forcing him to follow, get out of earshot. In a silent corridor, she turned to face him.

"I don't know what you are." Her voice shook despite all her training. "Your powers are astonishing and terrible. Your playing melts my heart. That's what I know. And I know that when we compete, all the lies you hide yourself behind will vanish; only the music and the power will be left. I will give you back the very best I have. But I think it will be only a trifle, a handful of wild-flowers, a shiny copper or two, compared to the terror and the treasures that will come out of you. That will be as it will be. So. There's no need to wear that face with me now. It's just another lie. Grant me that much, before you change at last into something I won't begin to recognize."

She turned again without waiting for him to answer, made her way to the main doors, listening, all the while, for all he did not say.

The new dawn broke with a ray of light and a shout of trumpets across the plain, summoning the bards from inns and mansions, from school and court, from tents, skiff bottoms, and tavern floors, to gather under the golden eye of the midsummer sun and play until only the best of them stood alone: all the rest were silent.

Chapter Twenty-three

Phelan woke the sleeping princess with a kiss. She stirred, blinked puzzledly at his bedroom ceiling, then rolled over swiftly, groping for her wristwatch.

"What time is it?"

"The trumpets just sounded. I have to go." He didn't move, sat there in a riffled puddle of purple silk sheets, watched her push her tangled curls out of her eyes and smile at him, a little, private smile full of memories. Then the memory changed, and she sat up abruptly.

"I must have heard them in my sleep. I dreamed that my mother was competing to become the Royal Bard. She was playing an antique ear trumpet. She won."

He laughed. "No."

"Yes." She was silent, then, her smile fading, studying his face. She put a hand on his bare shoulder, kissed him gently. "I'm glad you can laugh. If I were you, I'd be terrified."

He shrugged the shoulder under her long fingers, slid his own hand over them. "I don't have such an exalted opinion of my gifts to be afraid of losing. I'm just there to keep Zoe's mind off Kelda."

"Kelda." She shivered lightly; he drew her hand from his shoulder, kissed her palm. "Will he win?"

"My father says over his dead body. That sounds like wishful thinking to me. And my father can't play even an ear trumpet. He doesn't have a chance of stopping Kelda."

She drew her knees up under the sheets, dropped her face against them. Her voice came, muffled by silk and her disheveled hair. "I'm still trying to absorb what he told us. It's hard not to want for him what he wants, but it's also the last thing you or I would want."

"Yes," he said softly. He touched the band of lace and satin that had slid off one shoulder, added, "I would never have imagined you in that color."

"What color have you imagined me in?"

He opened his mouth, stopped himself, and smiled. "Well. Not orange."

"Tangerine," she amended. "My lady-in-waiting refuses to let me wear the color in public. So I have to keep it hidden in my underwear." She raised her head, sighing. "We have our scant hours between the trumpets and the tide this morning. At least I'll be able to come for the opening ceremonies. Then I really must put in a few hours at the site. And then go home and face my mother."

"My father doesn't expect you to—"

She shook her head quickly. "I know. But I want to, today. I have explored every curve of the great dour keep where kings used to imprison recalcitrant nobles. I want to understand what we've found before I get locked up."

"I'll come and rescue you."

She gave him her sidelong smile. "You'll be busy helping Zoe. Surely I've learned enough working for your father to dig myself out of anything."

He dressed hastily and left the princess in Sophy's amiable care, discussing whether they should chance the traffic in Beatrice's car or take a barge upriver. As usual, Jonah was nowhere in sight. Phelan hoped his father hadn't gone after Kelda with a cobblestone. He took a tram crammed with whey-faced musicians and musical instruments of every size and shape to the huge stone amphitheater on the north edge of Caerau, built by the school four hundred years earlier for bardic competitions and used, between times, for everything from early steam-car racing to coronations.

The elaborate scaffolding rose like a wedding cake out of the center of the amphitheater to support the stage, the whole festooned with banners and garlands, and littered with equipment so that even those ensconced on distant hillocks, under the shade of a solitary tree, could hear the musicians compete. Even that early, the sheer numbers spread out over the grass looked like an invading army, laying siege to the old stonework. The thousands waiting to be seated inside spilled beyond every gate but two: the Royal Gate, from which a long purple carpet ran halfway to the barge docks, and the Musicians Gate. Phelan joined the crowd making for that humble entrance, on the shadowy side of morning. Around him, the competitors were mostly silent, bleary, and grim, some looking as though they were about to lose their breakfasts. As they entered and gave their names, they were handed a schedule. Phelan cast a glance over it and almost lost his. By some twisted luck of the draw, he was scheduled to play first.

He wandered inside dazedly, made his way through the laby-rinth of instruments strewn all over the floor and musicians wak-ing up their fingers and voices. The place sounded like a flock of demented mythological birds. He finally found an empty corner, put down his instruments, and looked around for Zoe.

As though he had made a wish, she was there beside him: an eyeful of bright multicolored silks, colors such as only ancient Royal Bards were once permitted to wear.

He smiled, dazzled by crimson and purple, gold and orange. Tangerine, he amended, and wondered if Beatrice would be there long enough to hear him play.

"I wore them for luck," Zoe said, reading his thoughts. "And hearing you will give me courage. I don't play until after noon." She stopped, studying him silently, quizzically, until he felt him-self flush. She said slowly, "No one has ever put that expression on your face before. Not even me."

"How can you even pay attention to such things," he de-manded, "at a time like this?"

She shrugged, her own warm skin ivory around the edges. "I can't help what I see, especially in those I love. I can't stop notic-ing, can I? What are you going to play?"

"One of three things."

She laughed, an incongruous sound among the broken flut-ings and tunings and ragged runs of notes. "I suppose you'll make up your mind at the last moment." Her lips brushed his cheek lightly, a kiss from the dead, judging from the chill in them. "Stay with me," she pleaded. "Give me something to think about be-sides Kelda and Quennel."

He glanced around for the big, dark-haired bard who, sched-uled to play later that morning, would no doubt choose his own moment to appear. "I will," he promised, though how, he had no idea; he fully expected his first song to be his last, judging by the music coming from the formidable court bards around them.

An hour later, he sat among the hundreds of musicians grouped around the foot of the scaffolding, gazing up through the layers of ornate grillwork to the top, where a master from the school gave a brief history of the competition, then the king welcomed everyone to Caerau, and, finally, Quennel repeated the traditional summons to the gathering of the bards, thanked them for coming, and wished them well. Phelan had been sent up the stairs during that, an endless walk into the welkin where he waited, wondering what he thought he was doing there, hovering between earth and sky, in a position he had never in his life intended to put himself.

Somehow, among all those faces, numerous as the stars and as remote, he caught sight of Beatrice.

She was sitting near the top beside Sophy, under the Royal Pavilion, leaning forward in her seat as though to see him better, the morning sun illumining her pale green silks, the wind blowing her hair into a froth. He couldn't see her expression at that distance, except in his mind's eye: her blue eyes very dark, calm, one corner of her mouth quirked upward in her familiar slanting smile.

In that moment, he knew what he would play for her.

He scarcely heard himself; the scant moments passed like a dream as he harped an old love ballad and sang to the woman who had wakened with the dawn beside him. He heard little of the applause afterward, just assumed everyone was relieved that he hadn't forgotten his words or lost his voice but had given the competition an opening note of grace. He passed the next musician at the top of the stairs, one of the court bards from Estmere, who ignored him entirely, then another on a landing, whom Phelan had seen piping along the river road and who looked as though he might topple over the scaffolding out of terror.

At the bottom of the stairs, he found his father, who drew him with a compelling hand away from the musicians, back into the stone archway from which they had emerged.

"What are you doing?" Jonah demanded, when they were out of earshot.

Phelan gazed at him wordlessly, seeing again that strange double vision of his father: Nairn the Deathless, the Unforgiven, imposed over the father he had grown up with, history pleated endlessly across a moment in time.

"Nothing," he said finally. "Just playing. Zoe asked me to."

"Get yourself disqualified," Jonah said succinctly.

"Oh, I will. I probably already have."

"Not playing like that you won't."

Phelan looked at him silently again, trying to imagine what Jonah thought he saw. "I played it for Beatrice," he said finally, his only explanation for any power the ballad had beyond the ordinary. "What are you afraid of? There are court bards here who play songs as old as the five kingdoms. They could blow me off the scaffold with a riffle of flute notes."

"That's not the point," Jonah said irritably.

"What is the point?"

"If Kelda is who I think he is, you could be in grave danger, that's the point. He destroyed my music. I won't let him take you from me as well. That would destroy me all over again. I couldn't live with that, and I am not able to die. So stop playing to the princess. Stop playing with your heart."

Phelan opened his mouth; nothing came out. He shook himself out of Jonah's grip, finally, and pulled his father back to the end of the archway, where they could hear the court bard playing above. "Listen," he said fiercely, trying to keep his voice down. "Listen to that." The bard was playing three instruments at once, it sounded like, and singing at the same time. "That's what he plays every morning for the Duke of Estmere's breakfast. Do you think that any world exists in which I can compete with that?"

"His heart's not in it," Jonah muttered doggedly.

"You're being unreasonable." He heard himself and laughed shortly. "What am I saying. You've been unreasonable all your life. Now I understand why, but Kelda isn't interested in either one of us. He has his eye on Zoe, and I promised her I'd give her all I had just to stay in the competition." Jonah groaned. "I barely remembered I had a heart, then," Phelan added dryly. "Even so, nobody has ever suggested that it's any kind of substitute for skill."

"How could you fall in love at a time like this?" his father said, exasperated. "Anyway, that's not the point, either. The point is—"

"I don't see the point of arguing about it," Phelan said, exasperated himself, "if you can't tell me what the point is. Sit with me and listen to the music."

"I've heard it all before," Jonah said inarguably.

Phelan sighed. "Well, I haven't. Try to stay out of trouble while I listen."

He saw Beatrice leave at midmorning. He watched the empty place where she had sat for some time after, hoping she would change her mind, decide not to join the digging crew and reappear as the one point in the dizzying multitudes of faces where his eyes could rest. Attendants passed among the musicians, offered water, fruit, tea, juices, and more hefty fare for the nerveless. Phelan, sipping chilled citrus juice, listened to Kelda work his magic over the crowd, causing vendors roaming the tiered stone walkways to stop in their tracks as the deep, honed voice flooded the amphitheater and the plain, until the distant hillocks seemed to take up and echo his song. Phelan, moved in spite of himself by the unfortunate lovers in the ballad, searched for Beatrice again and found his father instead, sitting beside Sophy and drinking something no doubt forbidden to the vendors to sell. Or maybe it was just tea; he offered the flask to Sophy, and she accepted it. Phelan's attention lingered on his father, as applause roared like a sea-wave around him. Still stunned by Jonah's tale, and hopelessly trying to imagine such a life, he knew that it would be his own lifelong predicament to wonder at the mystery until he watched Jonah watch him die.

He was rescued abruptly from such dark thoughts by the first wild, exuberant note out of the next musician's throat. He felt his skin prickle. He barely recognized the voice; it seemed as though one of the ancient stones, warmed by the bright smile of the sun, had broken into song. It made him yearn for an instrument— anything, a blade of grass, a singing reed—to play along with her. She seemed as serenely confident of her powers as a full moon drifting to airy nothing above the horizon, as strong as an old oak tree carrying generations of nests in its enormous boughs or a mischievous wind blowing any thought of death away as lightly as last year's dried leaf. He laughed, even as tears stung his eyes. Kelda could not matter against this. Nothing mattered, only the exhilaration and generosity in the voice that must have swept across the plain to startle the eagles on the crags of Grishold and make the old stones dance along the edge of the northern sea.

The musicians rose, clapping for her, even Kelda, as she came back downstairs. The unfortunate who had to follow her dropped a kiss on Zoe's cheek, laughing as they passed on the stairs. Zoe found Phelan; the musician beside him moved aside for her to sit with him.

The little, taut smile on her face, the absolute fearlessness in her eyes made him stare at her with awe.

"You've declared war," he breathed.

She shook her head. "Not war," she whispered tightly, as the musician on the stage above them began her song. "Not yet."

Late in the afternoon, the last of the competitors played, a dilettante so inept he didn't bother to finish his song, just broke off with a laugh and a wave. The musicians stretched their legs, had a bite to eat, talked tensely as they awaited the first round of eliminations. The amphitheater began to empty. An hour later the list of the musicians requested to return on the second day was read by one of the masters on the stage.

To his surprise, Phelan was among them.

"Good," Zoe said simply, when they heard. "We are allowed to play with each other and against each other, tomorrow, if we request it. I'll put us down together."

"Why bother?" Phelan asked. "You should play against some-one who might win. One of the court bards." She only laughed at that. "Kelda, then."

"That will come," she said softly, seeing it, her smile gone for the moment. Then she looked at him again, and it returned. "Who would you rather lose to, than me?"

He smiled. "All right. Just tell me what to practice."

She told him, then left to find Chase in the crowd lingering outside the amphitheater. Phelan looked for Beatrice, saw only Jonah, and went out another way to elude the argument waiting for him outside the Musicians Gate.

Chapter Twenty-four

The princess looked reluctantly up from under the earth toward the end of the day, deliberately not thinking of what lay ahead, only wondering how Phelan had fared. He had sung to her all afternoon, the tender ballad echoing in her head, in a lovely diversion, like a songbird on her shoulder as she brushed and probed and sweated under the cascade of midsummer light. Finally, the light faded, went elsewhere; around her, tools began to slow.

The work crew stood silently, pondering the mystery pulled deep underground by its own ponderous weight.

"It has to be," Campion said tiredly, leaving streaks from his fingers across his face as he rubbed an eyebrow. They all wore a pelt of dust over clothes and skin, as though they were slowly turning into strange burrowing creatures who measured their days by the hours they could spend underground and left their thoughts there when they came up, blinking, into the world.

The massive wall of yellow stone was riddled everywhere

with runes, except for what they called the door stone; the center of that squat, massive oblong held only one symbol: a dot that coiled around and around itself until it ended in a perfect circle. Ida had uncovered it earlier, absently chattering to them all the while, telling some story of a disastrous party while her vigorous brushing was revealing another story entirely.

"Why," she asked plaintively, gazing at the door. "Maybe it's a sort of pantry. Or some kind of sweat lodge, an early spa—"

"Could be, I suppose," Hadrian said dubiously, bending his thin frame backward and forward to unkink his spine.

"Doors," Curran pointed out, "are meant to be used. Unless they're meant to open once, then close something inside. Has to be a tomb. Likely we'll never know, the way that stone is wedged in there now—looks so old it's slumped and melted into itself."

"A king's tomb, maybe," Beatrice murmured. "All that writing, that special mark on the door . . ."

"Well." Campion reached for his tool belt, slung it over his shoulder. "Jonah will know. Odd he hasn't come to look at it yet."

"He's been at the competition," Beatrice said, adding as they looked at her questioningly, "Phelan is playing." She felt the warmth in her face as she said his name; luckily, she was so grimy nobody noticed.

"Does Jonah even know about this?" Curran asked.

"Oh, yes. I told him."

Campion grunted. "Phelan must be good, to keep Jonah's mind off his digs."

"He roams at night," Curran said wryly. "Along with the standing stones. Likely he's already seen it."

They clambered out then, leaving the mystery to the moon. They washed their faces in water and leftover tea from the thermoses, and pounded the dust off their clothes. Beatrice gave them a ride across the bridge, dropped them to catch their various trams, and turned reluctantly toward the awaiting squall. The last she had seen of the queen had been at the garden party. Beatrice had sent her a message from Jonah Cle's house that evening, a rather incoherent one, she recalled, but who could be entirely rational after emerging in tattered stockings and a party dress out of a sewer in the company of a thousand-year-old legend?

The answer from the castle had been ominous silence.

She had time, at least, to wash and change before the summons came. Unexpectedly, it was from her father.

She found the king pacing among his antiquities, tossing comments over his shoulder to Master Burley.

"Beatrice. Your mother told me to talk to you," he said brusquely. "Do you have any idea why?"

She smiled, enormously relieved. "Nothing to be concerned about," she answered.

"Good. She said that you ran away after a party two days ago and were seen this morning in the company of Sophy Cle." He picked up an ancient bone rattle, shook it absently, the whirling bones clicking wildly, to Master Burley's consternation. "Anything you need to talk about?"

"I don't think so, really. I think—somehow I might have fallen in love with Phelan Cle."

His brows rose. "Phelan." He gave the rattle a final spin, put it back down. "H'm."

"Yes."

"Well." His hand hovered over a fine, very early piece of pottery. Master Burley closed his eyes. Beatrice watched her father's expression change slowly, as he mused. He dropped his hand abruptly, leaving the pottery intact. "Well," he said again, looking hopeful. "That could work. Couldn't it? It gets tedious, trying to discuss antiquities with your brothers and Marcus. Anything else upsetting your mother?"

"Not that I can think of."

"Good. Then we can move on to what you've unearthed in that dig of Jonah's. Your mother said it was all you could talk about at her party. What on earth did you find?"

"Father, it's the most amazing thing," she told him eagerly. "A great creamy yellow stone tomb-looking sort of thing completely covered with runes. Except for the door. At least we think it's a door. There's only one symbol on that."

"What symbol?" both the king and the curator demanded together.

"A circle that coils inward to a dot. Or maybe the other way around."

"A coil," her father murmured, and glanced at Master Burley. "Anything come to mind?"

"Nothing immediately, my lord. Perhaps the princess could draw it."

"Of course."

"I'll find some dictionaries."

He disappeared, came back with pencil, paper, and an armload of books. Beatrice drew the spiral within the circle, and they all pored among the books, draping themselves in various positions over the collection cases: Beatrice with both elbows on the glass covering a case of early spear and ax heads, studying a translation from the runic; the king leaning against a cupboard full of pottery pieces and flipping through a dictionary of early symbols.

"Anything?" the king murmured. Master Burley, poised like a bookend on the other side of the pottery cupboard, shut one book, opened another impatiently.

"You would think that such a simple, memorable symbol would be more easily found."

"Not like 'bread,'" Beatrice commented absently, twirling the pencil through her hair. "Perhaps it's someone's name?"

"Lucien!" the queen said despairingly, and the cases rattled alarmingly as they all straightened. She eyed her daughter frostily, then tossed her hands. "I give up, I really do. Have you even tried, Lucien? Have you spoken to your daughter at all?"

"Of course I have. She says everything is fine. Oh, and that it may well be a tomb." The queen stared at him. He smiled at her. "Shall I take your brother there tomorrow, show him what Beatrice has found? He fell asleep during the bardic competition today. Perhaps he prefers tombs."

"Bards," Beatrice echoed abruptly. "Kelda will know."

"What?"

She gazed at her father without seeing him, seeing instead the dark, mystifying face of the bard, his teasing smile hinting of ambiguities. "What the symbol is. He knows them all, the old runes."

"Good. We'll invite him to supper tonight and ask him. That is, unless Jonah is joining us," he added. "There seems some odd tension between them. Do you understand it, Beatrice?"

"Ah—"

"Of course not, how could you? Some sort of misunderstanding, very likely." He glanced around at a strangled sound from the queen. "What is it, Harriet? Are we late for something?"

Neither Jonah nor Kelda appeared in the hall that evening. Quennel played alone, slow, old ballads and ancient court dances. There was an odd, distant look on his face, as though, beneath his own music, he could hear the music all over the plain as bards contended in private bouts in taverns, on hillocks under the moon, among the standing stones. His brows were drawn; his expression, on one of his final nights as Royal Bard, seemed more harsh than nostalgic. Beatrice guessed whose music he listened for, drifting across the long summer evening, and was both relieved and disturbed that the young bard with his raptor's glance, his perceptive smile, was nowhere in sight.

It was a smaller family gathering than usual around the tables. Charlotte and her family had left for the country, the queen told Beatrice, who was sitting in her sister's customary place beside their mother. Damon and Daphne were at yet another engagement supper; even Harold was out somewhere. The king was left to make desultory conversation with Lord Grishold. The queen's voice, carefully modulated, had lost some of its implacable resolve. Beatrice wondered if she was already regretting the loss of Quennel, who had played at every important occasion in the castle since her marriage. Even Lord Grishold, the most unmusical of men, seemed to respond to the change in the Royal Bard.

"I understand I might have to find another bard myself," Beatrice overheard him say to her father. "I've heard the odds are on Kelda to win. People tell me his voice is magical. I can't hear it myself; music all sounds alike to me, like bees—can't tell one note from another. But Petris and our daughters will miss him."

"Charlotte's invitation to you still stands, of course," the queen murmured to Beatrice. "In the event that, after a little time, you need a place to think things over."

About Phelan, her mother meant. In case he turned out to be as exasperating as his father, and Beatrice, having lost her heart to one who broke it, lost her job as well. How her mother imagined that Beatrice could have a solitary moment to trail through dewy mornings, scattering wildflower petals and brooding, with Small Marcus and Tiny Thomasina always with her, she had no idea.

"There are other digs," she answered calmly. "I think quite clearly when I'm working." She heard her mother's sigh under the genial clatter of cutlery, and added, somewhere between humor and exasperation herself, "It's what I do. If you don't want to look at me in my dungarees, I'll go up north. They're digging up an entire ancient village in the Marches." The queen flung her a horrified glance. "I am sorry, Mother," Beatrice added softly. "Truly. But, honestly, how long could you stand living among country roads and cows and hobby farms? If you insist I go there, I'll only find the nearest dig site and disappear into it. There are some wonderful barrows and tombs in that part of the country."

Her mother's knife scraped gracelessly across the porcelain. "At least Charlotte talks about shoes at the supper table," she said darkly. "Not tombs. You really are hopelessly like your father."

"I suppose so," Beatrice agreed amiably, while on her mother's other hand, Lady Petris picked the word eagerly out of the air.

"Shoes?" she exclaimed, actually drawing a second syllable out of the word. "I adore them, don't you? I have so many I had to turn the old nursery into a closet. Tell me, Harriet—"

Jonah found the princess at midmorning the next day, alone

at the site except for the guard in the car, who glanced up from his book and recognized the interloper. Everyone else had gone to the competition for a few hours, to experience the historical anomaly of it, as Campion put it. Beatrice had been drawn back to the runes. Only for an hour, she told herself, brushing dirt out of the deep scores in the stone. They had haunted her dreams the night before, like mute faces trying to speak. She searched for the rayed circle within the silent, continuous chatter patterning the face of the tomb. The sudden shadow falling over her startled her as deeply as if one of the runes had spoken.

"Master Cle."

"Phelan sent me to get you," he said, stepping onto the ladder and descending. "So this is what you've found. Where is everyone?"

"They went off to hear the music. I just came—I had to see this again." She gestured inarticulately at the mystery. "I couldn't help myself. Master Cle, have you ever seen anything like this?" He did not answer; she took her eyes off it finally to glance at him. "Master Cle?"

He was utterly motionless, not even breathing, as far as she could tell, his face so white she thought he might collapse there at the bottom of the dig. She touched him. He moved then, gripped her fingers.

"Yes," he said harshly. "I have seen it before. Or something very like it." He dropped her hand, turned abruptly toward the ladder. "Come with me."

"But what is it? What does it say? I don't recognize that symbol at all. We searched for it—my father and Master Burley and I—in all the runic dictionaries, and we couldn't find it."

"Of course not."

"But—"

He was halfway up the ladder; he gestured for her to follow. "There's no time. I think Phelan may be in terrible danger."

"From what?" she asked bewilderedly. "An old tomb door?"

"Don't ask."

She guessed anyway. "Kelda," she said abruptly. "You think— Master Cle, I have no idea what you're thinking. What would happen to Phelan in front of everyone in the middle of the competition?"

"What happened to me," he answered grimly, and she felt her throat close, dry with fear.

"Is Phelan that good?" she asked shakily, starting up the ladder.

"Only when he thinks of you. I want to be where I can see him. And Kelda." He gave her a hand onto the upper ground, paused briefly to take in her impossible attire.

"I brought clothes in the car," she told him quickly. "I'll change at the amphitheater."

"Good," he said with relief, and added, dourly, "If it's still standing. Kelda has already played once this morning. The place might be a heap of rubble by now, with all the shouting and stomping he caused."

"Magic?"

He shook his head, the lines on his face as rigid as the runes. "Not yet. He doesn't need it yet."

Beatrice told the guard to park the car down by the royal barge, got out of her dig clothes and into a frock in the private rooms reserved for king and courtiers. She went outside and climbed to the highest circle, at a level with the stage on its scaffolding, where she found Sophy under the flapping pavilion. It was Quennel's preferred spot as well, Beatrice noticed; the old bard sat along the rim, wearing his formal robe of king-fisher blue, his ivory hair in a tuft, his expression as tense as Jonah's.

"He went to speak to Phelan," Sophy told her, before she could ask. "Isn't that your aunt Petris under that wonderful hat? All those plumes look as though they're about to fly away with her."

"How is Phelan?" Beatrice asked anxiously.

"Better, I'm sure, now that you're here. He's playing—" She paused to put her spectacles on, study the program. "Quite soon, I think. With Zoe."

"There's my mother," Beatrice breathed, startled as she recognized the flowery hat next to the plumes. "I hardly thought she'd be interested . . ." She applauded at the sound of it around her, as one bard's song ended and a court bard took her place, wearing instruments like body armor that flared with light at every note, as though the sun played his music for him.

Her thoughts strayed again; she tried to find Phelan, sitting in the shadows under the scaffolding. She missed him; maybe he was somewhere with Jonah. But Jonah had come back, sat down next to Sophy, before the sun's song came to an end. Beatrice's hands moved mechanically; her face turned to Jonah's grim, closed face, a question pending for when the noise died down again. She drew breath to ask it, then lost it again as Zoe began to sing.

Beatrice stared at the stage, forgetting entirely to close her mouth. Two figures, one dark-haired, dressed in silks like blow-ing flames, the other pale-haired, in blue shot with silver threads down which light rilled like water, seemed to pull music not from their voices, their instruments, but out of the grass roots of the plain, the lichen on the ancient stones, the words carved into them as old as Belden. She felt her eyes burn, put a hand to her mouth. Surely, that was the sound of the spiraling circle on the tomb: that was its voice; the music pouring into her heart was the word itself, saying its name. The world blurred around her, flashing, melting. As the tears finally fell, she heard Jonah's sudden exclamation.

She could see again, but in what world she had no idea.

Chapter Twenty-five

Another harper played with them. Zoe heard the sweet, exuberant run of notes like a stream rilling and splashing into her music, then merging with it, sometimes deep, secret water, sometimes leaping into light. Phelan, attuned to her, eyes lowered to his hands, did not seem to notice at first. Then his head flicked up; he glanced at her. His eyes grew very wide; Zoe heard his fingers slow, lag after a beat, a sudden, startled absence before his fingers caught up with her.

She was beginning to falter herself: a breath instead of a sound now and then, her skin prickling cold under the midsummer sun. The amphitheater seemed to have grown incredibly high. The plain shimmered beyond it, green and gold and blue melting into imprecise horizons, behind an endless rise of stones spiraling around them. A dream of stones, she thought. A memory of stones. The plain seemed oddly empty, the sentinel tree on the crown of the hillocks scattered hither and yon on the plain no longer shaded colorful gatherings of listeners. Caerau itself seemed to have vanished into a silvery mist on both sides of the river.

She felt more breath than music flow out of her, a long, cold flash of river mist; even her bones had gone cold.

"Don't stop," a voice said cheerfully between verses. Kelda, she thought at first. She heard Phelan beside her, fingers laboring doggedly, as though his quick, skilled hands had turned stiff as wood. The harper drove them now, kept the beat, chose the song they slid into, helplessly caught in his current, held them in the bright web of his strings.

The amphitheater seemed empty, too. There was no amphitheater, she realized. The transparent stones surrounded them; they stood on a knoll somewhere on the plain, somewhere in time or memory, playing to the whims of the harper, who was not Kelda, she realized. He was no one she had ever met, an aging, craggy figure, like a battered old stone, one eye pale blue, the other twilight dark, his voice like the deep drag of waves on a rocky shore. She turned her head to see him more clearly, and he smiled.

She recognized that smile: the kelpie's fearless, teasing, perceptive glint.

She could hear Phelan's breathing begin to grow ragged with shock, fighting itself to finish the song. She waited. When the harper began yet another rollicking ballad, she wrested the notes away from him, slowed them into a wordless court dance to free their voices.

The odd eyes narrowed at her, but the harper's dancing fingers did not argue.

"Phelan," she said softly, letting her fingers carry the slow, lilting melody without her.

He was looking around bewilderedly; she wondered if he saw what she did, or if he had summoned up a private vision. He answered finally, huskily, "This is—"

"Yes."

"How did we—"

"I don't know."

"You must have— I could— I could never have—"

"You're here," she said inarguably, and he was silent again, face the color of bone, fingers loosing notes like a scatter of gold into the air.

"Well, how do we— How do we get ourselves out of this? My father couldn't find his way out."

If she had been singing when he said that, her voice would have shriveled with wonder and shock. Her throat closed; she couldn't breathe for a moment. She could only keep playing until her wordless, frozen thoughts thawed out a word or two, dredged up a memory.

"Not—" she whispered, her voice still trapped. "Not—"

"Yes."

"Nairn?"

"Yes."

"Oh," she said soundlessly, the word like a smooth, cold river stone in her mouth. The harper, restive or mischievous, tried to pull out of her rhythm suddenly. She fought him stubbornly, held him to her beat. He could be patient, she thought. He had nothing to fear. Nothing to lose.

Or did he? She looked at him again, sitting on a stone merging like an old tooth from the grass. "Who are you?" she asked, with or without words; she wasn't sure. "Are you Kelda?"

"Welkin?" Phelan echoed incomprehensibly, and the harper

only smiled, and played a note that melted Zoe's heart, kindled it to flame, and then to poetry.

"Oh," she said again, astonished, and he nodded at her.

"Play with me," he said in his voice like the broken shards of the world.

"Yes," she said, or her heart answered; there was nothing in that moment she wanted more than to spin all the music she knew into that power, that gold, then to give it all away.

Phelan felt the change in her: the dancing rill turning suddenly into such a deep, strong, overriding current that he could barely keep himself afloat. He let his fingers think for him, move to her music while his brain told him he could never possibly do what he was doing, which was akin to keeping himself adrift by clinging to a leaf sailing above the current, balancing his life on a passing feather, letting a twig pull him through the swift, wild, frothing waters of the music that came out of her. He played accidentals, it seemed, hitting notes out of nowhere by the skin of his teeth, pulling music out of his prickling back hairs, out of runnels in his brain he never knew existed. It wasn't fear of his father's fate that kept them coming; he had no time even to think of that. He was grasping the lowest thread of Zoe's hem, catching the edge of her shadow with his fingernails. There was no letting go; he could only go where she led him.

So when what he thought was a standing stone on the crest of a nearby hill shouted his name, he rolled an eye at it confusedly and did not stop. The Oracular Stone, he assumed, though it sounded oddly like his father.

"Phelan!"

His fingers skipped a beat. It was his father, calling from the other side of the Turning Tower. Jonah shouted something more that got tangled up on Zoe's voice. Phelan ducked his head, concentrated. If his father had any good advice, he thought grimly, he would have given it to himself all those centuries before. As though Jonah had read his mind, he began walking toward Phelan, a tiny, impossibly distant figure who would take days, years, eons, maybe, to cross the distance between them.

The harper wrestled the next song out of Zoe's closing notes and leaped away with it, nearly snarling Phelan's fingers as he scrabbled to keep up. Something strange came out of Zoe. He saw her voice curl out of her in long banners of color, fluttering and dissolving into the wind. Her harp notes scattered like tiny, glittering insects that spread bright, metallic wings and swarmed away. He laughed suddenly, breathlessly, and tried to make that magic with his fingers. Nothing sparked to life from his notes, but she smiled at him anyway, all flaming silks and windblown hair, stepping out of her shoes then to stand barefoot in the long grass. How could she smile? he wondered. How could she not be afraid, caught in that dire web of power and poetry, with his father's fate looming like a vast doorway into timelessness and trouble in front of them both?

The harper spun the song away again; he and Zoe sang it together, voices swirling like wind songs over the plain, his deep, rough-hewn, blustery, hers soaring above it, the golds and reds and deep gray-blacks of clouds gathering to kindle the tempest. Phelan's notes scattered like birds before the storm riding on their tail feathers.

"Phelan!"

Jonah's voice sounded out of the weltering. Phelan couldn't see him clearly through the blinding shafts of sunlight spearing through mists and billowings across the plain. He sounded closer, or else his voice had gotten stronger. What he could possibly do that wouldn't plunge them all more deeply into the inexhaustible cauldron of time, Phelan couldn't imagine. He wished Jonah would stop shouting. The incongruous sound, like a sudden voice breaking in upon a dream, made his fingers falter, miss the note that led to the next, then the next, until Zoe caught him out of his flailing, set him back where he was, balanced on the cliff's edge by a breath, trying to keep time itself motionless beside him.

The next time Jonah shouted, he was very close, and whatever word he loosed across the plain was not Phelan's name.

It cracked through the music like an oak bough breaking, and it silenced the old harper's voice in the middle of a word.

The brief hesitation was astonishing enough to freeze Phelan's fingers as well. Zoe, fending for herself, seemed impervious to the disruption. She only glanced at Jonah when he appeared on the crest of the hill beside Phelan and pulled the harp from his hands.

"What are you doing?" Phelan cried at him, wrenched off-balance and feeling as though his own misguided father had pushed him the wrong way over the cliff edge. "You can't even whistle! Strings break when you look at them."

Jonah ignored him. The harper flung his glinting smile at them and found his voice again; Jonah's fingers leaped after him. Phelan stared at him, sweating, trembling, torn from the embrace of his instrument, from the embrace of the whirling, deadly current of music, to stand empty-handed on the shore, music still clamoring in his head with no way out.

Then he heard Jonah's music melding with Zoe's like silver braided with gold, like sunlight with sky, small birds flying out of his harp, and butterflies out of hers, their voices winding together, sweet, sinewy, strong as bone and old as stone. Together, they transfixed him, spellbound in their spell, his mouth still hanging open, and all the unplayed music in him easing out of his heart with every breath.

He didn't notice when the old harper stopped playing. Sometime before that, the mist of stones around them had begun to float away, like clouds breaking up after a maelstrom. Phelan, sitting on the ground by then, watched wordlessly as the harper slipped the harp from his shoulder, reached for its case. Phelan saw the markings on the harp then, secrets all over it, whittled into the wood.

He found his voice finally, whispered, "Who are you? Are you Kelda?"

"Sometimes. Sometimes I'm Welkin. Sometimes..." He shrugged. "I go where the music is."

"What is— What is your true name?"

The paler eye narrowed at him, catching light. "Ask your father. He knows."

Phelan gazed up at his father, who was still playing as though his fingers were trying to let loose a millennium's worth of unspent notes. "What did you do to him? He couldn't play a blade of grass before today. He couldn't find the beat in a pair of spoons."

"I didn't do anything. You did." He slid the harp into the case, fastened the old leather ties, and patted it fondly, whereupon it disappeared. Phelan stared at the nothingness where it had been; his eyes were pulled away to follow the harper's gesturing arm. "He's been trapped in this tower since he tried to kill me with his music. That time, he only brought down that old watchtower. This time, he found a better way to deal with me. He turned his heart inside out to rescue you from his fate. Not," he added, as Phelan opened his mouth, "that you were anywhere near it. But he didn't know. He pulled down the tower walls with his music for you."

Phelan felt his skin constrict. "Who are you?" he asked again, his voice a wisp, a tendril of itself.

The harper smiled. "Just an old stone," he said, and became so, a weathered boulder embedded in the crown of the hill, scaly with lichen and the faint patterns of what might once have been words, drowsing in the afternoon sun.

Phelan shifted to lean against it after a while, as he listened to his father and Zoe. After a longer while, he heard the stone prophesy:

"She'll be the next bard of this land. She'll sing the moon down and the sun up, and not a bard will be left standing against her magic."

After a time even longer than that, Beatrice found him.

She came up the knoll, carrying her high-heeled sandals, looking windblown, uncertain, even, he saw with astonishment, as he rose, somewhat fearful. He went to meet her, saw the tears still drying on her face. He put his arms around her, felt again the strong, sweet embrace of the music in her.

"I couldn't see you," he said.

"You're all I could see. I was so frightened. I've never been so frightened. Everyone else had faded away, and I knew from your father's tale where you and Zoe had gotten to. Kelda tricked you—"

He started to shake his head, then stopped and smiled crookedly. "Well. I suppose he did."

"I tried to follow your father into the tower. But I couldn't find my way until now. What happened to them?"

"My father managed to topple the right tower this time."

She turned her head, looked over his shoulder; he felt her indrawn breath against his ear. "That's Jonah. All this time I thought it was Kelda, playing with Zoe. I couldn't see anything very clearly until now. I've never heard your father play before."

"Neither have I. He finally remembered how."

Her hair brushed his mouth as she shifted again. "Where is Kelda?"

Phelan hesitated, found it easiest just to say it. "He turned back into Welkin and reminded my father how to play again. Then he turned himself back into that."

He gestured to the boulder breaking out of the ground. He felt the princess's tremor of astonishment. She loosed him slowly, dropping her sandals, all her attention on the stone now, he noticed wryly, with the labyrinth of weathered lines on it.

She knelt beside it, touching it, caressing it, her splayed fingertips finding and tracing the ancient scorings, smiling even as her mouth shook with wonder and tears fell onto the sunlit stone. "The oldest words," she whispered. "The oldest magic . . . Oh, Phelan, look at this." He crouched down beside her, drew a salty kiss from her, wishing he lay under those gently searching fingers and wondering if, in whatever dream the old bard inhabited, he felt them. "It's the spiraling circle."

"The what?"

"There." She took his hand, guided his fingers around a circle, then into smaller and smaller rings that wound down into its heart. She looked at him, laughing through her tears. "It's the symbol on the door stone of the tomb we're unburying. I've never seen it anywhere else. I wonder if that's his name."

"He's a ghost?"

"Well, maybe the tomb isn't a tomb. Or maybe it's still waiting for him—he hasn't gotten around to dying yet."

Bemused, he thought of the word Jonah had shouted that made the bard's sure fingers skip a note with astonishment. Hearing your own name after who knew how many millennia might have that effect, he thought. He took the princess's fingers, raised them away from the battered face of the stone to his lips, moved that she could see so clearly the words engraved in stone and all the worlds within the words.

Behind them, the music had begun to slow, fray into an unfinished phrase, a scattering of notes. Jonah laughed suddenly, a free, wondering sound unlike anything Phelan had ever heard from him.

Then the amphitheater thundered, roared, wave after wave of sound rolling across it from every point to crash together, unwieldy echoes rippling back again to meet the constant noise. They stood on stage and scaffolding again, musicians turned to stone in the suddenly appearing world, the princess looking around bewilderedly for the vanished stone, the knoll, the secret world, the ancient word beneath her hand.

Zoe came back to life first, managing a smile across the distance at Quennel, on his feet like everyone else in the place, and clapping so hard she thought his hands might fall off.

Then she turned to Jonah, held him in a long, incredulous gaze before she spoke. "Nairn?"

He looked back at her silently; Phelan glimpsed the shadow of the endless road in his eyes.

"I was young and foolish then," he answered finally, and she shivered.

"So are we all . . ."

"Maybe," he said more gently. "But you recognized Kelda before I did. Welkin. All the magic and the poetry, the ancient voices of this land come to life, with two feet to roam on, a harp, and a pair of hands to play it with. You heard that true voice."

Her eyes clung to him. "You played that true voice today," she whispered.

He smiled. "I hear it every time I listen to you. You were born with it. There are always ulterior motives in mine." He reached out to Phelan, drew him close. "I thought I was rescuing my son. That wily harper fooled me again. I seem to have rescued myself instead."

"My father," the princess murmured, looking over the edge of the scaffolding, "is on his way over here. And Quennel. And my mother. And my uncle, probably wanting to know where Kelda is. And my aunt. Is there anyone who particularly wants to explain all this?"

"I don't," Zoe said adamantly.

"Nor me," Phelan breathed.

"That leaves me," Jonah said dryly. "But not just this moment . . ."

"The school refectory," Zoe suggested tiredly. "I put a stew on to simmer this morning, and I don't think I've ever been so hungry in my life. It will soon be the only quiet, empty place in this city. Come back with me, and I'll feed everyone. Phelan, what is so funny?"

"The Inexhaustible Cauldron," he told her, throwing an arm around her and dropping a kiss on her sweat-soaked hairline. "The final detail. I wondered when you'd get around to that."

"I'll drive," the princess offered promptly, looking a question at Jonah, who nodded after a moment.

"For a little while . . . Then I will need to go and find the moon, drink a cup of moonlight with her."

"You will come back," Phelan said abruptly. Jonah gave him a bittersweet smile.

"This time," he promised. "And all the nights that I have left . . ." He tightened the hand on his son's shoulder. "Don't grieve for me yet, boy; I've simply returned to the land of the living. I may never get used to it, and what a wonderful change that will be. Ah—" he added, at a thought, and slid the harp from his shoulder, held it out to Phelan.

Phelan shook his head, slipped the strap back over Jonah's shoulder, "Keep it," he said huskily, smiling crookedly at his impossible father. "Celebrate with the moon for me. You've finally given me an end to my paper."

Chapter Twenty-six

The great bardic contest held on Stirl Plain on Midsummer Day at the request of King Lucien's bard Quennel raises far too many questions to answer here. Like the precise location of Bone Plain and the origins of the poetry it engendered, the event will keep scholars as well as students working on their final papers busy for decades, if not centuries. Why did Kelda, who by most expectations would win the contest, vanish so completely at the end of it that not even the Duke of Grishold could say what happened to him? How did Jonah Cle, who by all accounts failed spectacularly at his bardic classes as a young student, end up accompanying the next Royal Bard of Belden with such stunning skill and passion and knowledge of his art that only his absolute refusal to accept any such title and responsibility kept him from being scheduled during the third and final day of the competition? And what of all the persistent, vague, and peculiar rumors about that second day? That there was yet another bard, with "a voice like a landslide and songs coming out of his fingers that only scholars could name"? A bard without a name, who vanished as completely as Kelda did? Who was this stranger? That the mysterious crack across the stonework of the amphitheater was not caused by the sheer numbers sitting in it, but by a shout so loud it became the stuff of instant legend? And what are we to make of the complaints, not only from dubious sources but from those, like the queen herself, who would be completely unlikely to be drunk at that hour of any day, of the strange mist that flowed into the amphitheater and stayed, it seemed, for a very long time, during which the music was played by unseen musicians? The few, like Quennel, who could see through the mist, could describe the musicians playing then, from which we recognize our mystery guest. What of the rumors of standing stones appearing in odd places? And the persistent smells hinting of a wonderful feast wafting through the amphitheater so entrancing that they sent any number of people adrift through the mists, bumbling against one another, falling down steps, and stumbling headfirst into vendors' trays? And what, one might finally wonder, as the mists cleared, was the princess doing on the top of the scaffolding?

But we can only push our way through the cloud of questions, keeping our eyes stubbornly on the business of this paper: Nairn. Who, we are prepared to prove, returned after so many centuries to the site of his dismal failure to redeem himself at last and find what he had been searching for so long, and which we will describe only as what we might wish for him, though at this point the two words may be synonymous in his mind: Peace.

To that end, I have persuaded Nairn to tell us his own story, which began so long ago in the Marches. Let it stand, as does the very earliest of our poetry, as a cautionary tale for the ambitious

*and the powerful, as well as a glimpse into the infinitely faceted
face of the past.*

> *He sang with her like silver,*
> *And she sang with him like gold,*
> *Together they sang the tower down,*
> *And the Old One back to stone.*

> *O the Cursed is Free and the Lost is Found,*
> *And the Fool can play again.*
> *He freed himself and his son from the Turning Tower,*
> *O what shall we sing of now?*

ANONYMOUS: STREET BALLAD HEARD THE MORNING AFTER ZOE WREN
WAS DECLARED ROYAL BARD OF BELDEN

PHELAN CLE: "AN EXPLORATION OF THE UNFORGIVEN"